IN HARM'S WAY

Book 5 of the Lone Star Reloaded Series

A tale of alternative history

By Drew McGunn

This book is a work of fiction. Names, characters, places and incidents are the product of the author's overactive imagination or are used fictitiously. Any resemblance to actual events, or locales is coincidental. Fictional characters are entirely fictional and any resemblance among the fictional characters to any person living or dead is coincidental. Historical figures in the book are portrayed on a fictional basis and any actions or inactions on their part that diverge from actual history are for story purposes only.

Newsletter Sign Up/Website address:
https://drewmcgunn.wixsite.com/website
V1

ISBN: 9781791816919

ACKNOWLEDGEMENT

To my first group of beta readers who encouraged me with "Hurry up and post the next chapter." Thanks for encouraging me to continue past the first book. Special thanks to Grue, Butchpdf, Perfectgeneral, and others at the AH forum for excellent feedback that improved the story.

Table of Contents

The Story So Far

There's a scene from William Goldman's *Princess Bride*, where the intrepid hero Wesley asks, "Who are you? Are we enemies? Why am I on this wall? Where is Buttercup?" To which the Spaniard, Inigo replies, "Let me explain... No, there is too much. Let me sum up."

After four books, there is too much to explain, so allow me to sum up. Our intrepid hero, Will Travers, veteran of the Second Gulf War, finds his mind and soul cast back through time to 1836 into the body of William Barret Travis. With only weeks to avoid a martyr's death at the Alamo, Will contemplates fleeing from San Antonio de Bexar but realizes he can't abandon men like James Bowie and David Crockett to die at the old Spanish mission. Instead, he crafts a plan that is both daring and a little bit crazy to defeat Santa Anna long before the Mexican dictator can consolidate his army. Will manages to scrape together nearly every Texian soldier west of the Brazos River and meets Santa Anna on the Rio Grande River where Texian arms bleeds Santa Anna's vaunted Vanguard Brigade, before strategically retreating to the Nueces River, where the Texians destroy much of the Mexican army and capture the hapless dictator.

Once independence is secured by treaty with Santa Anna, Will joins with other famous Texians like Sam Houston and David Crockett to form a constitution for the nascent republic. He helps the constitutional convention craft a document avoiding the worst of the Southern slave codes, and which allows a path to citizenship for the Cherokee.

After narrowly surviving an assassin's bullet, Will takes command of the entire army of Texas. But he has barely begun to transform the army when the frontier erupts into violence as the Comanche ride out from the Comancheria and attack Fort Parker, on the edge of the Texas frontier.

Despite an early defeat at the hands of the lords of the Great Plains, Will eventually drives the Comanche to the peace table. In the ensuing years, he refines both the tactics his army uses as well as its weapons.

Despite a fragile peace between Texas and Mexico, the treaty signed by Santa Anna has never been enforced until President Crockett orders Will to take the army to secure Santa Fe and Albuquerque for the Republic, in accordance with the treaty from six years before. The army is more than eight hundred miles away when Santa Anna sends a force under Adrian Woll to capture the Alamo.

Total annihilation at the Alamo is only stopped by A. Sidney Johnston's arrival with every army reservist he can scrape together, while Will is still hundreds of miles away with the regular army. After burying the dead, Texas prepares for total war with Mexico.

Total war is expensive, and a long campaign will destroy the fragile republic. Will has every expectation of a quick war. The Mexican commander is rash and headstrong, but before the campaign can begin, he is killed in a freak accident and his cautious second-in-command, Juan Almonte takes charge and changes the Mexican strategy to one of defense.

Almonte forces Will into several pitched battles, where the Texian army's skill, tactics and superior weaponry are pitted against Almonte's defense in depth and tactical retreats. Months drag by, and inflation and debt eat away on the Homefront as Will's Texian army grinds down Mexico's Army of the North.

Santa Anna, exasperated by the glacial speed of the campaign, sacks Almonte for failure to produce a victory and takes command, as he brings north another twenty thousand men. In a battle that dwarfs every previous conflict between the two nations, Santa Anna tries to overwhelm Texian defenses only to come up short. In the ensuing retreat, the dictator once again falls into Will's hands.

Meanwhile, back in Austin, President Crockett resigns his office and turns over command of the Republic to his vice president, Lorenzo de Zavala and heads into the west with a column of Texians, which includes Will's son, Charlie, who runs away from home to have an adventure. Crockett easily defeats the lightly defended garrisons of Mexican California, but before he can enjoy the fruits of his labor, he is gunned down, and Will's son is kidnapped.

Chapter 1

He heard the creaking sound of wood as his eyes fluttered open. Panic squeezed his heart when he saw nothing but darkness. His heart raced faster when he tried running his tongue along his teeth and found a rag wet with his own saliva stuffed into his mouth. He twisted and realized he couldn't move his arms. They were pulled behind him, bent around a wooden dowel rod and tied securely in place. The rod extended beyond his arms another foot to either side.

As panic set in, he tried kicking his feet, only to find his legs were tied together. He tossed and turned, but the ropes were securely fastened. The rod hit against the wooden flooring, as he rocked back and forth. He tried to cry out, but the only sound was a faint muffled moan. His heart raced as, wide-eyed, he turned his head in the darkness and saw nothing. It felt like his heart was trying to climb out his throat as it thundered in his chest. Mercifully, he slipped back into unconsciousness.

When he came to, the youth heard the creaking of wood against wood. He was on his side, rocking as the flooring beneath him gently pitched side to side. He was still tied and gagged. He breathed in deep through his nose, willing the echoes of panic from earlier to stay under control. At first, the darkness seemed complete, but as they adjusted, his eyes saw a few narrow cracks overhead where light shone through. From there, he studied the ceiling and saw an overhead hatch next to a wall. As he focused on the opening across the room, his eyes acclimated to the darkness and he saw a narrow, steep stairway leading to the hatch.

"I'm on a ship," Charlie Travis finally managed to think.

Slowly, memories pushed their way into his consciousness. He recalled sitting at a breakfast table with his Uncle Davy. Then all hell broke loose. He remembered men crashing through the door of the hotel's common room and then being knocked to the floor. Then the room was filled with gunshots and acrid tasting gunpowder. Rough hands had yanked him to his feet, and he saw his grandfather curled in a ball as someone kicked at him. Charlie's head had been covered in a burlap bag as he had been hustled from the common room. A moment later there was a final shot. And then cursing as he landed heavily in the back of a wagon.

A high-pitched voice said, "He shot me, and I shot him."

The wagon sagged as someone climbed into the seat. A moment later Charlie heard the crack of a whip, then the vehicle lurched forward.

The memory brought unbidden tears to his eyes. Overhead, on the ship's deck, walked David Crockett's murderer. Tears, especially when one is fourteen, burn. Charlie struggled against the ropes which secured him to the wooden rod through which his arms were tied, causing the ends of the rod to knock against the planks on which he lay.

Hinges groaned in protest as the overhead hatch was thrown open. Intense light flooded the hold, and Charlie turned his head away and screwed his eyes shut. He heard leather soles slip down the narrow stairs and then a voice said, "Lookee who's back in the land of the living."

Hands grabbed at the rod and propelled him to his feet. "Move it, kid. Give me any shit, and I'll cut your throat and toss you overboard." A moment later his legs were untied, and he was shoved toward the light.

Charlie tripped against the stairs and with the low, sibilant voice behind him propelling him forward, he stumbled upwards. Once he reached the deck, from behind, he was shoved to his knees. "Give me one good reason, and I'll gut you like a pig, boy." The tone shifted, and the voice said, "That poppy juice finally wore off, boss. The boy was rolling around below."

Another voice, deeper and more resonant spoke. "Young master Travis. Welcome aboard the *Orion*."

Charlie stayed still on his knees until his eyes adjusted to the light. He saw a man a couple of inches shy of six feet. Brown hair waved in the wind. He wore a plaid waistcoat and a white muslin shirt, with sleeves rolled above the elbows. One of his forearms was scarred, the skin appeared twisted in on itself.

He saw the scar tissue up close as the man stepped forward and removed the gag from his mouth. "That can go back in if you can't keep a civil tongue in your head."

The boy felt as though he had a million things he wanted to scream at his captors. But the cloying taste of the gag had left his tongue swollen, and he merely stared at the man.

"Smart, like your Pa, I'd imagine. Look around, boy," he said, his arm revolving around the ship. "There ain't no place to go."

Charlie could barely see a smudge to the east. Land had to be a dozen miles or more away. Still not trusting his voice, the youth said nothing.

"You give me your word you'll behave, or I'll have Mr. Williams tie you back up. I'm sure you've noticed he can be a might rough."

His heart raced at the thought of being cut free from the painful binding, where his forearms were bent around the rod. He hated the taste of the word on his mouth as he bobbed his head, "Alright."

The man behind him, Williams, made quick work of the knots tying his arms around the rod. Finished with the rope, he hissed, "I'll hurt you bad, boy, if you don't do as Mr. Jenkins says."

For the first time in he had no idea how long, Charlie was unbound, but as blood flowed back into his arms and legs he gingerly stepped over to the portside railing. The shore was only a speck in the distance. Despite being free from the rope's restraints, he felt more trapped than ever.

9 August 1843

The taste of salt stung Obadiah Jenkins' lips, as mist wafted over the ship's bow. He peered over the gunwale and watched the hull cut through the choppy water. Nearly three weeks had passed since they had taken passage on Captain Palmer's *Orion*, and Jenkins was ready to get ashore. In the far distance, he could see the Central American shoreline. The captain had told him he expected to drop anchor in Ciudad de Panama's harbor later in the afternoon.

In the amidships, Hiram Williams was watching their prisoner. Jenkins had misgivings about the volatile gambler watching over Charlie Travis. But Jackson and Zebulon had already taken their turn. Williams had stolen the single greatest act of revenge Jenkins had ever considered when he killed David Crockett in the hotel's common room back in Los Angeles. He had meant for the former president of Texas to suffer the humiliation of having his grandson kidnapped from under his nose. It was a fitting revenge for Crocket's customs agents killing Nancy a few years before. Williams' erratic act of violence still chafed him.

From the deck below, he heard Williams' voice. "You got no idea how lucky you are, boy, that I ain't gutted you yet like I did your grandpa."

Charlie Travis was sullen. The boy had been depressed since they had hauled him onboard. That didn't bother Jenkins in the least. Boys his age were prone to mood swings. But they would soon be on land,

and he needed the boy to understand his life was in Jenkins' hands.

He leaned over the railing below the pilot's cabin, "Hiram, Leave the boy be. He's worth more to us alive than dead. If you damage the merchandise, it'll come out of your hide. Kill the boy without my leave, and I'll extract the ransom from your hide, you hear?"

Williams returned a knife he'd been playing with to its sheath and spat a stream of tobacco juice over the gunwales. "Yeah, boss. Just having a bit of fun with the boy."

He turned and leered at the boy. "Right, Charlie?"

The youth inched away from him in response. Williams burst out laughing. "See, Ob, I told ya."

True to Captain Palmer's word, the sun still lingered over the Pacific Ocean when the *Orion* dropped anchor.

They stayed that evening in a derelict building passing itself off as a hotel. The room was small, made all the smaller by four men and a boy crowded together. Jenkins tied Charlie's hands together. It wouldn't do for the boy to escape.

Elizondo Jackson, his longtime associate from Florida, woke him up sometime after midnight. "Ob, your watch." Jackson had taken the first watch. Jenkins tossed aside his blanket and stood. The remnants of a candle flickered. He dug another from his pack and lit it using the last of the old candle's wick before he sat in a rickety chair and looked at his prisoner.

The boy's ginger-colored hair reflected the candlelight. At fourteen, Jenkins guessed he still had a few inches left to grow. For the moment though, the boy's chest rose and fell. As the son of one of Texas' most notable and well-off personas, Jenkins was certain William Barret Travis would pay the ransom. But much rested on his and his compatriots' ability to get back to South Carolina. If he gaged the tea leaves right, several men would shelter Jenkins' crew, merely to hurt an abolitionist like Travis.

The boy shifted, and his eyes fluttered open, revealing blue irises. After a few blinks, the boy glared at Jenkins.

Softly, the kidnapper said, "Go back to sleep, boy."

Charlie shifted his glare to the ropes binding his hands. "You could untie me. I can't go anywhere."

Chuckling, Jenkins shook his head. "No. You're too valuable for me to risk."

"My father will find you."

"False hope will do you no good. Now get some rest."

Briefly, the boy's eyes closed, but then tears seeped from the corners of his eyes. "Why did y'all kill my grandpa?"

Jenkins flinched. "That wasn't supposed to happen. I wanted him to suffer the failure of knowing we kidnapped you under his nose."

The boy's voice was flat and emotionless. "Bastard."

Jenkins laughed, the bitterness was sharp enough for his own ears. "You can't even begin to know. Your grandpa caused the death of my Nancy. She died in a fire when customs agents raided my house. They might as well have pulled the trigger."

"But you must have done something to bring that down on you."

The kidnapper grimaced. "Just peddling a bit of paper. Folks needed titles to their land, and we were happy to oblige."

"Forger," the boy spat out.

"What do you know about that?"

The youth said, "Enough. My pa said folks like you were the reason the courts are clogged with conflicting claims."

Jenkins sighed. "Go back to sleep, kid." Charlie Travis was right. Two men claiming the same land, both holding deeds they thought were valid had caused more than a bit of conflict across East Texas.

The next morning, Jenkins left the boy in the room with Bill Zebulon. The burly man had been with Jenkins since before he had first crossed the law. Although not the sharpest of the group, Bill's size was intimidating. He was more than six foot tall and broad across the shoulders. Over the years when he needed to flex his muscles, Jenkins would send Bill in. Zebulon could lay a man out cold with one hit.

At least with Bill watching the boy, he didn't have to worry about Williams doing any physical harm to Charlie. The fiery gambler's temper was a liability, but his ability to ferret out information was second to none. It was that ability he was now relying on as he followed the small man down a narrow, muddy street.

Williams stopped at a run-down stable, on the edge of town. The building's wall was weathered and warped planking. The walls had once been painted white, but only curling chips remained, flaking from the wall.

A corral held a dozen donkeys. They were crowded around a long trough on the side closest to the stables. Williams waved at a man who hobbled from the dilapidated building. "Amigo," he called out.

The man appeared as run-down as his building. He wore a scruffy beard. It covered the collar of a once white shirt. The wrinkles on his swarthy face nearly covered a long scar which stretched from his right eye down to his jawline. He shook his head. Williams had a knack for finding the right sort of men for the work at hand.

The old man said, "I hear you're looking for passage across the isthmus. Hell of a time to go, during the rainy season, but if you're of a mind to do it, me and my boy are for hire."

Years of living in Mexican territory had honed Jenkins' Spanish. He said, "How much?"

"Three of you?"

Jenkins shook his head. "No, there'll be two more."

The old man scratched at his beard and eyed Jenkins, appraisingly. "Fifty pesos, señor."

Jenkins blanched. Seventy U.S. dollars was a lot of money. He sputtered, "That's more than three month's wages. You're daft."

The man's weathered features hardened. "As if you ask for much? Crossing the isthmus during the rainy season is dangerous. The vapors alone might kill any one of you. The risk to my son and me is great. Take it or leave it."

Williams sidled next to Jenkins. "Boss," he hissed, "I done checked with two others, and he's the only one willing to take us at all."

Paying the fee would put a significant dent in their finances, and he still needed to figure out how to get from Chagras, on the Caribbean to Charleston. He glared at the old man. "Twenty-five pesos."

The old man's laugh sounded like glass breaking. "Fifty pesos. If you don't like my rates, you're welcome to talk to someone else."

Jenkins frowned. Williams' warning echoed in his ears. "Fine. Fifty pesos. When can we leave?"

"Saturday."

That meant two more days in the tight confines of the hotel room. Reluctantly, Jenkins nodded.

Charlie rested the paddle on the canoe's gunwales and rubbed his wrists. His captors still tied his hands each night, even though they had left the road a week before and were paddling east on the Chagres River.

From the start, the trip had been a nightmare. Ten days earlier, the weathered old guide, Julio Sanchez had led the party east from Ciudad Panama, in a torrential downpour. The first leg of the trip had been along a muddy track. It had taken them four days to travel twenty-five miles. Charlie was convinced they had only managed to stay on the road because of Sanchez's surefooted burros.

When they had arrived at the Chagres River, they stayed at a dilapidated shack, which made the hotel back in town look like the proverbial Taj Mahal, about which Charlie's pa had told him. The shed masqueraded as both hotel and stables for the burros. From there, they continued on the river in canoes.

"Quit your lollygagging, boy, and paddle," Hiram Williams snapped at him.

"God damn you to hell." Charlie's voice didn't carry enough for the irascible gambler to hear. Sandro Sanchez, who dipped his paddle into the swiftly moving current, grunted a laugh. The son of their guide, Sandro had been assigned to Charlie and Williams' canoe. Charlie sighed in resignation. The young man, only a few years older than Charlie's fourteen years, was affable, and if he had to stare at the back of someone's head, better Sandro's than anyone else's.

Switching to Spanish, Williams said, "Hey, pretty boy, shut the hell up."

Charlie bit his lip as the young man, sitting a few feet away, cursed under his breath at Williams. The young man's mustache and beard were more scruff than stubble. Charlie nearly stopped paddling, tempted to rub at the peach fuzz above his upper lip, but thoughts of Williams hitting him made him dig into the murky water with his paddle.

His shoulder muscles ached as he dipped the paddle's blade into the river. He hated all of his captors, but Hiram Williams he hated worst of all. He had a mean streak a mile wide. If Charlie slacked on paddling the canoe, Williams was prone to leaning forward and cuffing the back of his head. Sometimes he just did it for the hell of it, too.

Less than a hundred yards ahead, Charlie watched Jenkins and Julio Sanchez, in the first canoe. The guide waved toward something out of view. Sandro turned, warily eying Williams. "My father says we'll reach the village of Chagres soon. There's a spot ahead of where we can stop and eat."

Williams, sitting in the back, steered the canoe into a shallow beach next to the others. Jenkins and Sanchez were pulling food from a small crate as Charlie splashed ashore. He dug his toes into the soft sand and rolled his shoulders, when he tumbled to the ground, pain exploding from his head.

Charlie lay sprawled on the sand, his mind confused. His eyes squeezed shut as a wave of pain washed over him. He cracked open his eyes, and stars weaved around. Brown feet, belonging to Sandro knelt beside him, "Are you..."

The words were cut off by a sharp thwacking sound. "Get your ass away from the boy, you greasy *puta*!"

The young guide leapt up. Charlie wasn't sure what happened next. There was a flying fist and then a splash as Williams landed in the water. Sandro stood over the boy, his fists raised.

"Call me *puta* again, and I'll kill you."

Williams sputtered. "Nobody hits me, boy."

Jenkins dropped the food and stepped forward, "Hiram, enough!"

Williams crouched in the knee-high water, shifting his attention between Jenkins and Sandro. His eyes burned with hatred. Charlie cringed as he yanked his revolver from his holster. He pointed it at Sandro and fired.

A puff of smoke escaped from the chamber as the percussion cap detonated. But the gunpowder was soaked. Screaming with rage, Williams hurled the useless weapon at the young guide. Sandro dodged the heavy gun. Charlie heard a startled grunt and turned to see Sanchez sink to the ground, his face a bloody mess. The weapon had crushed his nose.

Charlie scampered over to the old guide. Sanchez was dazed. His eyes were unfocused, blood seeped from a deep gash on his lip, dripping into his graying beard.

He heard Jenkin's voice, "Goddammit, Hiram, stop!"

The youth turned and saw Williams tackle Sandro, who was gripping a knife. As the two hit the ground, Williams drove his fist into the young man's face, cutting his cheek.

From under Williams, Sandro slashed with his knife, missing the gambler's face by a hair's breadth. Williams used his elbow to block the next swipe and the blade sunk into the sand.

Charlie shouted, "Sandro!" as Williams grabbed the young man's throat and squeezed. Both combatants' faces turned beet red. The guide's from the hands gripping his throat, and Williams' from the adrenaline-fueled exertion, as he squeezed the life from the young man.

His voice was hoarse, as Charlie screamed, "No!"

The blade slipped from Sandro's hand as he lost consciousness.

Jenkins and Jackson rushed over to Williams and dragged him from the young man, but Charlie knew it was too late. The color was fleeing the young guide's face, as it turned a waxy pallor.

Before anyone could react, Williams shook loose the hands holding his jacket free and fetched the knife lying next to Sandro's limp hand. He pushed Charlie to the ground and leaned over old, dazed Sanchez. With a steady hand that spoke of practice, he slit the old man's throat.

"What the hell did you do that for?" Jenkins screamed. "We need him to get us out of here."

Glowering at the forger, Williams reached into the old man's jacket and fetched out a jingling pouch and threw it at Jenkins' chest.

"You said we didn't have enough money for passage to Charleston. Now we do."

Chapter 2

1 September 1843

The dust cloud gradually dissipated as President Herrera's coach and armed escort returned south. Now that peace was at hand, the Mexican president raced south to put down a Centralist rebellion. Will Travers stood next to Lorenzo de Zavala, the president of Texas, until even the dust cloud disappeared.

Zavala was the first to break the silence. "Now that we've won the war, it's time to focus on winning the peace, Buck. Let's get out of the sun and discuss which units we can safely put on the road back to Texas."

Buck? That wasn't really his name, but he'd gone by it for more than seven years. Will Travers shook his head. Even all these years later he marveled how God or fate had taken an infantry grunt who was just doing his duty on a supply run in Iraq and dumped his mind and soul into the body of William Barret Travis a few weeks before history would have recorded his death at the Alamo.

After all these years as William "Buck" Travis, so many of his past memories were hard to recall, but he'd grown used to that. The mind is a resilient thing, and Will had adjusted to his new world, even as thoughts of the world he had left behind faded from his conscious memory.

Will had put down roots in his new reality. He had taken responsibility for William Barret Travis' young son, Charlie, who had been shipped off to Travis as part of a divorce settlement with his ex-wife from Alabama. He had also married his best friend's daughter, Becky Crockett.

He turned to follow Zavala, and his heart felt like it was about to explode. He could scarcely believe David Crockett was dead. With no massacre at the Alamo, Crockett had gone on to become Texas' first president in 1836. As commander of the small, professional army of Texas, Will worked closely with Crockett to stabilize the young republic. Will had only learned of Crockett's murder the day before, and he was still in shock. If anything could be worse, though, it was the news his son, Charlie had been kidnapped by the former president's murderers.

He didn't want to deal with Zavala at the moment. He burned to know what happened to his son. But duty demanded he follow the president back into Saltillo's governor's palace.

Zavala led him into a small library he had taken as his office. Instead of books piled high, the desk was loaded down with reports and papers.

"I plan to head back to Austin within the next few days, Buck," Zavala said as he settled into his chair. "I'd like to get your thoughts about how large of an army we need to keep in Mexico. I'm not convinced Herrera will be able to push the treaty through as soon as I'd like. I want a physical reminder left behind of Mexico's obligation before withdrawing the entire army back. But heaven help us, we need to demobilize as many battalions as soon as possible."

Will wanted to scream. God and the kidnappers alone knew where Charlie was, and David was dead. Why didn't Zavala understand that? He collapsed into the chair opposite from the president and shook his head. "I've got to find Charlie. I should have forced him to come home when I got his letter."

Zavala shifted a stack of papers out of the way, clearing his line of sight. "Would it have changed anything? It's hard to compel a young man of Charlie's age from a thousand miles away."

Will shrugged. "I don't know. But that doesn't matter. The only thing that does is finding him."

"Once things have settled down here, why don't you detail a few of Hays' boys to track down the kidnappers?"

Will winced. "That could take a while, sir. I can't imagine waiting for that. If anyone is going to find my boy, it's going to be me."

A look of alarm crossed Zavala's features. "We have men trained to follow Indians across the plains; I'm sure they are the sort who could track Charlie's abductors. Buck, I need you here."

"No, Lorenzo, you don't. Not as much as Charlie needs me. Sidney can take over command of the troops here in Mexico and Ben can take the reserves back to Texas to be demobilized." A. Sidney Johnston commanded the army's 1st brigade while Ben McCulloch commanded the 2nd.

Zavala rose to his feet, "They're fine officers, but this is the army you built. As we absorb California, I want a strong hand overseeing military matters. You're that man."

Will shook his head. "God help Texas if I'm the only man who can command the army. Don't sell Sid Johnston short. With your permission, let's fetch him. I'd like his input on which battalions to keep here."

A few minutes later, the brown-haired commander of the army's 1st brigade leaned against one of the bookshelves. Will said, "Sid, we need a plan to return to the army to a peacetime footing. What are your thoughts?"

Johnston ran his finger down the leather spine of a book as he said, "There are more than ten thousand men active right now. If it were me, I'd demobilize in two stages. First, I'd send most of the 2nd brigade back to Texas. I'd demobilize the 5th, 8th, and 11th Infantry battalions once they're back across the Rio Grande. I'd send the 2nd Cavalry back, too. That's more than two thousand men."

Zavala grimaced, "We need a lot more men back on the farms than just a couple of thousand, General. Can we cut anywhere else?"

Johnston said, "The 10th and the 12th Infantry are currently protecting our supply route back to the Alamo. We could shift the Ranger's frontier battalion from Saltillo to cover the supply line between Monterrey and the Rio Grande. That'll get you up to thirty-two hundred now."

Begrudgingly, Zavala said, "I guess that's a start."

Will said, "Until the treaty's ratified we don't want to be unable to continue the war if it were necessary."

"Michel Menard is right," Zavala said, "We're balancing on a knife's edge, and if we can't find a way to get as many of our men back home and farming again, we run the risk of folks going hungry."

Will could only nod. Menard was the Secretary of the Treasury. The former Quebecois had managed to keep the economy afloat, if just barely, during the war.

Zavala said, "That'll get us started, but what about after the treaty has been signed? I don't want us to fall into the same trap we found ourselves when General Woll invaded last year."

Will glanced at Johnston and gave a slight nod.

"We trim down to two infantry battalions. Right now, the 1st and the 6th are made up entirely of regulars," Johnston said. "I propose we keep them. We rebalance them, and we'll have two units of eight companies each, about twelve-hundred men between them.

"I'd keep a single battalion each of cavalry and artillery. I was impressed with Hays' special Ranger command, and I'd recommend we keep a company or two of them active. Currently, there are over six hundred men between the engineers and the quartermaster corps. We can probably reduce that to a couple of hundred."

Johnston paused, his expression thoughtful. "That will reduce the army to brigade strength, around twenty-four hundred men."

"Will that be enough to cover our new territory?" Will said.

Johnston shrugged. "I can't say for certain. I do know that, as of last year, the United States mustered less than six thousand regulars."

Zavala interjected, "One thing I do know. Twenty-four hundred men will still put a sizable dent in the treasury."

Will's duty done, he said, "Mr. President, I told you Sidney was more than able to handle things. I know I'm leaving you with a capable commander to wind down the war and set the army on a peacetime footing."

Johnston looked confused while Zavala was alarmed. He said, "The nation can't afford to lose you, Buck!"

Will smiled sadly. "I'm sorry you feel that way, Lorenzo." He dropped the formality of rank. As far as he was concerned, he was addressing an equal. "For the sake of my family, I resign my commission. I've got to find Charlie."

He hadn't stayed in his tent since the army arrived at Saltillo back in June. Will thought it best to give the president some space. He hadn't taken Will's resignation well. The side walls of the tent were rolled up, letting warm tendrils of air waft through. He sat at the cramped camp table, cleaning each piece of his revolver separately.

"Taking that peashooter with you?" Will looked up and saw Sid Johnston standing by the tent's pole.

"I don't fancy on remaining around for long. Is Lorenzo still spitting nails?"

Johnston sat on a cot and ran his fingers through his sweaty hair. "He'll calm down. Eventually. I shouldn't be surprised, Buck. I can't imagine what I'd do if I found out my son had been taken."

Will pursed his lips as he began reassembling the gun. "How is Preston?"

A smile lit Johnston's tired face. "My sister says he's growing like a weed. He's already thirteen. I can scarcely believe it."

He fished into his pocket and brought out a small metal case and handed it over. Will opened it and saw a solemn boy staring back at him. Photo studios were becoming more popular in large cities across the United States. His heart threatened to break as he recalled the last night he had seen his own son. He handed the daguerreotype back to Johnston. "Fine boy you've got, Sid. You, of all people, should understand why I need to do this."

"Understand and agree, I just wish it wasn't necessary," Johnston said. He paused as he tucked the picture away. "With the war over, what were your plans for the gun works on the Trinity River?"

Will said, "According to the rolls there are more than twenty thousand men in the militia. If I were you, I'd keep the contracts coming. If war comes again, I'd like all of our men to have breechloaders. Beyond that, there are two other developments they're working on worth following. They are trying to mechanize the production of brass cartridges. They've developed a new version of our revolver that uses them. The problem is that each round is handmade right now. They're horribly expensive. But if they can work the issues out and develop a cheap cartridge, you'd do well to convert the revolvers.

"The second item is one we've been playing very close to the vest. Near the gun works, we're experimenting with nitrogenated cotton. The stuff's explosive but unstable as hell. If Mr. Borden can stabilize it, it could transform all of our weapons," Will said.

There was a noise from outside the tent. A moment later Major Jack Hays came through the opening, “General? You wanted to see me?”

"Jack, just the man I'm looking for," Will said with a weary grin.

“Uh-oh. That’s the look you’d give me when you were sending me and my Rangers on dangerous missions. Last I heard, the war’s over.”

Johnston stood and moved around Hays, heading out. “Major, make sure you tell General Travis goodbye.” With that, he started back toward town.

Hays colored at the comment. “I, ah, heard about your resignation, sir. I hate to see you leave, but I’d do the same thing in your shoes.”

Will’s smile widened. “I’m glad to hear that, Jack. I’d like for you to join me. I need steady men beside me, and there’s none better.”

Hays flushed at the compliment. “Aw, hell, General, I just did my duty.” With his remaining arm, he pointed at the empty left sleeve. A few months earlier, he had been the lone survivor when Mexican lancers had stormed a ranch house he and a company of Rangers had fortified. He had lost one of his arms there. “But I’m washed up now. There are plenty of men with two arms who’re better than me.”

Will’s smile faltered. “Jack, you’re one of the best men we’ve got, one arm or two.”

Hays dug the toe of his boot into the hard dirt, “Hell, it ain’t like it’s easy for me to do this, but my Ranging days are behind me. I've been chewing over what you said about California. And I've a mind to go back home, find a few boys who want to go prospecting. I can get me a grant of land, and if there's any gold or silver, maybe I'll be the one to find it."

Will was desperate, "Are you sure I can't change your mind? I need help finding Charlie, and you're one of the best."

"Tell you what I'll do, General. Let's see my boys. You can have any of them as wants to volunteer. Just don't take them all. Lorenzo would shit a brick."

Later that evening, Will was looking over the four men who had volunteered. The first was a young Cherokee, Jesse Running Creek. Like the other men, his uniform was battered and torn, but he carried two pistols at his belt. They were clean and well cared for. Next to him was another Ranger, who stroked his luxuriant brown mustache. "Jethro Elkins, General," he said.

The third man said, "Ranger Dempsey LeBlanc, sir." His Cajun accent made it sound like "Rahnzher." Like the other two, he was festooned with a couple of pistols, and the long bowie knife at his belt glimmered in the firelight.

The last of the four wore the black chevrons of a sergeant. His gray mustache drooped, as though tired of life. But the man's eyes were hard. "Major Hays said these boys needed a steady hand, so I thought I'd come along if you'll have an old hand like me."

Will couldn't place the accent. It wasn't quite German. The man continued. "Sergeant Maartin Jensen, sir."

"What did you do before joining the Rangers, Sergeant?"

"I served in the first United States Dragoons before coming to Texas. Before that, I served in the Danish army at the end of the Napoleonic wars," the graying sergeant said.

Will studied the four Rangers. He would miss the brash young major, but Hays had come through. The four men carried themselves with the casual air of veterans. *"Yes,"* he thought, *"They would do."*

Will slid the rifle into the saddle scabbard and checked the straps, making sure they were cinched. The four Rangers were checking their mounts, too. Rays of sunshine blazed over the eastern mountains, and despite how early it was, it promised to be a hot day.

"Hell of a day to ride out of here, Buck." Sid Johnston had come to see him off.

Will slid his eyes to the eastern horizon and squinted. He reminded himself he'd dealt with hotter days back in Iraq. "I'm not going to melt, Sid. Has Lorenzo cooled off yet?"

Johnston shook his head. "By the time he gets back to Austin, he'll be fine. He'll see that I'm a hell of an officer and forget he ever knew you."

Despite his worries, Will laughed like he hadn't since word of Charlie's kidnapping had arrived. He dabbed at his eyes and reached into his jacket. "Would you see that this gets delivered to Becky? I can't imagine what she must be going through right now. If time weren't critical, I'd go back to see her and the children and explain myself."

"There's nothing to explain. She'll understand. It's Charlie. I'll send the letter back with Ben."

At that moment, words failed him, and Will came to attention and saluted his friend and fellow officer. Johnston, a graduate of West Point, returned the salute. Then he grabbed Will by the collar and hugged his neck. "We'll be praying for you and Charlie. Come back safe."

As Johnston moved away, Will saw several more men approaching. In the vanguard was a slightly built man with graying hair, dressed in civilian clothes. The former commander of the Mexican Army of the North, Juan Almonte was followed by several other men. From the way they carried themselves, Will guessed they were men who had served under him in the late war.

"I'm glad I was able to find you before you left, General Travis."

Will offered his hand. Despite the tenacious defense Almonte waged across northern Mexico, Will had come to respect the exiled officer. "With Santa Anna deposed, I'm surprised you're still here, General."

Almonte spread his hands wide, in resignation. "President Herrera didn't see fit to overturn my exile. I'll be heading north with General McCulloch's brigade. I'll stay in Texas long enough to send for my wife and daughter. From there, I'll probably return to Washington. I've friends there." Before commanding the Army of the North, Almonte had served as Mexico's minister to the United States.

"Good luck, sir," Will said, with feeling. Almonte didn't deserve the condemnation of the Mexican government. Will didn't think it fair. Texas' superior weapons and tactics had won, despite the masterful defense Almonte had orchestrated.

Almonte frowned. "It sounds like you'll need it more than me, where you're going. I'm sorry for your loss. President Crockett was an able leader. I hope you are able to find your son." He paused and looked at a young man standing behind him who wore a shabby officer's coat. Will recognized the jacket as belonging to the Cazadores regiments. The rifle-armed Mexican light infantry had stymied Will's advance for much of the way to Monterrey from the Rio Grande earlier in the summer.

"Going across Mexico to the port at Mazatlan is dangerous. Bandits make passage treacherous for anyone," Almonte said, redirecting his attention back to Will.

Will shook his head. "It's that or take a route twice as long to San Diego. I'm left with bad options and worse. I'll take the bad, General."

Almonte waved the comment away, "As would I, were I in your shoes. I've no doubt you and your Rangers would give a good account of yourselves should you run into trouble. My young friend, Captain Morales and one of his men, who is familiar with the area east of Mazatlan are willing to travel with you if you're agreeable."

Will searched Almonte's eyes, looking for the reason he would help. "Why?"

"I'm a father, too."

Shaken by Almonte's admission, Will shook his hand and struggled to keep his emotions together. "Thank you."

As they prepared to depart, Will studied the two Mexicans. They were a study in contrast. The former officer, Morales, was fair skinned. As the sun rose in the sky and reflected off his hair, there were hints of brown mixed with black. The Mexican army was rigidly separated by caste. The officers, like Morales, were the descendants of Spanish immigrants. The conscripts who filled the *soldados'* ranks were Mestizos and full-blooded natives. Morales' companion was dark skinned. When he spoke, his Spanish was so rapid Will had a hard time understanding him. The young officer introduced him as "just Lobo."

As he swung into the saddle, Will sketched a salute as Almonte stood on the Saltillo road. With his six men, he felt better about his prospects of making good time crossing the Western Sierra Madres. Will cast a final look behind him, dug in his heels, and guided his horse westward. He would find Charlie or die trying.

Chapter 3

Tendrils of fog laced around his feet. Charlie was alone in the jungle as the mist encircled his legs. Vines and branches sagged under the weight of heavy dew and he felt them closing in around him. He twisted his head around as he heard footfalls approaching. But he couldn't see anything other than foliage and white mist.

In the distance, he heard a faint echoing call. It was indistinct. Was it Hiram Williams? The thought sent chills up his spine. He took a step away from the call. His feet felt heavy. He looked down but could only see the mist as it reached his torso. Another step and he felt as though he were wading through water, so dense was the thick fog.

The call was closer. It had to be Williams getting nearer. Like fighting against a heavy current, Charlie took several more steps and tripped over something. He put his hands out to break his fall, and they landed on something soft. Within the mist, his fingers closed around something cloth, and he lowered his face and saw the buttons on a shirt, his face only inches away from the object. His hands reached above the shirt and felt something ice cold. He jerked away, but the mist was so heavy, he was held in place.

A breeze, with the smell of decay on it, cut through the fog and he saw Sandro's face materialize from the thick vapor. Eyes, pale white, stared back. A shrill scream broke the silence.

He felt something heavy strike him in the ribs and realized the scream he was hearing was his own. A harsh voice cut through. "Wake up, kid."

Charlie's eyes sprang open. He saw the dark grizzled features of Jenkins hovering over him. "You must have been dreaming again. You were screaming."

Remnants of a candle dripped onto a nightstand. The hotel room in the town of Chagras on the Caribbean Sea was small, but the minor port town catered to a few more ships than Ciudad de Panama on the western side of the isthmus had, so it wasn't as run-down as the other had been.

Charlie croaked, "Just a nightmare."

Jenkins settled back onto his pallet, grumbling. "That's the third time this week, kid. Get back to sleep."

Charlie rolled over and stared at the wooden wall. Bits of wallpaper, gray with age, clung to the wall. He followed the grain on the wood. *"I'll be damned if I'll go back to sleep."*

The dream had been so vivid and real. The last thing he wanted was to return to it. But he was tired and the patterns on the wall eventually blurred, and he finally returned to his troubled sleep.

A door slammed, and he heard William's voice, "Boss, there's a Spanish flagged merchantman just put into the harbor."

The voice droned on, Charlie opened his eyes and pinched himself. Ouch. He was awake, and Williams' voice wasn't a dream. He cursed below his breath as he imagined what it would feel like to sink a knife into the wretched little man.

Jenkins said, "Is it going to Charleston?"

"No. Havana. Heading that way to pick up tobacco, I'd imagine. He dropped off a few passengers here, so I imagine there's room for us."

Jenkins' voice sounded hopeful. "Shouldn't have any trouble getting to Charleston from Havana."

Elizondo Jackson and Bill Zebulon were sitting on the narrow bed, listening to them when Jackson frowned at Williams. "Unless you decide to kill the captain and navigator. We're lucky we didn't get lost in the jungle, Hiram."

Williams sneered. "We needed the money to buy passage to Charleston. We managed to find Chagras without those dirty dagos."

"Yeah, and what happens when you lose your cool again? When some fool on the ship calls your mother a whore, are you going to gut the poor bastard and start a fight we can't win?"

Charlie moved against the wall as he saw Williams grow tense and flex his fists. "Watch it, Eli. I might forget whose side you're on."

Jenkins stepped between them, his hand resting on a knife at his belt. "Knock it off." With his other hand, he retrieved a bag of pesos from the nightstand, "Hiram, go on and book passage for the five of us."

Williams left, slamming the door behind him. Charlie heard his heavy feet stomping on the stairs as Jenkins collapsed into a chair, "Damn that man to hell."

Agitated, Jackson paced the room, "Ob, Hiram's crazy. We got lucky finding Chagras after he lost his temper and killed the guides."

"Don't I know it. The problem is, he's right. We'd have been out of luck when we got here if he hadn't got the money back from them."

Jackson wagged his finger in Jenkins' face. "I don't mind killing anyone who needs killing, but what he did was stupid and impulsive. Ride herd on him if you've got to, but from here on, if he does something that risks our lives, I'll kill him myself."

Jenkins lowered his head into his hands, "Eli, you know it's not that easy. He's got a knack for finding stuff we need. Can you do as well?"

"We've been together for a lot longer than Hiram's been with us, so we can make do without him like we did before." He paused and pointed to Charlie, "When his daddy comes through with the ransom, I'm done with Hiram. Until then, I'll try to keep my powder dry."

14 September 1843

Obadiah Jenkins adjusted his footing as the vessel rolled in the gentle swells of the Florida Straits. The provincial Spanish capital, Havana appeared low on the horizon, growing slowly as the ship tacked back and forth against the light southerly breeze. The past eight days had been uneventful. Between him, Jackson, and Zebulon, they had kept a weather eye on the boy. Williams was just too unpredictable to trust him not to hurt the boy.

From his place next to the ship's gunwales he saw the boy, untied, standing next to Jackson on the opposite side of the vessel. To occupy himself, the half-breed was carving a piece of wood. The boy leaned against the railing, staring westward. The Gulf of Mexico flowed into the Florida Straits. In that direction lay Texas.

Whether the boy ever saw Texas again wasn't of concern to Jenkins. But until Travis paid the ransom, he was too valuable a chit to let Williams' fecklessness run amuck. Now they were back on the right side of the continent, and it was time to notify General Travis of the ransom. The previous evening, Jenkins stood over the boy until he had penned a letter to his parents, telling them he was alright. Jenkins would see it posted in Havana on the first ship to New Orleans or Galveston, along with the demand for fifty thousand dollars. Split four ways, it was still more money than a laborer would see in a lifetime.

Because the wind was blowing from the south, the sun was setting before the *Santiago* dropped anchor in Havana harbor. The next morning, Jenkins and his companions were rowed ashore.

Once upon the cobblestone street running alongside the harbor, Jenkins was nearly run over by a slave on horseback, pulling a two-wheeled carriage. A prosperous merchant and his wife sat comfortably in the contraption. Wagons laden with sugarcane were creaking and groaning under the weight, as oxen pulled them from a warehouse toward the docks. As Williams clambered onto the road beside him, he stuck his hands into his pockets and sniffed the air. “Smells too much of dago and nigger for me.”

Jackson, holding the boy by the scruff of the neck, joined them. “No, that’s the smell of whiskey and sweat. If you’d bathe that smell would go away.”

Williams turned on him and put his hand on the butt of his revolver. Jenkins swore and turned to the two of them. "Enough!"

Heads turned in their direction as people heard Jenkins' angry shout. "Hiram, if you reach for that pistol one more time around us, I'll kill you with my bare hands if I have to." He shifted his glare to Jackson. "Eli, you go off and poke a bear and one day that bear's gonna claw you good and proper. Let Hiram be."

Jackson said, "If I have to listen to that *puta* say one more word about dagos, you'll have to kill me to keep me from gutting him like a pig."

Jenkins winced. He'd known the half-breed Floridian for more than half his life. Typically, Jackson was oblivious about his Spanish blood, but Williams' constant harping about dagos had crossed a line. He turned to Jackson, "Take Bill and the boy and find a tavern. Me and Hiram are going to mail the note for General Travis and find a ship bound for Charleston."

He grabbed Williams' arm and hustled him away from the rest of the group. When they were alone, he turned on his sullen companion, "You've got to stop this palaver with Eli."

Williams huffed up. "He started it, calling my ma a whore. I'd a put a hurt on him the likes of which he wouldn't soon forget."

What could he say? Jackson had only spoken the truth about William's mother. "You'll not be putting the hurt on anyone else without my leave, Hiram. If you ever forget that I'm the biggest toad in this puddle, you'll find yourself on a lee shore."

The unkempt gambler's eyes flashed for a moment before Williams plastered a smile on his face, "Hell, Ob, a week on a ship and you've gone all sailor on me. I know who's in charge."

Jenkins continued walking along the road, "Don't forget it. Now, help me find a ship going to Charleston."

25 September 1843

A ship was fast approaching from the stern. Charlie strained his eyes, trying to see the speck of a flag flying from its yardarms. He felt the presence of Bill Zebulon on one side of him and Williams on the other. The gambler rested a hand lightly on his shoulder. Since embarking on the *Palmetto* several days earlier, his captors had kept an even closer watch on him. He wasn't allowed to talk to the ship's American crew.

As the ship neared, Charlie saw an American flag streaming over the pursuing vessel. What would a US flagged ship want with a merchantman chock full of goods from Europe? Charlie heard the ship's captain tell Jenkins, "She's likely part of the slave trade patrol. She's a bit far to the north of the regular routes in the Caribbean."

Charlie recalled his father telling him about the British and US-led efforts to choke off the slave trade from Africa. While the British and American governments had made the transatlantic slave trade illegal in 1808, much of South America ignored the law. It was frequently violated in the Caribbean, too. Every once in a while, smugglers would attempt to offload slaves in the American South.

Charlie's hope soared as the captain ordered the ship to reef the sails. If the warship sent over men to search the *Palmetto*, he would find a way to get their attention!

Jenkins came over. In a low tone, he said, "Take the boy to our cabin and hide him there. Tie him up and gag him if you have to."

His disappointment must have been written large over his face as Williams cackled, "You're stuck with me, kid." He dug his fingers into Charlie's shoulder and steered him below decks to one of the cabins.

Bolts secured the table to the floor, and two narrow bunks were fixed to the cabin walls. A lantern swung from the low ceiling, casting a flickering light onto the walls. Williams leaned against the table, playing with a sharp knife. Charlie eyed the deadly weapon in the hands of the unstable gambler. Why did Jenkins send him belowdecks with Williams?

He despised all of his captors, even the slowwitted Zebulon, who had treated Charlie better than the other kidnappers. But he loathed Williams more than the others combined. Loathed and feared the little man. The nightmares hadn't stopped since leaving Havana. He was haunted by the ghastly image of Sandro's empty eyes staring at him. He prayed the dreams would leave him alone, but so far, his fervent prayers had gone unanswered.

A thump on the ship's hull announced the warship's longboat arriving alongside the *Palmetto*. Charlie's eyes involuntarily swung to the cabin door.

"Don't even think of it, boy. You ain't got Eli or Ob to save your shitty, little ass now." Williams stood and brandished the knife in front of him. "If you so much as squeak, I'll make you bleed."

Charlie retreated from the bunk to the wall closest to the hallway. He tried breathing, but his chest felt constricted. The feeble light from the lantern gave

Williams' eyes a reddish hue. Charlie felt like he was looking into the pits of Hell.

Overhead he heard leather-soled shoes pounding on the deck. Williams's toes touched his, and the smelly gambler's face was only inches from his own. The stale stench of an unwashed body mixed with garlic and fish threatened to overwhelm Charlie. He couldn't back up, and he couldn't step to the side. He looked down, Williams held the knife, the blade missing his shirt by a hairsbreadth.

He raised a finger to his lips, as they heard booted feet walking along the hall outside the cabin. A voice called out, "Everyone topside, by order of Commander Tidwell."

The tip of the blade poked through Charlie's thin shirt and pressed against his stomach. "Shhh."

The footsteps retreated to the ladder leading to the deck.

Charlie scarcely breathed as the minutes ticked by. In his mind, he could see the sailors or marines from the US warship going through the ship's hold, comparing it to the manifest. Unless they decided to go through the cabins, they would find things in good order. The only thing out of order, he thought, was a homicidal maniac holding a knife on him. As he tried to suck in his stomach, he recalled the conversation between the ship's captain, Anson Tremont, and Jenkins when they had first come aboard.

"I don't traffic in contraband slave trading, Mr. Jenkins. I'll not risk my ship to line a few planters' pockets." Tremont's soft Georgian drawl was unmistakable. Charlie had heard Pa talk about how the United States outlawed the importation of slaves from

Africa. An American ship caught transporting slaves from Africa would be seized by the government.

The heavy footfall of boots on the stairs indicated someone was returning to check the passenger cabins. The door to the room next door opened for a brief moment and then closed. The steps echoed off the wooden planking. Silently, Williams slid beside him, and Charlie felt the icy touch of steel at his throat. "Not a word," Williams hissed in his ear.

His heart was beating so loud, surely whoever was approaching would hear. The doors to the cabins all swung inward. Unless the person checking the cabins looked behind the door, he wouldn't see Charlie or his knife-wielding captor.

The doorknob twisted and the knife against his throat pressed harder. The door swung open. Could he kick at the door and get the sailor's attention? He inched his foot forward. His neck stung as the knife pressed harder.

A moment later the door closed and the footsteps retreated again. The knife stayed at Charlie's throat. Instead, the stinging continued until the light from the lantern went dim. Then, there was nothing.

Chapter 4

20 September 1843

Becky Travis watched the back of the uniformed messenger as he retreated to the street where his horse tore at a clump of the neighbor's shrubs. In one hand, she held a letter, her husband's neat scrawl on the envelope's face. Her other hand cradled little David. A few months shy of a year old, the baby grasped a wooden toy in one of his chubby hands while the other was in his mouth.

"Who's at the door?" her mother called out. Elizabeth Crockett had been staying with her daughter since David Crockett had resigned as president the previous year.

The door closed behind her, and Becky handed little David to her. "A rider. He had a letter from Will." His friends might call him Buck, but to her, he was her Will.

David fidgeted in Elizabeth's arms until he discovered the brooch at her throat and then he became enamored with it. She said, "Well, open it."

Becky tore the letter open, and her eyes settled on the first words, "Dearest Becky." Her heart felt like it was stuck in her throat. Seeing her husband's words for the first time since learning of her father's death and her stepson's kidnapping brought home how much she missed Will. With her mother and Henrietta, a freedwoman who cooked and cleaned for the family, nearly always present, she was hardly alone. She'd never tell either of them how many times she had soaked her pillow with tears at Will's absence.

She continued reading, "I pray every day for you and your mother's comfort. Your father was my best friend, and I miss him terribly." She choked back a sob. Will had to be torn up over Charlie's kidnapping, but he took the time to tell her how much she was on his mind.

She blinked away the tears threatening to spill down her cheeks as she continued to read, "Given our heartache, I'm thankful to a merciful God that your mother is with you, that you may both be of comfort and strength to each other. Above nearly all other duties, I wish I could return home into your loving bosom now that peace is at hand, but I have hope that, with God before me, I will find the men who killed your father and kidnapped our son."

The dam broke, and the tears slid down her cheeks. Since her marriage to Will, his duties in the army had kept him away from home more than either of them would have liked, and she had been the only mother Charlie had. The woman who had given birth to him had sent the boy to live with his father after their divorce. Inside of the first year of marriage, Charlie had taken to calling her "Ma." She thought it generous of Will to acknowledge that bond.

Her tears concerned her mother, "Becky, is everything alright with Will?"

She nodded, and read the rest of the letter, "President Zavala is not happy with me, because I refuse to put Texas above my family. But, my love, you and the children are my Texas, without you I am nothing. I resigned my commission and am, by the time you read this, hot on the trail of our boy's kidnappers. Pray that I find success, my beloved Yellow Rose of Texas. Your loving husband, Will."

She handed the letter to her mother and grabbed a towel from the table, to dab her eyes. She had heard the story about how he had penned the song the soldiers loved to sing on the march about the yellow rose of Texas. He had said she was his inspiration for the song. She found comfort in knowing that even as he raced off in pursuit of Charlie's captors, she was still his inspiration.

That evening at the dinner table, Becky reread Will's letter for the dozenth time. Her mother said, "It's still the same words. Nothing's changed. Lordy, I hope he finds the boy soon."

With a hint of reproach in her voice, Becky said, "He'll be home in no more time than it takes to find Charlie, Ma. We've managed alright since he went away to war, we'll be fine until he comes home."

Elizabeth's smile was forced, "I'm sure we will, Becky. But those payments from the army aren't going to continue. What happens then?"

The idea that Will's monthly pay from the army would stop hadn't crossed her mind. Will had set up an account for the household at the Commerce Bank's San

Antonio branch. Becky had deposited his pay into that account since he rode south with the army. She was confident there was enough for several months.

She glanced over at Henrietta, who was washing dishes in the corner of the great room, in the kitchen. Henrietta's monthly wage was her single most significant expense. On Will's pay as general of the army, the twenty dollars she was paid was a small enough luxury. Becky's heart beat faster at the idea of losing Henrietta's help. With two small children under the age of four, her help was nearly indispensable. If she was careful with the money in the bank Hattie's employment shouldn't become an issue.

"If we need to tighten our belts a bit, I'm sure the three of us can figure it out." Elizabeth raised her eyebrows at Becky's remark. But as she wiped a pan dry, the relief on Henrietta's face was plain to see. Becky continued, "I'll go to the bank tomorrow and see how we're doing. If it takes a bit of time for Will to return, if any of the men Will's done business with owe him any money, I can collect." There was no doubt in her mind Will would agree with her.

Wind whipped the tops of the oak trees as rain lashed the riders. Will was drenched entirely, like the rest of the party, but he nudged his mount with his spurs. They had left the village of Concordia de San Sebastian earlier that morning, but dark clouds now raced across the sky, obliterating the sun.

The wind was fierce. As a native Galvestonian, he should have recalled September was the height of the hurricane season. He tossed his head, sending torrents of water onto his mount's neck. What would that matter? Would he have changed anything had he recalled the risk of hurricanes during the fall? No. He wouldn't have changed his mind. Behind the party, he heard a loud crash. He pulled the reins and looked behind. A large palm tree had toppled.

He cursed. The winds were growing stronger. They needed to seek shelter soon. If this was a full-blown hurricane, he knew the wind's power could continue rising until the lives of the men traveling with him would be at risk. He amended the thought, more at risk than they already were.

The former *Cazadore* lieutenant, Javier Morales cantered over to him, his poncho proving the limits of waterproofing, "General, we should seek shelter until this storm blows over" He had to shout to be heard.

Will scowled. As close as they were to the port of Mazatlán, he hated the rain. Apart from the raging storm, they would have arrived before nightfall. Now, it was anyone's guess how long the storm's fury would last. Through the din of the wind, he heard another tree topple nearby.

He sawed on the reins, bringing his mount to a stop on the muddy trail. "Very well, Lieutenant. Let's find a place to get out of this soup."

"The trail's blocked back to Concordia, sir. Maybe Lobo knows of a place." His voice was hesitant as the rain came down even harder. He nudged his horse forward. Lobo, the other Mexican traveling with the party, was riding point along with the Cherokee Ranger, Running Creek.

According to Morales, Lobo had lived in this part of Mexico before being conscripted into the army. As a streak of lightning raced across the sky, Will was hopeful he would know of a place to escape the worst of the storm.

Will had sat on his hat to keep it from blowing away as the rain and wind whipped his ginger hair, while he waited for Morales to return. "There's a place a couple of miles up the way, where the army used to keep a relay station. Lobo says if we can get there, we can ride out the storm."

The rain was doing a thorough job of turning the trail into a mire, and after pushing his mount only a couple of hundred yards more, Will was forced to dismount and lead the horse through the muck.

The rain stung his face and hands, as it blew across the valley sideways. Treetops whipped back and forth. Will wiped the water from his eyes as the world exploded in a bright flash, and then darkness. He heard a loud crash and a sharp cry. "Help!"

He blinked and slowly his sight returned, white spots swirling before him. He wrapped the reins around his hand as his horse reared up and pulled on them. Another horse bolted by him, terrified by the lightning bolt which had struck nearby. A few yards away a stump of a tree smoldered. The rest of its seventy-foot trunk had fallen across the road.

The plaintive voice cried out again. But Will heard the Mexican lieutenant over the din of the storm, "General, the tree has fallen on someone!"

Will raced back to the tree trunk lying across the trail. Morales was kneeling next to a prone figure. As he pushed through the wind and rain, Will saw Ranger Jethro Elkins. The tree had fallen across his legs, pinning them.

He heard footfalls and turned and saw the Cherokee, Running Creek and Lobo slogging through mud puddles. "Get some rope; we're going to try pulling this thing off of Jethro here."

More splashing and a moment later, Will slid the end of a rope around the trunk. Several inches separated the log from the trail. Elkins cursed as Lobo pulled on another rope tied around the tree, "Sweet Lord Above, man. Go easy on that tree. If you ain't noticed, my damned legs have taken up residence down there."

Will hoped Elkins wouldn't lose his legs. As he tied the other end of the rope to the saddle's pommel, the thought of losing one of their own only twenty days into the trek to find Charlie chilled him more than the drenching rain.

Four ropes tied to four saddles and a moment later, Will and the other men guided their horses until they pulled the lines tight. "Easy goes it." Morales still knelt by Elkins' side. Will ignored the wind and the rain, both of which were getting progressively worse. Walking beside his horse, he urged the animal to pull the rope. With the help of the other men and their mounts, he heard branches breaking and felt the tree trunk shift.

More swearing from Elkins cut through the din of the storm. "A bit more and I'll pull him free!" Morales shouted.

Another lurch forward and Morales called, "He's out!"

Will splashed back to Elkins. He was still on the ground. One of the other Rangers asked, "Can you feel your legs?"

"Yeah, Sergeant, they hurt like a sumbitch."

Will said, "Can you climb onto your horse?"

Elkins grimaced, "You trying to kill me, General?"

Morales offered, "Why not build a travois?"

Although it was midafternoon, it looked more like twilight. Will glanced at the sky. Every time he looked up, it was worse than before. "Cut some boughs from the tree. We'll lash the branches together."

Building the travois in the rain ranked down at the bottom of Will's experiences. He had endured some hellish situations in Iraq before the transference into William Travis' body, but this was worse. The hatchet he used to strip the smaller branches from a larger one was slick in his wet hands. If it slipped, he could really hurt himself.

He forced himself to slow down. The idea of injuring himself, and what that would mean for his search, scared him. He finished and tossed the stripped branch to Lobo, who was tying them together. Within minutes, they were back on the trail, slogging through ankle-deep water, following the intrepid Mexican *Cazadore*, as they guided the horse pulling the travois.

An hour later, a stone wall built to cover an overhang, loomed into view. They led their horses inside, and the last member of the party, Running Creek, had no sooner closed the door behind them when the storm grew even worse.

26 September 1843

"How well did you say you knew these fellows?" Jenkins asked Williams as they stood outside a tavern in the port of Charleston. The building was run-down and reeked of stale sweat and fish, but at the moment, it was quiet. He sniffed at the offending smells. Evidently, its usual patrons were still at sea.

“Me and Zeke go back years, boss. We grew up in Charleston,” Williams said.

Jenkins cast a sidelong look at the smaller man. What was unsaid was more important than what was said. Before Williams had joined up with Jenkins, Jackson, and Zebulon, he had been one step ahead of the Charleston district sheriff. Of course, that was more than a dozen years before.

“We need a place to put the boy. It’s going to take a few days before he’ll be ready to travel. Wouldn’t have this problem if you hadn’t cut him so bad.”

Williams shrugged, “Wouldn’t have happened if he hadn’t tried to warn that Marine.”

"Come on, let's go see if your friend can find a place for us."

The tavern was old, but it didn't smell as bad inside as out. Large windows looked onto the street leading to the wharves. Jenkins had expected a dark and dingy bar area, but the taproom was well lit and airy from the open windows. An old slave, hair long gone to gray, was cleaning glass mugs in a bucket of soapy water, under the indifferent supervision of the barkeep.

Only one of the tables was occupied. An unkempt man, whose black hair seemed determined to flee into the rafters, nursed a glass of warm beer. As Jenkins approached, he saw the man's jacket had once been a vibrant forest green. It was now faded to nearly a dingy black. "Hell's bells, Hiram, I'd a thought you be hung by now."

“I was the hare, and the sheriff was the turtle. I was halfway to Saint Augustine before he hit the district line." Williams laughed as he took a seat across from the man. "Ob, this here rapscallion is Thomas Jefferson Hamilton."

Hamilton extended his hand. Jenkins had shaken hands with worse men, and he shook the proffered hand as he sat. "Hiram tell you we need a quiet place to rest?"

"Yeah. You're not on the run, are you?"

Williams's laughter sounded like a braying donkey. "Not so as you'd know it, T.J."

There was a glimmer of something in Hamilton's eyes that made Jenkins nervous. Hamilton said, "If you're still working your confidence games on folks, I might could help steer you in the right direction. The law ain't too particular about a bit of card playing."

Jenkins realized he had been holding his breath. He planned to be well hidden in the Carolina backcountry before news of Charlie's kidnapping and ransom became widespread. He exhaled as he grasped Hamilton only wanted to work a con with Williams.

When he had been in California, he had thought the hardest part of kidnapping the boy would be traversing eight thousand miles, but as he neared his goal of the Carolina backcountry, worry had begun to set in. What if someone found out while they were hiding in Charleston? Sure, General Travis would find very few friends in Charleston, but folks who thought themselves better than him could turn on him. "No," he thought, "It doesn't matter how crazy Travis' abolitionist views may be, those Holier-than-Thou, well-to-do Charlestonians, resting their fat asses in their pews would turn on me quicker than a blue tick hound could tree a coon."

Realizing he had been woolgathering, Jenkins said, "Can you find us a place for a few days? Just long enough for me to contact some friends of mine."

"I'm sure something can be arranged," Hamilton said. "For the right price."

Chapter 5

1 October 1843

"Don't that beat all?" Andy Berry said as he and Gail Borden entered Borden's laboratory. "How many orders did we take for the NPC?"

Borden cocked his head? "NPC?"

"Nitrogenated processed cotton. But that's a mouthful."

Borden set the booklet of orders on a table and chuckled. Over the past few months, the twenty-seven-year-old son of John Berry had turned into a valuable, if infrequent, assistant. Usually, he worked at the Trinity Gun Works, just a few hundred yards away from Borden's lab. Berry's interest in his gun-cotton experiments had led the younger man to experiment with using the explosive in the rifles his family produced for the army.

A few months before, it had led the young man to create a small bomb which he detonated under a stump. Despite the instability of the nitrogenated gun cotton, Berry's test had revealed a commercial use for the explosive. According to the Texas Land Bank, more than two million acres were under cultivation across East Texas. Clearing a field involved the time-intensive labor to remove stumps. The larger the tree, the more likely a stump became an obstacle a farmer just worked around.

He must have said that aloud. Berry nodded. "Not anymore. For a few dollars, a farmer can buy enough NPC and blow that stump to hell and gone."

In the back of his mind, Borden worried about the military application of the new explosive. Now, it was merely a new product sold to farmers and miners. But in time, there was no doubt they would harness the explosive as a weapon. He tuned out Berry, who was talking about the demonstration earlier that day as well as the money and the orders collected afterward. The entire enterprise had been started from a mishap in a hospital when his friend, Ashbel Smith, had accidentally mixed nitric and sulfuric acids together. The rag he had used to clean up the mess had spontaneously exploded after it dried. The results were too significant not to pursue, but with the army preparing to march into Mexico, Smith had enlisted Borden's help in experimenting with the unstable mixture.

Berry's words cut through, "Mr. Borden, I'm still not sure how we're going to take the next steps. I've taken the milled powder from the gun cotton and experimented with our rifles, but nothing I've done, from cutting the loads to putting them in metal cartridges has made a difference. Eventually, the stress on the rifle is too great."

Berry had been complaining of this issue since shortly after the first milled gun-cotton. Borden said, "Your iron is too weak. What are you doing to strengthen it?"

Berry set the papers down and used the table as a seat, "We melt the iron ore down and then use the water-powered hammers to hammer out the steel and then rollers to mold the iron into the barrels and other metal parts for each gun. Then we use the machines to drill the barrels and rifle them, as well as to cut the individual metal parts. We'd need to change the process to get stronger metal."

Borden tilted his head in agreement. "How?"

"Damned if I know. But it's something I'll discuss with our other gunsmiths. The method we use to roll our iron isn't the only method out there."

The laboratory was well illuminated, with windows every few feet on the walls. It saved on the amount of oil used to light the lamps. Borden crossed over to the nearest window. An extensive clearing ran between the lab and the test range. A tarp covered a large gun. "What about the artillery? Any luck with our gun cotton yet?"

Berry joined him and looked at the covered gun. "You know the reason General Travis bought all of the army's field guns from the United States?"

When Borden shook his head, he continued, "as early as last year there were no cannon makers west of the Mississippi." He pointed to the gun. "Not anymore."

Having read about Mexican artillery in the recent war, Borden said, "Mexico had several hundred guns. Surely they have some manufacturing?"

Berry laughed derisively. "Either left over from their days under Spain or imported from England. John

Bull was happy to sell all that surplus equipment they didn't need after they sent Napoleon into exile. Most of the guns were worn from heavy use before the Mexicans ever put it into service."

Berry continued, "That's the fourth gun we've cast here. Its bored for three-inch ordinance. It's the first gun we've manufactured I've succeeded at using the milled NPC in."

Arching his eyebrows, Borden said, "Really? How many rounds?"

Berry grinned like a little boy giving away a secret, "Over a hundred."

"Bless my soul," Borden said. "What about the other three guns?"

Berry's voice turned sheepish. "We melted them down for their bronze after they blew up."

A few days later in San Antonio

Becky stared at the shopping list. If she could find everything on it, she might avoid the need to venture onto Alameda Street for a bit. She shifted the baby from one hip to the other while her toddler, Liza pulled on her dress.

"Missus Becky, why don't you hand little Davy to me?" Henrietta, following a pace behind with a burlap bag in hand, offered. The little boy was still a couple of months shy of his first birthday, but like all Travis men, she thought, he was big for his age.

With an apologetic smile, she handed him over. "Thanks."

As she walked along the dusty street, she thought about the change Will had made to her life. She had grown up in western Tennessee among hard-working farmers and frontiersmen. Very few of her neighbors had been able to own a slave. Who had three hundred dollars to buy one?

She glanced back at Henrietta and realized how much she missed Will. He had employed the freedwoman before Becky had married him and she had learned of his disdain for the South's peculiar institution. To a young woman from hardscrabble Tennessee, his views were an oddity, but as she became familiar with Henrietta, not merely as a worker, but as a person, Becky began to appreciate Will's views.

She found herself standing before a sturdy brick building, one of the first red-bricked ones in a town full of brown adobe. A sign overhead declared it to be the San Antonio branch of the Commerce Bank. Will had partnered with some financier from Galveston named Williams to establish the first private bank in Texas a few years earlier. From the lone office on Galveston Island, it had grown to several more branches across the Republic, in Houston, San Antonio, and Austin.

As she led her little troop into the bank, her eyes took a moment to adjust. Sitting in a chair, next to the door was a guard. That was new. Slowly men were trickling back into jobs across the country as militia and reserve units were demobilized. He tipped his hat to her.

"Mrs. Travis!" a voice from within the gloom called out, "welcome. What can I do for you?"

As her eyes finished adjusting, she saw an older gentleman standing behind the counter. Iron bars ran from the countertop to the ceiling. "Mr. Higgins, how are you?"

“I’ve been worse. My rheumatiz is acting up again. Wouldn’t be surprised if we get a norther afore long. Would you like to deposit the general’s pay?”

Becky put on a brave face. "I'm afraid the general has resigned. Our son, Charlie, is in a spot of trouble, and Will has gone to fetch him."

The teller reached his gnarled hand through the bars and placed it gently on her own. "I'd heard about your son, ma'am. My Martha told me that she and her friends were praying for him. I'll make sure she knows the general needs their prayers, too."

“I need to withdraw our funds,” Becky said.

“Would that be five or ten dollars?”

Becky’s eyes widened, “We’ve got plenty in the account. Why so little?”

“I’m expecting more money to come from Galveston shortly, ma’am. But for the next few days, we’re limiting withdrawals so that folks with accounts still have access to some of their deposited money.”

Shocked, Becky said, “What has happened, Mr. Higgins? You’ve never been short of money before.”

The old man blushed. Then he said to the guard, “Pete, close the door and lock it.” Once Becky heard the lock snick into place, he continued, “I really shouldn’t say anything, but seeing as your husband is the bank’s largest shareholder, I suppose you should know. Mr. Williams has been using some of the deposits to buy the government war bonds. In the past, he’s been able to borrow directly from the Commodities Bureau if capital ran short. But now that the war is as good as over, the Secretary of the Treasury, Menard, won’t extend new loans.”

Horrified by the news, Becky said, "What is Mr. Williams going to do about this? I need to feed my children."

Higgins quailed before her as her voice rose. "Now, Mrs. Travis, you can withdraw ten dollars today, and next week, another ten if the bank's capital situation hasn't improved. But rest assured, once this matter is resolved, you'll have access to the entire balance."

Becky shook her head as tears ran unbidden down her cheeks. She took the money and hurried away.

That evening, after she had bathed and put the children to bed, Becky sat at the dinner table. Her mother sat at one end, and Henrietta sat at the other end. A pot of coffee and several mugs were in the center. Around her, Becky had spread Will's ledger of the family's expenses, bills, and receipts.

"It's late, Becky, why don't we send Henrietta home?" said Elizabeth.

Becky shook her head, "This concerns Hatti, too." She turned to the freedwoman, "I'd like it if you'd stay, but the choice is yours."

Henrietta smiled shyly and retrieved a mug and poured herself a cup of coffee. "Thank you, Missus Becky. I'd like to stay. Joe's been running supplies out to Ysleta, and it's just me at home. What y'all decide's gonna matter to me."

Becky picked up a mug and hid her smile behind it. Her mother had taken Will's views on slavery in her stride, but folks had their places, and she was a bit put out that Becky had included Henrietta like an equal.

"I've been looking over our expenses, and frankly I'm worried sick. The bank is short of money, and I honestly don't know when we'll get the money in the account. I've pulled the money from the egg jar and added it to the pittance from the bank. We've only got forty dollars to make it until the bank decides to provide a few more breadcrumbs."

She lowered her head into her hands and cried. "Oh, God, how I miss Will."

Her mother reached across the table and took her hand, "We'll manage. We Crockett women always have. Lord love your pa, but my David didn't know how to manage money, and as God is my witness, I managed to keep a roof over your heads when you and your brother and sister were young. We'll make do."

Henrietta nodded, "Amen."

Becky tried to smile through the tears. "Between our food, the note Will's been paying on this house, the cost of liverying our horses, clothes for the children and wages," she paused as she waved her hand over the bills and in a stereotypical Crockett way, said, "we've got too much month at the end of our money."

Elizabeth said, "How much gets paid to livery the horses?"

Becky sorted through a stack of receipts until she found the one for which she was looking. She whistled appreciatively, "Ma, we're in the wrong profession. We're paying Señor Lopez twenty dollars each month to stable two horses."

"Land's sake. That's highway robbery."

Until she and the children had been deprived of Will's army pay, it hadn't seemed significant at all. His salary was more than three hundred dollars each month. He used some of it to supplement the officers' mess, but most of it was used to support Becky and the children.

Henrietta earned twenty dollars per month. Becky had long thought it was a generous salary for a freedwoman, but the wage had been agreed to by Will before their marriage, and the truth was, she earned every penny.

Becky mused, "I wonder what kind of a price Señor Lopez would give us if we sold him one of the horses?"

"A good horse would fetch more than a hundred dollars," Elizabeth said. "But what would Will say if you do it?"

Without batting an eye, Becky said, "He'd want me to take care of our family, Ma. If I have to sell the horses or even the house, so that we have a place to sleep and my babies have food in their bellies, he'd tell me well done."

Elizabeth gave a sharp look at the end of the table, where both women had heard another faint, "Amen." It was all Becky could do to keep from laughing.

Before her mother could respond, Becky said, "Will's got investments and money tied up in that farm on the Trinity River. I'll send a letter and ask about any payments he may be due."

Forgetting her displeasure, Elizabeth said, "Will's been a general since the end of the revolution. Surely the military owes him a pension now. I can think of several men in Austin you could ask"

Becky's eyes lit up, "Oh, Ma, you're right. I'm sure Will's got friends that could help me get his pension." She smacked her hand on the table, making the other women jump in surprise. "Once we sell one of the horses, I'll take the stage to Austin and ask for Señor Seguin's help."

Elizabeth reached over and rested her hand on Becky's, "I'll pray that Erasmo can help, dear."

From the other end of the table, Henrietta echoed, "Amen."

Chapter 6

5 October 1843

Charlie scratched at the bandage around his neck. Elizondo Jackson had told him the wound would itch as it healed. As if he needed anything else over which to resent his kidnappers, the only doctoring that was done to the gash on his neck was provided by Jackson.

While the half-breed had cleaned the cut, he had told Charlie, "I've cut myself worse shaving." The worst of the doctoring had come when he had poured whiskey into the wound, and that, only after he had given the boy several swigs of the potent liquor. Charlie had writhed in pain, clenching his teeth on a small wooden dowel. He hadn't been in a forgiving mood when his captor had said, "I've patched all of us up at one time or another. If it makes you feel better, I've stitched up Hiram more than the rest of us combined."

The other men had been preparing to leave the ship when they had come into Charleston harbor. Charlie had been alone with Jackson. Generally guarded around his kidnappers, the whiskey must have had an effect on him, "I hate him so much. I wish he was dead."

"Get in line, kid. He's a mean one. Try to stay clear of him while this is healing."

Ten days later and Charlie had to admit, Jackson seemed to have done a tolerable job on stitching him up. Staying clear of Williams was harder to do. Charlie was convinced the little gambler enjoyed tormenting him whenever there was an opportunity. But since they had been taken in by an old associate of Williams, Charlie had shared a small room with Jackson and Jenkins, and his dealings with Williams had been blessedly few.

The door swung open, and Jenkins came in. Jackson set a carving he had been working on down. "Any luck?"

Charlie felt the older man's eyes fall on him for a moment and saw a look of calculation before he responded, "Finally. Hiram found Jason this morning at the docks. Said he'd been waiting on some furniture for Saluda Groves to come in. He'll be heading back tomorrow, and we'll join him."

Jackson went back to his carving, but stopped as a fleck of wood fell on the floor, "How many days till we get there?"

Another glance at Charlie and Jenkins shook his head, "I'll tell you later."

The next morning Charlie was jolted awake by the slamming of a door, and then Williams and Zebulon crowded into the room. Williams said, "Mr. Lamont's ready. He's got his wagons close at hand."

Williams gave him an evil grin as he strode over to the sleeping mat and jerked Charlie up by his collar. His hands brushed against the bandages around his neck, and a wave of pain and nausea washed over him.

"Not a word, boy. I'll finish what I started if you're louder than a church mouse."

As the pain subsided, he found Jackson holding him up on the other side. "What the hell would you know of a church mouse, Hiram? The last time you went to church, you stole the communion set and locked the priest in the confessional."

Williams flashed a smile, "He had it coming."

Manhandled by the two men, Charlie was hustled out of the room and outside. The road was dark. The good folk of Charleston saw no reason to place street lamps along a stretch of road with such run-down houses.

Two large freight wagons filled the road. Atop the first sat a well-dressed man of middle years. Next to him sat a man whose skin was dark as coal. Another white man sat on the second wagon's seat. He wasn't as well dressed as the first. Another black man was perched next to him.

Jenkins waved, "Morning, Jason. Ready to roll?"

The well-dressed man said, "There's been a change of plans, Obadiah. We'll take the train to Columbia. I don't fancy being on the road with you and your cargo for the next ten days."

Jenkins appeared confused, "What cargo?"

"The boy. Last night a schooner put in from New Orleans. Seems someone's been holding out on me."

While he detested Jenkins for the horror of the past couple of months, Charlie begrudgingly admired the staged look of confusion Jenkins wore. "I've done nothing of the sort, Mr. Lamont. I told you we needed a place where folks didn't cotton to abolitionist views, where we'd be safe. Surely you understood a need such as ours had its reasons."

"Reasons, yes. I figured you might have kicked up a catawampus with some abolitionists in the North. Hell, man, you've kidnapped the son of the biggest abolitionist in Texas. That's no mean thing."

Jenkins' studied look of confusion was replaced by alarm, "Shhh. Do you want our business to be the talk of Charleston today? We had a deal, sir. Will you honor it?"

Lamont held a horse whip and used it to point at Jenkins. "My honor is good, Mr. Jenkins. Would that I could say the same about yours. You've flown a false flag, asking for sanctuary."

Jenkins became angry, "Don't play that game with me, Mr. Lamont. I told you what you needed to know. What you didn't know you couldn't tell. Do we still have an understanding?"

"Fifty thousand dollars? You're a bold man. I'm of a mind to wish you well and send you on your way."

A calculating look came over Jenkins, "But you'll not be doing that. How much?"

"The reward must match the risk, which is great. I'll shelter you and make sure the boy's whereabouts remain secure."

"How much?"

"Twenty-five thousand."

Jenkins cursed. "That's highway robbery!"

From his perch on the wagon's seat, Lamont's laughter sounded like a braying donkey. "That's rich. Don't talk to me of robbery, given your own sins. Take it or leave it."

"You've got me over a barrel, Mr. Lamont. But if our refuge is compromised, you'll pay old scratch his due before us."

Lamont gave a single nod. "That won't happen. My men will see to that. Load the boy in the second wagon. We've got a train to catch."

6 October 1843

The port of Los Angeles didn't look like much, Will thought. A single building was visible from the ship's pilot house. From where he stood next to the ship's wheel, the flag flying over the building was little more than a speck. Even though his time as general was over, he found himself wondering about what the 9th Infantry had been up to since arriving in California a few months earlier.

David Crockett's second-in-command, Major Henry McCulloch would be in charge of the 9th. If Crockett had followed the plan he created, the Major would command a force of seven or eight hundred men. Will would learn soon enough. The Mexican captain of the merchant schooner, *Maria Teresa,* was waiting for clearance to use the sole dock. Will and his party had brought their horses from Mazatlán. He was uncertain where the kidnappers had gone since leaving Los Angeles. The only report was a ship had taken them away, one step ahead of Crockett's men. If the kidnappers were somewhere along the Pacific coast, better for Will's men to keep their horses, he thought.

As he waited for the port's pilot to bring them permission to dock, Will looked over his men. Jesse Running Creek, the Spanish speaking Cherokee, was playing a card game with Jethro Elkins. A crutch lay beside the mustachioed Ranger. The tree which fell on his legs during the cyclone broke one of them. A doctor in Mazatlán had told them he was lucky it was a clean break. Once he had set it, he tied a splint around the break and told him to stay off it for a couple of months.

Will's instincts were focused on finding Charlie. An injured man, even one as resourceful as Elkins, was a liability. When he asked Lieutenant Morales about the care Elkins would receive, the former Cazadores officer said, "A Texian stranded here, once word of the peace treaty reaches Mazatlán, would face danger. Take him with us."

"Us?" Will asked. "You and Lobo's assistance has been a blessing, Lieutenant. But you only agreed to travel with us to Mazatlán. You've done more than I could have asked."

Morales flushed at the compliment. "If it's all the same to you, I'd like to continue."

"Why?"

Morales picked his words with care, "Things here are likely to become uncertain. My men and I could be viewed as deserters if the government decided to make an issue of it. As interesting as it is traveling with you, it might still be safer than returning home."

Will smiled at the memory. Morales and Lobo were next to the gunwales amidships, fishing poles hanging over the railing. After fighting the Mexican army in a bitter contest for land, he still found the idea surreal that two of their party had once been part of General Almonte's elite riflemen. But any doubts he possessed had been blown away on a washed-out trail east of Mazatlán.

The last members of the party were overseeing the collection of gear on the deck. Sergeant Jensen and

Ranger LeBlanc were collecting saddles and other accouterments from the hold. Over the past few weeks, Will had come to understand what Jack Hays saw in Sergeant Maartin Jenson. The old soldier was a steady hand. During the cyclone, the sergeant's calm demeanor helped to steady all the men as they worked to free Elkins from under the tree.

A boat bumped against the hull, a moment later the ship's captain said, "We're clear to dock, General."

A few hours later, Will stood outside the city attorney's office, where Major McCulloch had established the office of military governor. A wooden shingle hung on the door. It read, *Oficina de Síndico Procurador.* At some point, someone had painted the text in gold leaf, which was now flaking. Below that, another shingle had been hung. In plain black ink, it read, *Texas Military Governor*.

Will rapped on the door. Nothing. He knocked louder. Still, nothing. A moment later a soldier in the butternut uniform of the Texian army came around the corner of the building and stopped when he saw Will and his companions.

Will didn't recognize the private. The army had ballooned in size since the previous year. A thousand faces had been nearly impossible to recall, ten thousand would have required a miracle, and Will didn't walk on water. "Where's Major McCulloch?"

The soldier eyed the men before him. Will had to concede, his volunteers were a motley crew. He and the Rangers wore the same uniform jacket as the private, but there the resemblance ended. Will's once black wide-brimmed hat held little resemblance to its original regulation shape or color. The Rangers wore whatever headgear they had been able to find along the route as their hats fell apart. The former *Cazadores* had long since replaced their navy-blue jackets. In Mexico, it might have marked them as deserters or bandits, now in Texian California, it would have raised more questions than Will had the patience to answer.

"Uh, he expecting you?"

The thirst for information about Charlie's kidnappers made Will's temper short. He snapped, "Fetch him now. Tell him General William Travis is waiting on him."

The private stared at Will for several seconds before deciding the situation was above his pay grade, and said, "Yes, sir."

Minutes passed. Will was pacing in front of the office, battling his impatience when an officer came around the corner. Will's eyes fell on the shoulder strap, where he saw the golden oak leaf. "Major McCulloch?"

The clean-shaven major bore a passing resemblance to his brother, Brigadier General Ben McCulloch, whom Will knew well. "General Travis," McCulloch's voice held a note of uncertainty, "I thought you were down south in Mexico."

Will struggled to put a smile on his face as he mentally tamped down his impatience. "Some bastards have kidnapped my son and killed my father-in-law, Major." Will nodded toward the door, "Why don't you offer a bit of Texian hospitality and we can talk."

Blushing, McCulloch unlocked the office. Will accepted a glass of an amber liquid as he settled into a chair. He took a sip, and the fiery liquor burned his throat. "What can you tell me of the attack on my father-in-law?"

McCulloch said, "We're not really sure what to make of it, sir. The party that killed the president had their hands in forged land titles. Mostly petty stuff like that. I looked around the room where President Crockett was killed, and I have to tell you, I'm not sure they went in to kill him."

Will set the glass down after a second sip, "Are you saying they were trying to capture him?"

"No. President Crockett was beaten pretty bad before he was shot. I think your son was the target."

Will felt like a stake had been driven through his heart. "My son? What the hell would a group of forgers want with Charlie? That doesn't make any sense."

McCulloch dipped his head, "Oh, I agree. No matter how much it doesn't make any sense, it's where the arrow keeps pointing. We interviewed several Californios who saw the bandits rowing out to a ship in the bay. They saw a youth with a burlap bag over his head being manhandled by the men who killed the president. Can you think of any reason they'd want to kidnap your son?"

Will's shoulders sagged, "Since I first read your report, I've been wracking my brain, why anyone would want to hurt Charlie unless they're trying to get to me?"

"Colonel Crockett said you made a few enemies when you all were putting together the constitution. Quite a few of the delegates favored more protections for our peculiar institution. You've got your share of enemies."

"Robert Potter and James Collinsworth may be ardent supporters of slavery, but both of them had managed to work with David when they were in Congress. They might hate me, but kidnapping Charlie like they're some kind of Comanche Warband isn't their style."

"Hold on," McCulloch said. "Why do the Comanche kidnap folks?"

Will shrugged, "I suppose to expand their tribe or to extract a ransom from us."

McCulloch's chuckle held no warmth. "I think we can dispense with the first. But what if the purpose is to ransom the boy?"

For a moment, Will hated the young major. The idea of Charlie being a pawn to get at Will had been his greatest fear. Hearing McCulloch put words to that fear scared him. The plains tribes, like the Comanche or the Apache, had kidnapped to expand the tribe or to extort a ransom. In the years since his transference, he had never heard of a child being abducted by white renegades. Gangs kidnapping for ransom was a twentieth-century crime.

Will rested his head in his hands as he was forced to accept the probability of the reason for the kidnapping. "Dear God, how do I get him back?" Was it a prayer or a question? Even Will couldn't answer.

"I don't know if this will help," ventured McCulloch. "The *Orion* is a merchant schooner that has sailed a Pacific route between Panama City and San Francisco for a few years now. Captain Palmer commands the ship."

Will perked up at the news. "That's something. Has anyone seen Palmer or his ship?"

The major spread his hands, "No one has passed anything along to me, yet. But this morning a ship has anchored in the harbor, a US warship. The *USS Cyane*. Talk to the captain before you plan your next step."

The next morning, Will climbed onto the deck of the *USS Cyane*. Captain Thomas Jones stood aft of the ship's wheel, "You asked to speak with me?"

For the first time since his transference into the body of William Barret Travis, Will stood on US territory. After seven long years, he was surprised by his own indifference. Fleetingly, he recalled a conversation he'd had with the driver of the Humvee while they'd been driving in convoy in Iraq. He had told his driver, he'd love to see what Texas would have looked like if it had never joined the United States.

As he strode across the deck, he stifled a smile. Things for an independent Texas were certainly looking up. Then the idea of Charlie being forced into a boat focused his attention on the reason for his visit. "Captain Jones, my name is William Travis. Major McCulloch indicated you might have news of a ship called the *Orion.*"

The naval captain's eyes widened at Will's name before he grimaced. "Nasty business that. We heard about Davy Crockett's death. You're looking for your boy?"

The irony that his father-in-law had hated being called *Davy* wasn't lost on Will. But he suspected the legends that had been common in the world Will knew from his own childhood would pale in comparison to how Texas would eventually eulogize the first president of the Republic.

"Yes. What word do you have of the *Orion*?"

Captain Jones' eyes swept toward the open water beyond the bay, "Before putting into port here, we patrolled up the coast all the way up to Port George, where we showed the flag to John Bull. I made a note in the ship's log of all ships we've seen, and we haven't seen that one in several months."

Will was alarmed by the news, "What does that mean? Did they go into hiding?"

Jones wagged his head, "Not likely. While there are a dozen rivers a ship could go up, there's nothing up those rivers other than a few fur trading camps. Have you considered Panama City as a place your son's captors may have gone? It's the quickest way back east."

Will wanted nothing more than to scream in rage at the men who kidnapped his son. All he could do was shake his head. "Not yet. I guess I'll head that way next."

Will turned to leave, but a word from Jones stopped him. "If I might, General Travis." Will wore no markings on the well-worn butternut jacket of his former rank. The American officer chuckled at Will's surprised look. "What American hasn't heard of the victor of the Battle of the Rio Grande?"

Will smiled ruefully as Jones guided him to the ship's port side. "In the past when we put in here, we'd routinely refill our water-casks under the watchful eyes of the Mexican garrison. A bit of silver traded hands, and both governments officially looked away. Now that California is under new governance, I wonder if I might offer something a bit more valuable than a bit of silver for water." The officer paused for what Will thought might be dramatic effect, "My patrol route usually takes me down to the isthmus of Panama. If it would help your quest, I'd happily give up space on my ship for you and your companions in exchange for water."

Will was stunned by the offer. While Texas had enjoyed excellent relations with the United States since before the Clay administration, he hadn't expected such a proposal.

"How will you explain that to your superiors?"

"If they even bother asking, I'll just tell them the truth. I was assisting you in hunting down pirates."

Will blinked back tears. The offer nearly overwhelmed him. He had worried about how to get on the kidnappers' trail, and Captain Jones offered what he considered a fair trade. Despite a voice brimming with emotion, he said, "Thank you."

Chapter 7

Charlie shifted in his seat. His backside was sore from the six hours on the train. He felt as if the walls of the passenger railcar were closing in on him as he was squeezed between Jackson and Jenson on the narrow wooden bench. The seating arrangement wasn't of his choosing, but it beat sitting next to Williams. He'd prefer being thrown into the locomotive's firebox than sitting next to the vicious man.

He closed his eyes and the image of being thrown into the firebox, added to the continuous rocking motion of the railcar lulled him into a stupor. He dreamed he was one of the three children of Israel being cast into the mighty furnace because he refused to bow down and worship Nebuchadnezzar's golden idol. In the dream, the fire licked around his feet, and he turned and looked at the Babylonian king. Leering back at him was Hiram Williams. "Burn, boy! You'll burn before your pa comes for you!"

Charlie jolted awake and looked around the car. Williams was across the aisle, looking out the window at farmland passing by. "Watch it, kid." Jackson edged away. Charlie sucked in a large gulp of air. *"It was just a dream."* Only a dream? The furnace's heat had seemed so real, at least until Williams appeared. He shuddered at the memory.

Coming down the aisle was Jason Lamont, "Train'll be in Columbia in a few minutes. Once the slaves have unloaded the supplies, we'll be on our way."

Charlie heard the squeak of the iron wheels as the train slowed. The teenager leaned forward and looked out the window. He saw tall wooden poles, evenly spaced every so often. He recognized them. He had seen them first when he was still little, running around the Alamo, back when his Uncle Davy had agreed to be an incubator for Samuel Morse's new telegraph. Nowadays, the wires connected San Antonio to Austin. It looked like the inventor's technology was quickly following the railroads.

"End of the line," the conductor said as he swayed down the aisle. "If you leave anything behind, you've contributed to the South Carolina Railroad Conductors' pension fund."

Once the train lurched to a stop, Charlie was hustled from the train by his captors. His skin crawled when he heard Williams voice softly in his ear. "Make a noise, and I'll open you like a gutted deer."

Despite the fear Williams tried to instill in Charlie, what the boy could see of the city from the railroad platform looked nothing like San Antonio. He was used buildings clad in brown adobe. Clapboard and red brick buildings sprawled away from the station. The town, while not any more significant than San Antonio, felt different. San Antonio's architecture borrowed heavily from its Spanish colonial past, while Columbia carried a hint of self-awareness at its status as the capital of the Palmetto state.

Another difference was the sheer number of slaves. He was fifteen, and no stranger to slavery. As men had immigrated to the western parts of Texas, a few had brought their slaves with them. As one member of their congregation had told his pa, "A gentleman needs his servants." Even then, slaves were a small part of San Antonio's population.

Columbia was a different world. Other than a few men, like Jason Lamont, who watched over the men unloading the wagons from the freight cars, nearly everyone on the platform was black.

Before long, Zebulon thrust Charlie into one of the wagons, and he heard whips crack over the backs of the mules. The heavy wagon pitched forward, and the boy barely avoided falling into Jackson, who sat beside him.

After he righted himself, he leaned against the side of the wagon and looked at the land they passed through. Townhomes gave way to small farms. Charlie watched families working to get in the harvest. On some farms, he saw the farmers and their families working alongside slaves. The further away from town the wagons rolled, the larger the farms became.

The road ran through one such farm. A whitewashed railing ran along both sides of the lane and slaves were hard at work in the field. There were men, women, and children and each had a burlap bag tied to the waist. They slowly walked along the rows of cotton, picking bolls, and stuffing them in the bag.

A horse cantered up to the wagon. Jason Lamont said to Jenkins, who was sitting on the bench, "Some of the best farmland in the Midlands, and it's mine."

He pointed to the fields, "All that cotton, it's mine too. All them niggers, they're also mine. Everything you see around you is mine. I've got the power to keep you safe from any outside interference while arranging things with General Travis."

Charlie was bone tired from the long day spent on the railroad and then on the wagons, but he tried to stay awake as he recalled the moment when Lamont had taken them to the slaves' quarters and pointed to an empty cabin, "You and your prisoner will stay there for now."

Jenkins had been too stunned to respond, and now after several slaves had cleaned the cabin, he said, "Damn him if he thinks he can treat us like this and still demand half the ransom."

Jackson looked around the room, "Well, Ob, it ain't as bad as those little rooms onboard the boats."

Jackson dodged the thrown hat. "It's the principal of the matter, Eli. Lamont's saying we're no better than the darkies working in his field."

Charlie retreated from the men to a pallet on the dirt floor. "*No*," he thought, as he wrapped a threadbare woolen blanket around him, "*these poor wretched slaves are far better than you'll ever be*." Exhausted, he fell asleep.

20 September 1843

The bells in the tower of San Fernando were chiming noon as Becky and Elizabeth left the Methodist church with Liza in tow and little David asleep in Becky's arms. The worst of summer was over; the temperature was only warm, instead of scorching hot. Even so, dust swirled around the hem of her dress as she walked down the street.

"Pastor Calvert was on fire today," Elizabeth said as she guided the eighteen-month-old toddler along the road.

"True, but I enjoy it more when he talks about love. Repentance is all well and good, Mother, but the folks most in need of that sermon don't usually darken the door of the church."

Elizabeth scooped up Liza as the little girl tried to run toward a horse tied to a hitching post. "I thought it was nice the pastor prayed for Charlie's safe return."

Becky bobbed her head as David stirred. "I'll be all the happier when Will and Charlie return."

She stopped in her tracks as they drew even with the Commerce Bank. The doors were closed tight, but something white caught her eye. "Hold on."

With that, she stepped over to the doors and read the note posted on the window. A moment later, she slowly returned to her mother, tears running down her face. "Lord have mercy. I wish to God, the pastor had said a prayer for us. The bank's closed all next week."

Later, when they had returned home, while they were preparing dinner, Elizabeth said, "There's not enough money next month for you to pay Hatti's wage. What are you going to do?"

Becky set a knife down on the table where she had been slicing a loaf of bread Henrietta had made the previous day. "Again? Ma, If she were working today would you say anything? I'm not going to get rid of her. Her husband is hundreds of miles away, delivering supplies to our soldiers out west. She needs this job as much as we need her help."

"Where are we going to find the money? With the bank's closure, we ain't got two pennies to rub together."

Becky giggled, "Balderdash. Ain't none of us going to go hungry, at least not this week."

Elizabeth smiled sheepishly. "You know what I mean. You need to make some hard decisions and do it soon."

Becky placed a thick slice of bread, smothered in a jam in front of Liza. "I know. I'm of a mind to talk to Mr. Garza at the stables about buying one of the horses. You said a good one would sell for a hundred dollars or more. If I can get close to that, we'll have enough money to weather the next month or two. Will should be back by then."

Elizabeth said, "Heavens, if I had a dollar for every time I thought David would come through the door, I'd be richer than the queen of England."

Becky teared up. The last thing she could imagine was Will staying gone longer than necessary. Despite her husband's duty in the army, he had been everything she could have wished. When in San Antonio he had spent as much time at home as his responsibilities allowed. The tears overflowed and ran down her cheeks.

"Oh, dear. As much as your Will doted on my David, the two men are as different as they can be, Becky," Elizabeth said when she saw the tears flow. "Your man will be home as soon as possible."

Becky dabbed her eyes. She smiled through her tears, "I know, Ma. But until then, we have to soldier on. Tomorrow, I'll go see Mr. Garza and see if he can give us a fair price on one of the horses. Once that's done, I'll go visit Señor Seguin. I'll get Will's pension paid, and we'll manage until he returns."

***

Becky took the carpetbag from the stagecoach driver with a murmured, "Thank you," and hurried toward the hotel. With every step, her relief increased. How Will managed to travel so much was a mystery to her. Twelve hours of hell is what she thought of it. There were six seats in the coach, and all of them were occupied. Most of her fellow travelers had been pleasant or aloof. Either was okay with her. The husband and wife Baptist missionaries had been chatty. Overly much, in Becky's opinion. A young officer from the Alamo garrison had also been onboard. If he had said more than a dozen words the entire trip she hadn't heard them.

The fifth passenger had been an elderly clerk returning to Austin. He had alternated between taciturn and conversational. He had eventually explained he had been auditing the Alamo garrison's finances for the Treasury Department. "Quite boring," he had said. "It only gets interesting when I find irregularities. A shame, really."

The sixth passenger was a young Tejano. He was well-dressed and carried himself with the confidence of a Hidalgo. Too much confidence in Becky's opinion. He had been as talkative as the missionaries. She had tired quickly of conversation when the young man had started trying to talk to her and ignoring their other traveling companions.

Now, as she reached for the door handle, another hand brushed by hers and grabbed the knob, "Allow me, *bonita señorita*."

Becky was tired after so long in the coach. She had had enough of his unwanted fawning. *"Manners be damned."*

"That is señora. Señora Travis." With that, she hurried through the door.

As the door jingled closed, she heard, "The pleasure was mine, *bonita señora*."

She ripped the pen from the hotel clerk's hand and scrawled her name on the registry. With more heat in her voice than she realized, she said, "I sent a telegraph. A room reserved for Mrs. William Travis."

When she heard the tremor in the clerk's voice, "Y-yes, ma'am," Becky realized the young Tejano had gotten under her skin, and she was taking her temper out on man behind the counter.

She took a deep breath and calmed her nerves. When she took the offered key, she gave an apologetic smile before climbing the stairs to her room.

The next morning after a tiring night of tossing and turning in an unfamiliar bed, she ate in the inn's common room with the other folks staying there. Although breakfast didn't measure up to Henrietta's cooking, she felt better than she had since leaving San Antonio the previous day when she stood outside the modest, wooden-framed building housing the Commodities Bureau.

While the building's window panes were spotless, the whitewashing on the building's siding was graying with age and was starting to flake under the hot, Texas sun. Stifling an uneasy feeling, she stepped onto the porch and entered the building. There were two desks in the narrow lobby, one on each side of the room. At one sat a man in civilian clothes, with a pair of pistols at his waist. His right leg was propped on the desk, wrapped in heavy bandages. He wore a badge on his chest. It was a circle, about the size of a Mexican peso. Within the circle was a five-pointed star. Becky nodded in the guard's direction. She had heard the Zavala administration had taken one of the Ranger companies on the frontier with the Comanche and had tasked them with policing the western settlements, like Austin. The Ranger dipped his head, "Ma'am."

A clerk sat at the other desk, "Mrs. Travis?" The clerk's mustache drooped, as though tired. Becky thought the hangdog appearance of his facial hair matched the dark circles under his eyes.

A moment later, he escorted her into a large room that took up the rest of the building. In the back corner sat a gray-haired man, hunched over a desk, reading. "Señor Seguin. Mrs. Travis to see you."

Becky studied the man she was there to see. Erasmo Seguin, at sixty-one, wore his gray hair long. It brushed the top of his shoulders. He kept his gray beard neatly trimmed. When he stood, she noticed he was more stooped than the last time they had met.

But his voice was as sonorous as ever, "Rebecca, child, I'm glad to see you again."

His wide-open arms welcomed her, and she gave him a hug before she took a seat before his desk. "Señor Seguin, I'm grateful for your time," she started. She settled into the hardbacked chair and launched into her reason for the meeting. "Until Will returns with Charlie, we're hard-pressed right now."

Seguin leaned forward and patted her arm in a fatherly way. "My Maria and I say prayers and light candles for your husband and son at Mass every time we go. I thought Will would make sure to provide for his family. How is it you find yourself hard-pressed?"

"We had more than enough to see us through, but the Commerce Bank held nearly all our money. It has been two weeks since their office in San Antonio has been open. Mr. Higgins has assured other people with accounts and me that our money is still there and safe, but that doesn't feed my children."

Seguin frowned, "I thought Will was the primary stockholder. Did this Mr. Higgins say why your money wasn't available?"

Tears were building in Becky's eyes as she explained how Will's partner had invested much of the bank's deposits in war bonds and that the Treasury Department was refusing to loan the bank any money.

Seguin stood and began pacing, "This is worse than I feared. Michel told me he was limiting any loans from the treasury now that the war is effectively over. I had no idea that the Commerce Bank had been using people's deposits to buy bonds."

He stopped his pacing and said, "I should have, I suppose. The war has been more expensive than I could have imagined. The treasury department wasn't able to pay for our army as taxes slowed with so many men away from their homes. We issued war bonds to raise the money. A few months before your husband's victory over Santa Anna we faced a crisis in selling the bonds. Our foreign bondholders were asking for steep discounts and high-interest rates. To stop the certificates from being devalued Mr. Williams bought several hundred thousand dollars in bonds. But I hadn't realized he was using his depositors' money. I thought it was investment capital."

"But why can't we get our money now?" Tears ran unbidden down Becky's cheek.

Seguin perched on the desk, "I warned Monsieur Menard his decision to stop loaning money would have a far-reaching impact on merchants and bankers who relied on treasury certificates."

It was clear Erasmo Seguin had already spoken to the Secretary of the Treasury about the problem resulting in the Commerce Bank's cash on hand. She still had one arrow in her quiver. "I'm sorry to hear about that. But what about my husband's pension?"

Despite Seguin's swarthy complexion, she saw his cheeks redden, as he became flushed, "I wish I had a better answer, Rebecca, but Lorenzo and Congress have suspended cash payments of pensions. Men who are owed their pensions can receive a grant of land for their service. I'd need to find out how much land Will's pension would amount to."

Crestfallen, Becky said, "More land ain't going to feed my babies. We need access to the pension the country owes my husband. Surely, there's something you can do to help us claim it."

There was sadness in the eyes of the director of the Commodities Bureau when he spread his empty hands, "I'm sorry, Rebecca. The government's cupboard is bare. But Will is like family. I'm glad to give you enough money until he returns."

Becky stood, tears streaking down her face, "Thank you, but I'll not be taking charity, even from you, Señor Seguin."

She turned and hurried out, running by engraving plates and currency presses. When she reached the street, her vision was blurred. She had taken only a dozen steps when she slammed into someone, and she felt a hand gripping her arm. Through the tears, she saw the same young Tejano blocking her way. "Ah, the *bonita señora*."

Becky wanted to scream, his grip hurt her arm. "Let go of me!"

His easy laughter angered her. “A kiss for Esteban from a pretty lady and I’ll happily step aside.”

She snapped. With her free hand, she reached into her purse and brought out a gift Will had given her on their first wedding anniversary. The .36 caliber revolver shook in her hand as she said, “You’ve got three seconds to let go of me, or I’ll blow your brains out.”

He let go of her arm and stepped aside, his face ashen as he stared at the gun. He stammered, “I was only playing.” He turned and hurried away.

Becky was shaking as she uncocked the gun and made sure the hammer lined up with the cylinder's empty chamber.

Chapter 8

Charlie's hands were blistered, and he had wrapped them in a rag as he gripped the shovel. His life in San Antonio was as far removed from Southern plantation life as imaginable. The thought about what slaves did after the harvest had been collected had never crossed his mind. Until now.

"Pace yo'self, boy." A slave pushed a wheelbarrow a few feet behind him. "You ain't gonna get a reward for first place."

Charlie used his shirt to wipe his face. Despite the crisp fall day, he was sweating. "Shit," he said. And he meant it. He dug the shovel into the wheelbarrow's pile of manure and then spread it over the soil.

"Truer words," said the slave.

They worked in silence until the wheelbarrow was empty. As they walked back to a wagon loaded with more of the natural fertilizer, the young man beside him said, "It'll be lunch soon. Slow down a spell, and with any luck, they'll ring the dinner bell around the time we get there."

"Alright, Cuffey," Charlie said.

Charlie slowed his walk a bit and looked across the field. Jackson was on duty. He was chatting with an overseer. Every day one of his captors joined the overseer, keeping an eye on him. At first, Lamont's slaves had avoided Charlie like the plague. On large plantations, a few white overseers kept a close eye on the field hands. But they didn't work beside the slaves.

Things changed a bit a week after they had arrived at Saluda Groves. Charlie had been forced to help pick the last of the cotton, and Hiram Williams was assigned to watch him that day. After half a day, Charlie's fingers were sore and blistered, but his bag was less than half full of cotton. Williams had been razzing the slaves until the overseers came over to him. Charlie couldn't hear what was said, but when the other white man strode away, Williams stomped over to Charlie and screamed, "What the hell's wrong with you? Less than half a bag, boy. Them niggers working rings around you."

He pushed Charlie to the ground and tore the bag from his waist. Then he upended it and poured it out on the boy's head as he lay in the dirt.

After that, Charlie found himself working beside one of the slaves each day. Most wouldn't say much, but Charlie liked Cuffey, who was only a few years older than him. It was from Cuffey he learned that even the overseers disliked Williams. Cuffey had explained it, "Them overseers, they usually makes sure we're getting the work done Marse Jason tells them to. They know if they treat us too bad, we have ways to be difficult. Ain't none of them like it when Mister Williams is around. He's just mean as a cuss."

Charlie said, "Is that why you're working with me?"

Cuffey offered a toothy grin. "Maybe. Or maybe I drew the short straw and nobody else wanted to spread shit with you."

True to the slave's word, the dinner bell was clanging when they arrived at the manure wagon.

As Charlie sat with Cuffey eating lunch, Jason Lamont rode up. "Jenkins! I want a word with you."

Jenkins had been eating with Charlie's other captors. He stood and said, "What's got your dander up? I'm right here."

Lamont threw a wadded-up piece of paper in front of him. "Your damned ransom note was published in New Orleans. Every Federal Marshal between the Sabine and the Potomac knows there's a ransom on the boy."

Jenkins jerked his head toward Charlie, "Well, at least the boy's pa knows our demands. No doubt he'll come through with the payment soon."

Lamont growled in frustration. "Do you think so? The newspaper in Columbia said that as of the first of September, General Travis was still in Mexico. Even if he's aware of your demands, it could be another month or longer before he can do anything. And, in the meantime, why did you tell Travis to post an advertisement in the *Charleston Courier*? Why don't you set up a lighthouse and flash a beacon to every marshal in the South that we've got the boy in the Palmetto state?"

Jenkins seemed affronted by the accusation. "What else was I supposed to do? I needed a way for the boy's father to contact us."

Lamont jerked on the reins, swinging around, "Keep the boy out of sight. Figure out where to stash him if any federal marshals come looking around. If anyone finds out the boy is here, I'll see that you swing."

2 November 1843

The door slammed open, and a young midshipman, no older than Charlie stood in the doorway, catching his breath. "Sir, the *Orion* is still in port. Captain's compliments, he'd like to see you at the helm."

When the door opened, Will was sitting on a bunk in the small cabin he shared with Javier Morales. Sergeant Jensen had joined him and the young lieutenant as they examined a borrowed map of the Isthmus of Panama.

As he followed the midshipman up to the deck, Will's mind was still analyzing the map. The isthmus was barely fifty miles wide but consisted of some of the worst jungles and swamps in Central America, as he recalled from the history he had studied before the transference. While a railroad had been built a few years after the California gold rush, the construction of the Panama Canal had been a harrowing experience for the men who created it. As he stepped onto the deck, Will recalled the French had failed in their attempt to breach the isthmus and had lost as many as twenty thousand workers during their unsuccessful effort. And if, as he suspected, Charlie's captors had taken his son across the isthmus, there was no choice but to follow.

Captain Jones handed him a spyglass and pointed toward a ship riding at anchor in the harbor. Wishing for his binoculars, Will looked through the monocular and found the American flagged schooner. Rope swings hung over the side of the ship. Men, clinging to the swings were working on the hull.

"What are they doing?"

Jones said, "It looks like they've just finished repairing the hull. Go too long without scraping the barnacles from a ship, and they can foul the bottom so bad that it slows you down to a crawl." He offered a half smile, "You probably got lucky. If the captain of the *Orion* hadn't decided to use Panama City for repairs, he'd have been gone for a while."

Will glowered at the distant ship. "We'll have to pay him a visit and thank him for waiting."

Jones offered a warm smile. "I think we can arrange that. Let's discuss our options in my cabin."

Windows along the ship's stern let ample light into the captain's cabin. Compared to the tiny cabins for the ship's other officers, the captain's cabin, despite its low ceiling, felt palatial. A table was fixed in the middle of the cabin, large enough for the captain and his officers to fit around. With just the two of them, the table felt wide open.

Jones took a chair at the head of the table and said, "It's a good thing the *Orion* is a US flagged ship. We'll be well within our rights to search it under maritime law."

Will flashed a nasty grin, "When me and my boys get ahold of the bastard captaining that ship, I'll make him tell me exactly where Charlie's been taken."

Jones raised his hand, as though flagging Will to stop. "Let's not invite more trouble than necessary, General. I can justify a search under the law, but to let six angry Texians board a US flagged ship, I'd rather not have to explain that if things get ugly."

Will frowned. His instincts were to race ahead. His men were professionals. In a firefight, he'd trust them above the sailors and Marines of the USS *Cyane*. When he told Jones that, the captain shook his head and said, "I'd feel the same way if I was in your place. However, on my ship, I'm god. We'll do this my way."

Will bit back an angry retort, realizing the US naval officer was right. He didn't have to like it, but he and his men were guests. "What do you have in mind, Captain?"

"I'll send over a squad of Marines under the command of Lieutenant Chambers. Pick one of your men, and the two of you can accompany them. Be ready to go at dawn."

Will's voice couldn't hide his disappointment, "We could be ready to go within the next hour. Why wait?"

Jones walked over to the stern windows and looked out on the falling twilight. "How often would you order a night attack, General?"

Will grimaced in chagrin. He'd not, unless it was absolutely necessary. "I take your point. Why take unnecessary risks? We'll be better rested at dawn, anyway."

Jones slapped him on the back, "That's the idea. In the meantime, I'll make sure the night watches keep an eye on the *Orion*. I doubt they'll try to leave, but if they do, we'll be on them before they clear the harbor."

The next morning, Will sat in the *Cyane's* longboat as it sliced through the harbor's still water. Next to him sat Jesse Running Creek. The young Cherokee Ranger examined his revolvers again. While the percussion caps were waterproof, the black powder charges were anything but. Will approved of the young man's diligence. The boat was crewed by a handful of sailors, the Marines crowded the inside seats, their bayoneted rifles pointing to the sky.

Will tugged at the revolver he wore on his belt. He had checked it before climbing into the boat. As agreed, he would scramble aboard the *Orion* last. Will respected the American captain's calm demeanor and desire to avoid escalating a high-risk encounter.

The boat thumped against the schooner's hull, and Will watched the Marines with their muskets slung on their backs, climb the ship's ladder. By the time Will and Running Creek reached the deck, the Marines had their weapons pointing at the ship's crew. From below decks, a Marine half carried, half propelled a man before him. Shaving lather covered his face.

"Lieutenant, here's the ship's master."

Lieutenant Chambers, wearing a dark blue fatigue jacket of the Marine waited until Palmer was standing before him. Once the Marine let go of him, Palmer wiped the lather from his face and glared at the officer, "What it is the meaning of this, Captain?" His voice echoed across the ship.

"That's *Lieutenant* Chambers, sir," the Marine officer stressed his rank. "By orders of Captain Jones of the USS *Cyane*, I'm to inspect your ship to confirm you're in compliance with public law nine-dash twenty-two."

Palmer wore a look of incredulity. "In Panama? I ain't ever shipped slaves aboard the *Orion*. You can search my ship until Gabriel blows his horn and you'll find nothing."

Chambers waved a couple of Marines to check the hold while the rest watched *Orion's* crew. Will took that as his cue, and approached Palmer and said, "You wouldn't happen to have any information about four pirates with a redheaded boy in tow?"

Palmer's eyes grew wide at the question before he looked down and studied his shoes, "No, why?"

Before Will could continue his questioning one of the Marines checking the hold tossed a long wooden rod and a coil of rope onto the deck. When the rod clattered onto the planking, Palmer flinched. A moment later a tin plate and a battered cup landed next to them.

From the hold, a voice echoed, "Hey, Lieutenant, someone was kept down here. There's a bucket of waste here."

Will lashed out, striking Palmer in the nose, knocking the stunned man to the deck. "What the hell do you know about my son?"

Palmer's eyes were crossed, and flecks of blood in his spittle covered his chin. As he regained awareness of his situation, he stared daggers at Will.

Will reached to grab Palmer and found Running Creek's iron grip on his arm, "General."

The words barely reached him as rage blurred his vision. This piece of filth had been aware of Charlie's capture, and he had provided his kidnappers with a means to escape Los Angeles.

The Marine lieutenant stepped between him and Palmer, "Sir, look to your hand, you appear to have cut it."

Palmer scrambled to his feet, "Are you going to let him hit me? I'm an American citizen."

The officer turned on Palmer, "The deck's slick, mind your step. It'd be a shame if you fell again."

With a firm grip on Will's arm, the young lieutenant guided him toward the ship's port side. "A wooden stave, ropes, and human waste in the hold. It's Captain Jones' call, General Travis, but we're either looking at slavery or piracy."

Will wasn't so sure about either, but he was sure Palmer knew more about his son than just the rod and rope on the deck. "Do you think either will stick?" Will said.

The other man shrugged, "Maybe, but what matters is what the *Orion's* master believes." He turned away from Will and ordered his men to secure Palmer. They eventually shoved a gag in his mouth when he wouldn't stop cursing them. A corporal's guard was left on board the *Orion,* and Will and Running Creek returned to the *Cyane* with the rest of the Marines and their prisoner.

Once back on board the US warship, Will watched the hapless Palmer dragged before Captain Jones. Will wanted nothing more than to beat the answers from the wretched man, but the authority Jones held aboard his ship was absolute.

"Mr. Palmer, my officer tells me that you've been transporting slaves in your hold. You realize that subjects your ship to seizure by the United States Navy."

Palmer rubbed his jaw, before he said, "I ain't ever trafficked in negro slaves. The risk just ain't worth it. My ship is my livelihood. Why'd I risk that?"

Jones paced in front of his prisoner, eying him each time he turned around. "If not slavery, then you've aided pirates."

Palmer tried to say something, and with his open palm, Jones slapped him across the face. "Shut up."

He stopped and stood toe to toe with his prisoner, "Which is it? Did you transport a slave from Los Angeles or did you consort with pirates, who raided and killed in Los Angeles and help them flee justice?"

Fear filled Palmer's eyes as he stammered, "I didn't do either of them."

Jones said, "Piracy it is."

He ordered a rope thrown over one of the yardarms before he turned back to Palmer. "Slave running is illegal. If we caught you trafficking in slaves, we'd haul your ass to Newport and convene a trial. If found guilty the government would seize your ship."

He waited until both ends of the rope snaked across the deck. "Piracy, though. That's different. Pirates I can take care of myself. Maritime law allows me to try and execute you here and now. I have the testimony the men you aided killed a former United States congressman and kidnapped his grandson and used your ship to escape. That's piracy, plain and simple."

A boson's mate tied a noose on one end of the rope while Jones spoke. "Do you have anything you wish to say before sentence is carried out?"

Will saw the horror in Palmer's eyes, "Dear God, man, you can't be serious. I didn't do anything other than take a few passengers to Panama City. You can't hang me for that. I had no idea they had killed some muckety-muck."

Jones frowned, "They killed David Crockett, man."

Blubbering, with tears streaking down his weathered face, Palmer said, "I had no idea. They didn't tell me. They just said, they'd pay me good to take them to Panama and ask no questions about the boy."

Jones waved the bosun's mate forward, and the sailor looped the noose around Palmer's neck. "I swear, I didn't do anything. The man you want is Obadiah Jenkins and his crew."

The sailor tightened the noose, and as the hemp rope scratched his neck, Palmer said, "Jenkins and his men took the boy into Panama City. I was curious, so I had one of my crew keep an eye on them. They hired a guide to take them across the isthmus."

"When?"

"Heaven help me, it's been almost three months."

Jones motioned for the bosun's mate to remove the noose and Palmer collapsed to the sloop's deck, sobbing uncontrollably. He beckoned Will over, "Is that enough information to go on?"

Will was stunned at how quickly Palmer had crumbled under the threat of hanging for piracy. "Uh, yes. I thought we'd have to beat the information from him. But, my God, he'd have confessed to anything."

As Jones and Will left the still sobbing Palmer on the deck, Will asked, "Would you have hung him if he hadn't talked?"

Smiling sheepishly, Jones said, "Not unless I wanted to face a board of inquiry when this cruise is over. No United States court would have bought the slaver argument and proving Palmer was complicit in the crimes committed by his passengers would be nigh on impossible to prove. But he didn't know that."

Will shook his head in admiration at the naval officer. "What'll you do with him?"

"I should toss him overboard. But, however loathsome he may be, he's still a United States citizen, and there are forms to observe. I'll send him back to his ship. He'll thank his lucky stars he escaped with his life and tomorrow, I suspect he'll take his ship to some other town that isn't on the Pacific Squadron's ports of call."

Before the sun had set, Will and his companions were ashore, hunting for the guide who took Jenkins' crew across the isthmus of Panama.

Chapter 9

8 November 1843

Will slapped his neck and looked at the mangled remains of the mosquito. Apart from an early rain shower, the day had been bright but humid. He had stopped wearing his jacket within a few hours of disembarking from the *Cyane*. Worse, the humidity forced him and his men to oil and clean their weapons more often. Now, five days later, their guide said they would reach Chagras in the afternoon.

Fifty miles in five days should have been easy. Will was no stranger to forced marches or long days in the saddle. But the isthmus of Panama was mostly jungle. The first three days had been hiking along a barely maintained trail until they arrived on the Chagras River. The last two had been on the river.

Will fretted about the malarial swamps they passed through. Every time he heard a buzzing near his ear he swiped at the insect. Will lost count of the mosquitos he'd killed. Unlike the men who traveled with him, he knew the cause of malaria and yellow fever. Until he had faced the prospect of traversing he had never thought about pointing Texian doctors like Ashbel Smith in the direction of the cause.

He swatted again, muttering, "If I survive this, I'll definitely get Dr. Smith to study the damned mosquito."

From the front of the canoe, Running Creek said, "Supposedly bear grease keeps the mosquitos away." He whacked at his exposed neck, "But the stuff smells something awful."

Will steered the canoe around a log, "I don't suppose you thought to bring any?"

The Cherokee chuckled as he dug his paddle into the water, "Sorry, General. Left it in my wigwam."

Will laughed. The Cherokee in Texas lived in villages similar to their white neighbors. Over the past few weeks, Will had gotten to know his traveling companions. Running Creek's father was a prosperous merchant, with a house more substantial than Will's place in San Antonio.

Thinking of San Antonio, his thoughts went to Becky and his kids. He missed Liza and little David only slightly less than he missed his wife. He hoped that things were going well for her, as he tracked his son's kidnappers halfway across the continent. He knew his pay would stop. Lorenzo had been in such a pique, he had no doubt his pay at the end of September would be the last. But he had left a sizable balance in the Commerce Bank, which she would be able to draw upon as needed. Even so, he offered up a prayer for her wellbeing.

The lead canoe drifted to the shore, and their guide climbed out. Will beached his canoe next to the guide's. He watched as the old, leather-skinned Panamanian called out, "We have a couple of more hours ahead. This is as good a place as any to stretch our legs."

Will mentally translated his words. He didn't speak Spanish often enough to gain Running Creek's fluency. He resented the guide's frequent stops along the river. What he wanted was to hasten toward the town of Chagras. What he needed to do, he set off for the tree line.

As Will walked back toward the canoes, the guide stepped out from the tree line and waved toward him, "Señor, you asked about the guides who led the men you're following. I think I found them."

Will followed the old guide back into the tree line. A few yards into the dense jungle Will came upon a shallow grave. Animals had disturbed the site. There were skeletal remains of two bodies.

In careful Spanish, Will said, "How do you know these were the guides?"

With a look of distaste, his guide knelt by the grave. He pulled a knife and used it to shift a bit of cloth away from the neck of one of the bodies. There was a small medallion made of iron on a chain. He slid it over the head and set it at Will's feet.

"I'd recognize that anywhere. It's St. George, the patron saint of explorers. I gave this to my nephew, Alessandro on his sixteenth birthday."

Will shuddered. He was no expert, but the bones gave up the trauma of the men's deaths. The guide said, "The men who took your son, they are the same men who killed my cousin and his son." His voice shook with emotion. "Find the men who did this and kill them."

The rest of the trip into the portside town of Chagras was uneventful, but the empty sockets staring back at him from their disturbed grave bothered Will.

What did this mean for Charlie? The men who kidnapped his son had killed his father-in-law for no discernable reason. Now, when they were within spitting distance of Chagras, they murdered their guides. The escalating behavior of Charlie's kidnappers left Will sick to his stomach.

Was one of their number a deranged homicidal maniac? Will wanted to dismiss the idea. But the evidence was too compelling to ignore. By the time he had paid off the guide, he was ready to find a ship and sail off in pursuit. The problem was there were no ships in port.

Will shaded his eyes from the sun as he scanned the houses along the harbor. They were thatch-roofed, wooden shacks. He frowned as he watched young children splashing in the water where the Chagres River flowed into the Caribbean. Their mothers watched them as they washed laundry. His thoughts turned to Charlie. Where was he now? He burned to know where the murderers had taken his son.

That they had come this way was undisputed. The impoverished town's harbormaster had confirmed their departure two months before. The redhaired youth had stood out in the harbor master's recollection. Will replayed the scene, "Señor, they arrived without a guide and stayed long enough to take passage on a ship to Havana."

Will shook his head, his eyes burning at the memory. Worse, there were no ships in the harbor to ferry him and his companions after Charlie's abductors. Despite the harbormaster's insistence on Chagres' importance to the trade route across the isthmus, which cut three months off the travel time around the Cape Horn on South America's tip, there was no telling when the next ship would arrive.

Only the desperate or those with an urgent need crossed Panama's mosquito-infested swamps. The dangers of sailing around South America were often preferable to the malarial swamps of Panama. The problem was that Will was running out of time. His boot kicked up dust on the hard-packed road. God alone knew when the next ship would arrive. He worried about Charlie. What were his kidnappers doing? His heart sank as he wondered if his son was still alive. The violence his captors were willing to mete out was startling in its savagery.

Once out of town, away from the playing children, Will turned, looking behind him. Chagres' few crude streets ran east to west, climbing a slope to an old Spanish fort. The Spanish had abandoned it in 1821 when Panama joined with her neighbors to form the nation of Gran Columbia. Although the state had been short-lived, Panama remained in union with Columbia.

Will cast a glance up at the fort atop the bluff overlooking the village. It was the Columbian flag that flew over the fort, which now housed a small prison. Squinting, he could see the red, blue, and yellow flag flapping in the Caribbean breeze. The flag's brilliant hues were in stark contrast to the steel-gray November sky. The normally azure water was choppy, matching the sky's dark shade. Despite this, the wind off the sea was mild.

As far as he could see across the water, the Caribbean was empty. Will's chest constricted as he felt hopeless. Nothing mattered more than tracking the kidnappers down and yet, he was stranded on a beach with nothing but endless seas at which to stare. Before returning to the town's lone inn, he pulled the binoculars he carried from the leather case. He lifted the well-made Italian glasses and scanned across the briny expanse hoping against hope he would see something. It was too much to ask for, but he made one final sweep when he caught a glimpse of a speck. He steadied the glasses and brought the tiny abnormality into focus. He gasped as he counted three dots on the horizon.

He stood on the shore until the tiny specks turned into ships. He lost track of time, as he felt hope rising. Every minute passing by gave promise these ships were coming toward the town. Eventually, he saw the colors flying above the nearest ship. He frowned at the green, white, and red. Those were colors shared by the Mexican flag. He strained his eyes, grinding his teeth in frustration. Mexico owned no navy, not after they lost their fleet at the Battle of Campeche the previous year.

The last ship stood out, as Will focused on the black soot swirling into the sky from its smokestack. As it came into focus, Will saw a few sails unfurled, gusts of wind billowed the canvas and pushed the ship through the water. Minutes passed by until he felt his heart skip a beat as the lone star flag of Texas came into focus. What was it doing so far south? Was it pursuing the other ships?

Refocusing on the first ship, the green, white, and red colors were not in the style of the Mexican flag. The green field held a circle of stars. Three horizontal bars, red alternating with white, filled the rest of the flag. Now Will recognized the flag flown by the rebel state of Yucatan. The Yucatecans were allies of convenience against Mexico. The Texas steamship appeared to be escorting the two sail-powered ships. A smile plastered Will's lips when it was clear the ships were heading toward Chagres.

With hope renewed, Will tore his tired eyes away from the oncoming ships and raced back toward town. His men were resting under an awning of a tavern next to the hotel. On a table stood an open tequila bottle. Sitting around the table, several of his companions played a round of poker. In a voice louder than intended, Will said, "I don't know how or why, but there's a Texas flagged warship sailing straight towards us."

The poker game disintegrated as the men leapt to their feet and followed him to the harbor.

Hours later Will climbed aboard the steam Schooner-of-war *Nueces.* Elias Thompson, the ship's captain, stood slack-jawed as Will's feet hit the desk. He recovered, saying, "General Travis? How'd you get here so fast?"

Will raised his eyebrows in surprise. The military of the Republic wasn't so large that he didn't know the names of all of the Navy's ship's captains, although he didn't know them on sight.

"Am I late? I wasn't aware you were expecting me."

The naval captain closed his jaw, as he regained his composure. "No, sir. I wasn't. But having just heard of the ransom, I assumed you had, too."

Will's heart skipped a beat. His unwelcome constant companion had been the fear gnawing away at his insides over what his son's captors intended. "Do you have a copy of their demands?"

Thompson turned to a midshipman, "Fetch the copy of the *Picayune* from my cabin."

A moment later Will devoured the article detailing the kidnappers' demands. He whistled low and offkey as he read the dollar amount the kidnappers were demanding. He handed the newspaper back to the captain, "Fifty-thousand dollars, they don't think small."

"No, sir." Thompson folded the newspaper and tucked it under his arm, "I take it that you didn't know about the ransom?"

Will shrugged, "After viewing the evidence in California I'd assumed they had kidnapped my son for a ransom, but this is the first confirmation I've received."

It was Thompson's turn to whistle. "That's a hell of a lot of traveling over the past couple of months."

Will's impatience crept into his voice, "What would you do if your child was taken?"

An apologetic look washed over the naval officer's face. "If I were in your shoes, I'd do the same thing. I'd have no choice but to hunt the bastards down. I'll never see fifty thousand dollars in my life."

Will turned his pockets inside out and chuckled ruefully. "I'm afraid I don't have that kind of money lying about, either. But I'm glad to know you'd chase someone down if they tried to hurt your family." He paused, searching for the right words. "I could use a favor. Your newspaper indicates the kidnappers took my son to Charleston. Can me and my boys impose on you for passage?"

Thompson said, "I've done my duty, escorting the Yucatecan ships this far. I think they can manage the rest of the distance to Gran Columbia on their own."

Chapter 10

12 November 1843

"Two days to get from San Jacinto to here!" Becky's back hurt as one of the coach's wheels lurched into a hole. When she had started out from San Antonio, she had admired the speed of the stagecoach. The idea of traveling more than seventy miles in a single day was hard to fathom. Growing up in western Tennessee, where roads were seldom more than meandering trails between homesteads and villages, distances beyond a dozen miles typically took longer than a day.

Even the stage from Austin to Houston was but three days. She glanced out the window and saw the elevated tracks. Only the bridge over the San Jacinto River remained to be completed. As the wheel jounced again, she winced and thought about how much faster it would be to travel between Harrisburg and West Liberty along the straight and smooth rails.

To listen to her husband, railroads were the future. Before the war, he had regaled her with tales of trains rolling out of New York and crossing the mighty

Mississippi before curving south and crossing the Sabine River, connecting San Antonio with folks on the east coast. It was only a dream, but as she saw the tracks, she wondered if perhaps he was right. Even in frontier Texas, progress marched ever onward.

Were it not for the other passengers Becky would have laughed. Everyone had their own idea of what progress meant. To her father, progress meant an ever-widening expanse of a new frontier. That idea of progress had kept her parents apart as often as they had been together. Her father's wanderlust was the stuff from which legends were cast. The memory of David Crockett brought an unbidden tear to her eye. She missed him something fierce.

Through the opposite window, Becky could see a plantation. Despite the lateness of the season, she saw slaves preparing the field for the spring harvest, still several months away. To the plantation owner progress meant the ability to move ever westward, opening up new territories to the slave economy. Growing up in Western Tennessee it wasn't that slavery wasn't present, it was just something she didn't give any thought to. Marrying William Travis had opened her eyes to his idea of progress. Railroads that crossed a continent, ships that could steam across the Atlantic without a stitch of canvas. Machines that would do the work of a hundred men, that was Will's idea of progress.

The coach was slowing, and a few minutes later, she saw clapboard buildings pass by as the coach rolled into West Liberty. In a way, it was Will's ideas of progress which brought her to this small town forty miles northeast of Houston. Will was a major stockholder in the Gulf Farms Corporation. In the years immediately following the revolution, he and several other veterans had pooled their land grants, claiming some of the most fertile farmland along the Trinity River. They had hired men who were struggling with their farms as well as families from Ireland, the Germanies, Mexico, and elsewhere to work the land. The hired men were not tenants, but employees.

Before the war, every few months Will received a check from the corporation. Dividends, he had called the money. It had been a while since Becky had seen any dividend checks and that's why she was here.

The next morning, she crossed the road from the boarding house where she had stayed the night. The house she approached was large, built in the Spanish Hacienda style. The President of the corporation was a man by the name of Don Garza. As Becky walked up the cobblestone path from the dirt road, the door opened. Standing there was an older man.

Becky eyed the man pensively. She judged he was closer to seventy than sixty. His black hair was streaked with silver. His face was lined with age. When he spoke, his voice was a deep, yet soothing baritone. "Señora Travis," he took her hand in his and raised it to his lips. "Your telegram arrived last night. Please come in."

After accepting a cup of hot tea from Don Garza, Becky settled into a leather chair in the hacienda's study. After she took a sip, she said, "Thank you, Señor Garza, for making time for me. I can only imagine how busy you must be."

The old man waved away the comment, "You haven't traveled all the way from San Antonio for a social call, although I would be honored were it so. Please accept my condolences on the loss of your father. President Crockett was a fine man. I am also troubled by the news of your stepson's kidnapping."

Despite every effort, a tear slid down Becky's cheek. Being so far away from her mother and children, she felt alone, notwithstanding the warmth of Don Garza's hospitality. Fearing her voice might shake, she nodded her thanks.

Garza filled in the silence. "Do you need any help, child?"

Becky swallowed her loneliness and offered a weak smile. "I understand my husband owns stock in Gulf Farms, Señor Garza."

The old man dipped his head, "Indeed. He's one of our largest stockholders."

Becky set the teacup down and asked, "Why did the dividend checks stop coming?"

Garza's smile faltered for a moment before he ruefully chuckled. "The company has to be making money to pay a dividend. Apart from the first couple of years, Gulf Farms has been profitable, and we paid dividends to our shareholders. At least until the recent war with Mexico."

Taking in Becky's silence, Garza continued, "When Texas declared war after the debacle at the Alamo last year, it wasn't long before the militia companies were called up and we lost more than half our men to the war effort. I had far more women and children working the land the past year than I had men. But we were forced to cut our cotton production back and grow food instead. Most of that was bought by the government with promissory notes."

He stood and walked around a long table at one end of the study until he stood at the window. He pointed down the road, "Because of those promissory notes, I am in arrears to the men and women who worked the fields this past year."

What had started as a single tear turned into a steady trickle. Becky felt powerless at the news. She needed to provide for her children and mother, let alone find money to pay Henrietta's salary. Garza's words held no comfort.

As she wiped the tears with a handkerchief, she felt Garza's bony hand on her shoulder. "Senora Travis, I may not be able to pay your husband's dividends, but I am not without means. There are homes here in town that are still vacant. I will gladly put you and your family in one of them until General Travis arrives back in Texas."

Becky reached up and squeezed his hand, "You're too kind, Señor Garza. But I won't be beholden to anyone. My husband wasn't without other investments. I will check on them before returning to San Antonio."

Becky bit her lip when she realized she had whistled when she saw the port of Galveston from the deck of the coastal schooner. She had read Galveston received seven hundred ships a year. She could believe it, looking at the forest of masts crowded alongside the docks jutting into the water. She repressed a grin, what would her mother think if she'd heard her whistle. Becky could almost hear her mother's voice, *Ladies don't whistle*, she'd say. A glance around the schooner's deck revealed no one had listened to her unladylike response to the bustling port.

As she waited for the longboat to be lowered into the water, she thought back to the short, hourlong ride on the train to Anahuac. Thirty miles in an hour. What a difference to the two-day trek from Harrisburg to West Liberty. Although she had been forced to stay overnight in the coastal town, waiting for the small ship to take her from Anahuac to Galveston, even the ride on the schooner had only taken a few hours. As the crew helped her into the boat, she decided, this was the type of progress she could support.

Later, she stood on a street where the signpost informed her she was on Avenue B. Someone had used some chalk and crossed out the words and in poor penmanship had written, "The Strand." Most of the buildings were wooden, but on both sides of the street, a few brick and stone buildings stood as a testament to the importance of Galveston's role as the gateway to the Texas frontier.

A sidewalk ran alongside the dirt street, and Becky was glad to lift the hem of her dress and step onto the wooden planks. As she walked by stores and offices, she was amazed at the many languages she heard. She recognized the guttural accent of a German speaker and the familiar sound of Spanish, but other languages were unrecognizable. Apart from when she and her mother had visited her father once while he was still a congressman in Washington City and when they had passed through New Orleans, this was the largest town she had seen.

Above one brick-faced building was a sign which read, "The Commerce Bank." A sign was posted in the window. She peered through the glass and read, "All deposits are guaranteed. Ten-dollar withdrawals are permitted every fortnight."

Unlike the darkened bank in San Antonio, when she turned this doorknob, the door swung open. A guard was posted nearby, and a young clerk stood behind a barred countertop. She had traveled a long way, and she wanted nothing more than to hold her children but she was determined to see the reason for her visit through to completion.

"Mrs. William Travis to see Mr. Samuel Williams."

Before the clerk could say anything, a head poked out from an office toward the back of the building. "Mrs. Travis, as I live and breathe." A body followed the head. Although she had not yet met Sam Williams, she recognized him from Will's description. Despite a youthful face, his hair was prematurely gray.

"Abel," he said to the clerk, "let Mrs. Travis through, and bring her back to my office."

As Becky settled into a chair across from a well-worn desk in Williams' office, he left the door open as he returned to his seat. After offering condolences on the death of her father, he said, "Yours isn't a face I expected to see today. To what do I owe the pleasure of your company?"

"Your bank in San Antonio has closed. My family's account is unavailable, despite the sign on the window to the contrary." Becky worked to keep her voice steady. Crisscrossing the republic to provide for her family was taxing, and she felt fatigue setting in.

Williams leaned forward, "It's a temporary setback. We're trying to arrange a loan from the Treasury Department to make sure we can cover any transactions our customers may need."

Becky was frustrated. "How did you allow things to get so bad?"

Williams' eyes widened at the words before he laughed. "Buck warned me you were a woman with your own thoughts and... dashed... if he wasn't right."

Becky's lips twitched upwards at Williams efforts to not offend her with profanity.

The banker continued, "Even though the war with Mexico wasn't long, it was disastrous for the nation's financial health. The president and Congress were forced to spend a lot more money than the government had coming in. To make up the difference, they issued bonds."

Becky said, "Isn't a bond just a loan by another name?"

"Exactly. Earlier this year, there was a threat that new bonds wouldn't be able to find buyers. That would have risked a collapse of the cotton-backs. Secretary Menard talked me into buying enough bonds to forestall collapse. The problem now is that we have very little cash on hand. To shore up the Republic's finances, Michel Menard has choked off new loans, which I need so that I can make sure depositors like Buck can have access to their money."

It was similar to what Señor Seguin had told her a few weeks earlier. Fearing despair would overtake her, she shoved her fears aside and refocused on Williams. "What about my husband's stock in your bank? Surely there are dividends owed."

Williams said, "Would that there were." He asked if she knew of the source of the loan with which Will had bought his interest in the bank. When she nodded, he continued, "We're two months behind in our repayment to our British friends. I've not heard any word from them about it, but I suspect they'll be eager for repayment to continue." He opened a drawer and pulled out a box. "Your husband doesn't really expect to receive payment on the investment for a while. But that doesn't mean I can't do something to help you."

He opened the box and pulled out a small stack of cotton-backs. "As the wife of my partner, I can extend one hundred dollars against your family's account. And more as soon as I secure a loan from the Treasury Department."

When she heard Williams' words, she realized she'd been holding her breath, and she exhaled. It was a small fraction of the money her husband had in the bank, but with it, she'd be able to take care of her family until the new year. The tension of weeks' worth of worrying ebbed away, and the strength which had driven her to leave her children behind in San Antonio was at an end. She blinked away the tears.

Williams pulled a handkerchief from a pocket and handed it to her, "I'd do more if I were able, Mrs. Travis."

As Becky dabbed her eyes, she prayed she'd find a way to provide for her children until Will returned with Charlie.

Chapter 11

20 November 1843

Will stood next to the bronze 18-pounder bow chaser as the *Nueces* steamed into Charleston harbor. From his vantage point, he saw a pile of rock and bricks at the harbor's mouth. Was that Fort Sumter? From the picture Will recalled from before the transference, Sumter looked half-built. A mile away from the half-complete Sumter stood another fort guarding the entrance to Charleston Harbor. A US flag flew atop the battlements of Fort Moultrie.

A noise from behind alerted him to another's presence. "General, Captain Thompson wishes to see you."

Will turned and saw the Cherokee Ranger, Running Creek. He had replaced his butternut jacket with a bright blue one. He had picked it up on the day the ship had stopped in Havana. All of his men wore civilian clothing. While the US and Texas were friendly, there was no point in drawing attention by entering the US in Texas butternut brown. "Lead on."

Captain Thompson stood by the helm, which was located behind the iron smokestack, "General, we'll be dropping anchor shortly. I'll be sending a party ashore to arrange for coal. I'd like to send you and your men ashore with them."

Will agreed. If Charlie's kidnappers were watching ships coming into port, slipping into port under the guise of a coaling party might let them pass under the noses of whoever was observing.

Thompson continued, "It'll take a few days to take on the coal. After that, I expect I'll discover some engine trouble that will keep me here until you return." The captain shook Will's hand, and a bit later he and his party were squeezed into the ship's longboat and shuttled toward shore.

Will looked his men over as they stepped ashore. The Mexicans, Lieutenant Morales, and the enigmatic Lobo carried revolvers and breechloading rifles obtained while the party was in California. The pistols they wore on their hips. The long-arms were wrapped in blankets. Behind them came Sergeant Jensen. Even in civilian clothing, he looked like a solider. No wonder, Will thought, the man had been one for more than thirty years. The Rangers Running Creek and LeBlanc brought up the rear.

Missing from their party was Jethro Elkins. Once Will's posse had reached Los Angeles back in early October, the Ranger's broken leg had prevented him from continuing. For the first time since he had received word of Charlie's abduction, Will felt his son was nearby. He wished the mustachioed Ranger was still with the party.

There was no shortage of inns along the waterfront. Some catered to well-heeled travelers, and others served sailors who were between ships. Will found one that seemed to fall somewhere in the middle. With some money he had received from Captain Thompson, he paid for a couple of rooms.

Once settled, he and the other five men crowded into one of the rooms. The window was open, and a cool Atlantic breeze rustled threadbare curtains. A newspaper lay on the bed.

Will pointed to it, "That's just one more proof Charlie's abductors came through here."

There was a reprint of the article from the *Picayune*, but a local reporter had added United States Marshals were searching in and around Charleston for the whereabouts of Will's missing son.

Leaning against the wall, Lobo spoke. His Spanish was inflected with a slow drawl. "General, these bandits, if they came through here, probably did so because they are familiar with this city. Before I was conscripted, I was a hunter. When my prey realized I was on their trail, they would seek familiar terrain. Let's search the parts of town where these forgers were likely to go. If there are no clues, then we can move on."

In the months since the party had left Saltillo, this was the most Lobo had spoken. Jensen's chuckle was dry, "The boy doesn't say much, but when he does, he makes sense."

Will agreed. It was sensible. They split themselves into three groups of two and waited until twilight to visit the taverns alongside the harborside.

Will arrived back at the inn a few hours before dawn. He and Morales had come back exhausted and empty-handed. When they walked into the room, tied up on the bed was a black-haired man, whose frizzy mane reminded Will of Albert Einstein.

Lobo and LeBlanc were standing over him. Black bruises around his eyes left Will suspecting the hogtied man had not come willingly. "What have we here?" he said.

"We were traipsing around one of the taverns asking about this Jenkins fellow when Mr. Hair here tried running away." LeBlanc leered at the captive, "One thing led to another and here he is. General Travis, allow me to introduce you to Thomas Jefferson Hamilton."

The fellow tied on the bed glared daggers at Will. "Take the gag out of his mouth. He'll not say anything with a sock in it."

A moment later, the man swore at Will. "You can go to Hell. I ain't got nothing to tell you anyhow."

"So you do know about Obadiah Jenkins, then." Will watched as the man's eyes darted around the room.

"I ain't telling you shit!"

Will picked the sock off the floor, "Put this back in his mouth. We'll make him talk." He turned and left the room.

Later, in his team's second room, the Danish-born Sergeant Jensen said, "I've served Texas in the Rangers and before that, I was in the dragoons out west. If we need to get him to talk, I can do it." In a voice just above a whisper, he continued, "During the war with the Blackhawks, we were on patrol in what is now the Iowa territory. Settlers were staking out farms when a Sauk warband raided a farm. They killed the man, but the woman and her children were taken.

"In our pursuit, me and a few other dragoons captured a couple of Sauk warriors. It was pretty clear they knew where the prisoners had been taken." He fell silent, evidently remembering something he'd rather forget. "This was before I saw what the Comanche could do to prisoners. But before we were finished with those two warriors, they told us what we wanted to know."

Jensen was staring at the floor. In a voice so quiet, Will could barely hear him. "I will make him talk."

Will stared at the modest sergeant. He had always assumed the quiet competence with which Jensen did his job masked nothing more than a stoic Danish attitude. He was moved that the old Dane was willing to revisit the demons he had carried with him for a decade to find out where the kidnappers had taken his son.

Will had been stranded in the body of William Barret Travis long enough to know torturing information from the human scum in the next room wouldn't involve waterboarding, loud music, or psychological mind-games. He's seen the horrors visited on his own men seven years earlier in the campaign against the Comanche warbands and had a good idea of what Jensen was capable.

Will walked to the window overlooking the harbor and clenched the old curtains, as he steeled himself against what was to come. He had grown up in a world in which "enhanced interrogation techniques" were hotly contested and of uncertain value. When weighed against his son, though, he realized he'd do anything to get Charlie back.

"If we're going to do this, let's get it done."

As he reached the door, Morales said, "Do what you must, General. If the only thing that will make our guest talk is force, then by all means, do what is necessary. But was it not your own William Shakespeare who said in *Henry IV* that 'a plague upon it when thieves cannot be true one to another?'"

Will's hand rested on the doorknob. "What are you suggesting?"

"Perhaps the information you seek can be obtained not by force but by appealing to his greed."

Will chuckled, "Perhaps. Maybe Shakespeare's right, there's no honor among thieves."

Back in the room where Thomas Jefferson Hamilton was tied and gagged, Will fished a small gold coin from his pocket and placed it on the bed. "My associates assure me that when they finish with you, you'll tell me everything I want to know all the way back to the name of the girl you first kissed. You may or may not survive the experience, but you'll talk before it's done."

Eyes that before had burned in anger were wide in fear as Will explained what would happen if Hamilton wasn't forthcoming with the location of Charlie's captors. "Or, you can tell me what I want to know, and, for your trouble, the gold is yours."

When the other man nodded, Will felt a burden lift. He hadn't been aware how deeply troubling the idea of torture had been until removed. The prospect of torturing the man, even for the noblest of reasons had weighed heavily on him.

With the gag gone, Hamilton said, "An old friend of mine, Hiram Williams reached out to me a couple of months ago, said he needed a place to stay while they were in town. I let him and his friends stay for a few days. They were looking for someone. Eventually, they met up with a gentleman who came for them in the dead of night. They took the train to Columbia."

"How'd you know they took the train?"

"These ropes are tight. Care to cut me loose?"

Will picked up the coin and made to stick in back in his vest pocket when Hamilton hurriedly said, “If they didn’t think I ought to know, I thought otherwise. I wondered if it might be valuable information. Is it?”

Will hated the man. Part of him wanted to see Hamilton pay. But he hadn’t forgotten the way the burden lifted when the man had caved.

He turned to Running Creek, “Cut him loose.” He tossed the coin in Hamilton’s lap and left.

Late November 1843

Had it only been two weeks since she had taken the stagecoach north? Thankful for a seat beside the window, Becky gazed across the prairie. In the distance, she could see the tall northern wall of the Alamo. By the time Becky had moved to San Antonio after the wedding, the crumbling adobe wall had been destroyed, and a long, two-story barracks was nearing completion. Made of adobe, in the evening sun, it reflected a golden hue.

She could scarcely wait to see Liza and David. Two weeks wasn’t long, but she wondered how much the baby had grown. As the sun dipped below the western prairie, she doubted if the trip had been worth it. Mr. Williams’ generosity notwithstanding, she had come back nearly emptyhanded.

The Travis family’s fortunes were a microcosm of Texas. The war had left both her family and her nation as poor as Job’s turkey. The thought brought a sad smile to her lips, as she recalled the expression was a favorite of her father’s.

As the coach rolled into San Antonio’s central plaza, she knew the hardest part of her journey was still ahead. Without knowing when Will would return with Charlie, she had no choice but to strip her family's finances to the bone.

With her carpetbag in hand, she hurried home. With each step, she alternated between elation at the thought of seeing her children and despair at the failure of her mission.

When she turned the corner from the plaza, she saw her home in the distance. She found her feet racing along the dusty street until she stood in front of her house. Despite twilight stealing the last of the light, she saw two figures sitting on the porch, in the shadow.

Unbidden, she called out, "Ma!"

"Lordy mercy," A familiar voice called out.

Becky burst into a run, holding high the hem of her dress until she threw herself into her mother's arms. All of the heartache of Will's absence, adding to the trials of her trip spilled down her cheeks as she hugged her mother.

Later that evening, she sat at the oaken dining table with her mother and Henrietta. She said "There's no money for a pension, not yet. Maybe never."

Elizabeth was pensive. "Is it just Will or is it all veterans?"

Becky shrugged, "I don't know. Señor Seguin was apologetic, even offered to help. But I get the feeling our government wrote checks it couldn't cover, and now the Treasury is stopping all payments that it can justify."

Becky accepted a cup of tea from Henrietta as she continued, "All that money Will invested in the big farm at West Liberty and the bank is tied up. Señor Garza and Mr. Williams were clear Will's investments were not profitable this year."

She folded her arms on the table and rested her head. “We can’t stay here. Sweet Lord above, I’m going to miss this place.”

While Henrietta studied her teacup in silence, Elizabeth placed her hand on Becky’s shoulder, “As long as we’re together, we’ll pull through.”

Fresh tears spill from Becky’s eyes. “I wish to God Will was back. None of this would be necessary.” She felt helpless rage as she gripped the table, “Damn all men who start wars to Hell.”

From the end of the table, she heard a faint, “Amen.”

Becky reached toward Henrietta and gripped her hand, her eyes begging forgiveness even as her words were stuck in her throat.

“I know you can’t afford a housekeeper, Miss Becky. Joe should be back soon. I’d go with you if I could, but my place is with him, even if he spends too much time away.” Henrietta’s voice was raw with emotion.

Becky dabbed her eyes, “You’ll always have a place with us if you need it.”

The freedwoman’s face glistened in the firelight, her tears still streamed down her face as she picked up the teapot. “I’ll be back in the morning, I’ll help til y’all have to move.”

Once they were alone, Elizabeth said, “Where are we going to go? Surely Will has friends who can help.”

Becky stubbornly stuck her chin out, “I’ll not be taking charity, Ma. You and Pa raised me better than that. Turns out there are a few houses for rent in West Liberty. I figure we can do laundry and sewing there. We’ll pay our own way until Will returns with Charlie.”

A few days later, she and her mother stood in San Antonio's main square. Little Liza gripped her grandmother's hand. Becky's arms were full, holding David. The house was locked. The furniture was still in it, and she didn't know when or if they would return to claim their property. The red Concorde stagecoach stood before the governor's palace, on one side of the square, waiting.

Becky had already said goodbye to Henrietta. No doubt some of the more proper women in town would be scandalized by their tearful hugs, but she couldn't care less. Over the years the black freedwoman had become more than just an employed housekeeper, Hattie had become a friend. Becky hadn't even boarded the coach, and she was missing everything she held dear in San Antonio.

Elizabeth handed her a handkerchief, "The driver's coming. Let's get the children loaded and get seated."

With a final backward glance at the city of the Alamo, Becky climbed aboard and waited for the coach to roll away.

Chapter 12

The iron wheels grated against iron rails as the train rounded the curve. A glance out the window revealed they were nearing the bridge over the Congaree. Will felt his heart rate pick up. Twenty-five miles until Columbia. The train slowed and began gently rocking side to side as he listened to the clackity-clack of the car crossing the river.

From the information wheedled from Thomas Jefferson Hamilton, he knew Charlie had been forced to ride this route. He shook his head; no boy's first railroad ride should be as a captive. As he stared out the soot-covered window, he pursed his lips. Will had grown up with cars and planes. Passenger railroads were already a thing of the past when he had been little. While such conveniences would be useful, he had long ago resigned himself to not living to see airplanes crisscrossing the sky. What he knew about engines wouldn't fill up a single page.

Maybe Charlie would live to see cars and airplanes, but he'd certainly see the railroads crossing the

Republic in the near future. The idea buoyed Will's spirits. It was the first time in several days where he considered Charlie's future. He would find his son and bring justice to the men who had kidnapped him.

The Congaree River receded behind the train. The tracks ended in Columbia. There were plenty of places where the kidnappers could have gone to ground. Was it possible they had used the capital of South Carolina as a jumping-off point to somewhere more remote? The Piedmont stretched to the Appalachian Mountains. Would Charlie's kidnappers take the boy further into the backcountry? Will didn't know. But the optimism he felt earlier vanished, like the coal smoke whisking by the window.

An hour later, Will climbed down the stairs, landing on the depot's wooden planking. To one side were a few buildings and beyond that, the Congaree River and then farmland. On the other side, behind the depot, lay the town of Columbia. As the conductor walked by, he said, "Welcome to the second largest city in the Palmetto state. Forty-five hundred souls call Columbia home. We hope you enjoy your stay."

A wide boulevard stretched north, heading to the city limits. The street running east to west had a signpost. It read, Gervais street. The South Carolina State House was a few blocks east from the depot. As Will walked along the side of the dirt street, he watched the folks who made Columbia their home go about their lives. He and his five companions walked by a blacksmith's shop. The smith, a burly black man, was shaping a horseshoe, using a hammer and anvil.

Next door, a sign over the building said, "Schneider's Fine Furniture." A workroom was visible through the windows. A middle-aged white man worked a piece of wood on a lathe while a black youth pumped the lathe's foot-pedal.

By the time the party found a hotel, Will was struck by the number of black workers in the town's business district. He doubted many were freedmen, like Joe. He wouldn't have been surprised to learn as much as half the forty-five hundred souls in Columbia were slaves. He shook his head as he entered the hotel.

Behind the counter, a clerk, who had been leaning over, reading a newspaper, straightened up, "Welcome to the Congaree hotel, gentlemen."

Will paid for two rooms, and as he followed the slave porter, he glanced back at the clerk. The man's black, curly hair and swarthy skin indicated he was of mixed race. But Will couldn't tell if the clerk was a freedman or slave.

Later, after dinner, the other five men joined Will in one of the rooms. "I feel we're close enough to the kidnappers to reach out and touch them," Will opened up.

Sergeant Jensen said, "We need to be open to wherever the clues lead us, sir. If we break up the town into a grid tomorrow, we should be able to search it fairly quickly and find out if our kidnapping counterfeiters stayed in the area."

Will tilted his head toward the Dane, "What do you have in mind?"

"We could pair up and search each section of the grid until we learn about the men who took your son."

Left unspoken was the risk they would search the town and come up empty. Will shoved the thought aside. *"We'll find the next thread in the tapestry, and when we do, I'll yank it so hard the whole damned thing will come unraveled."*

The next day Will and Lieutenant Morales walked into a mortuary. The undertaker was working on a casket. When Will described Charlie and the best description they had of Obadiah Jenkins the undertaker shook his head. "I ain't heard tell of them folks." He turned away from Will and yelled at the black man who had been holding a plank of pine. "Boy, set that down and run and tell the Widow Jackson the casket will be ready on the morrow."

For a moment, Will's singular mission to find Charlie was derailed by the command. Slavery was all too common in Texas, especially in the eastern part of the Republic. But in San Antonio and Austin, while it was growing, it hadn't become ubiquitous as it was in Columbia. Will's twenty-first-century views had taken a beating over the years, but not on slavery. If anything, he reviled it more seven years after the transference than before.

"Your slave have a name?"

The undertaker looked up, an expression of surprise on his face. "I'm sure he does. But he's not mine. I rent him from a planter after the harvest. Maybe if Mr. Lamont would send the same buck back each time, I'd bother to learn his name."

Will had assumed the black man had been the undertaker's slave. That he was rented out hadn't crossed his mind.

The undertaker continued, "If a slave does well, I'll pass him a couple of bits. I ain't going to be niggardly toward them."

The man's lips twitched, waiting to see if Will would react to the near-homonym. Will allowed a slight frown to crease his lips. He recalled hearing the word niggardly nearly cause fights back in the twenty-first century when he had served in Iraq. An officer, an Aggie from A & M, had explained the word was Scandinavian in origin, meaning stingy, and had entered the English language in the fourteenth century, long before English imported the Latin word for black.

Dryly, Will said, "You're a credit to South Carolina." With that, he turned and walked out.

As he and Morales reached the street, they heard a noise from a nearby alley. Turning, Will saw the slave who had left the building a few minutes earlier beckoning for them to approach.

"Y'alls was looking for some white men?"

The slave's eyes darted back and forth, fearfully.

"Yes."

The slave slipped deeper into the narrow space between two buildings. "I's not want anyone t' see us."

When he was hidden within the shadows, he said, "You got a boy named Charlie?"

Will's heart skipped a beat when he heard his son's name. "Where is he? Is he alright?"

"You didn't hear this from me, but Mr. Jason Lamont, he had a passel of men and a boy named Charlie who been staying at Saluda Grove. They treat the boy near bad as they treat me."

Will sagged against the wall of one of the buildings. He was torn between relief and helplessness.

"Are you a slave at Saluda Grove?"

The response was a single nod.

"Can you take me and my companions there?"

The fear returned to the other man's eyes as they slid toward the street. "Marse Jason will kill me if he finds out."

"We'll take you with us when we leave." Nothing was going to get between Will and rescuing his son.

Finally, the slave said, "Alright."

It took a couple of hours to find the others before Will's party was able to follow Henry, the slave from the alley, back toward Saluda Groves.

The plantation was upriver from Columbia, above where the Saluda River fed into the Congaree. They rented a skiff and with Henry's help, finding the place was easy.

Will and his companions were led to a place on the Saluda where they could hide in the cattails along the bank. Keeping low, he moved forward, until he used his hand to sweep aside the foliage. He raised the binoculars to his eyes and looked at the plantation. It was big. From his vantage, he saw fields, lying fallow in winter, stretching across the landscape, sprinkled with groves of white oak and dogwood trees.

In the distance, he saw split rail fencing. He marked that as where the road ran toward the Lamont mansion. Weeping willow trees were evenly spaced along the lane. Despite the binocular's range, he didn't see any buildings. "How big is this place?"

Henry, standing a few feet behind him, said, "Big. Marse Jason says he's got more than a thousand acres."

"How many slaves?"

"Close to a hundred."

Will lowered the glasses. "I want some eyes on the slave quarters and the plantation manor." He turned to the men, "I'd like Lobo and Running Creek to scout the lay of the land. Find out the best route to and from where they're keeping Charlie."

He knelt by the slave, "Can you take these two men with you, and show them the way to where they're keeping my son?"

Henry had been calm, as though his life didn't hang in the balance, by his association with Will and his companions. The question, though, reminded Will of a deer in the headlights. "We gets caught, and I'll hang. It's bad enough I brought you here."

Frustrated, Will ground his teeth. "You've got nothing to worry about here. We'll protect you. You've brought us this far. Help us the rest of the way."

Slowly, the other man nodded. He turned and beckoned to the Mexican and Cherokee to follow as he slipped out of the thicket of cattails.

Will watched the three men disappear into twilight's gloom before settling down to wait.

Chapter 13

From his seat on a log, Charlie observed a woman lift the cast iron skillet from the fire. His mouth watered as the aroma of fresh-baked cornbread reached his nose. Another woman stirred a large pot. He could hear the water boiling and imagined the small, cut potatoes bouncing in the boiling water. With any luck chunks of pork would be mixed in with the tubers.

Cuffey, the young slave who he had worked beside when he was still allowed, sat beside him. "That's gonna be some fine eating tonight, Mister Charlie. Winnie, she's a mighty fine cook. And say what you will about some of you folks," his eyes slid over to Hiram Williams, who was lurking near the fire, puffing on a pipe, "there's more food to eat while you're with us."

A stranger to plantation life before arriving at Saluda Groves, Charlie had been surprised to find the fare eaten by the slaves had been so plain. The plantation grew nearly all its own food. For every four acres of cotton, there was an acre for corn, wheat, potatoes, or other foodstuffs. There were gardens sprinkled around the slave cabins where squash, radishes, beans, and other vegetables were grown.

Cuffey had told him Marse Jason could get stingy with the amount of grain provided for the slaves, especially in the months between harvesting the crops and the planting season. He had told Charlie a few other nearby plantation owners had a few trusted men, some even who were slaves, that supplemented their rations with game. Not Jason Lamont, though. The idea of a slave with a gun was one Lamont rejected. It would have resulted in a dead slave on this plantation.

"Come and get it!"

The slaves held back as Jenkins' men and Charlie ladled food onto their plates. As Charlie was walking back to the stump he heard Williams' voice, "Now, Winnie, you're shorting me some pork there."

Charlie turned around in time to see Williams wrench the ladle from her hand and use it to fish another spoonful of pork and potatoes onto his tin plate.

He seethed as the hated man sauntered away from the cooking fire. His anger at Williams subsided as he dug into the food. It was bland, but he was hungry.

Charlie was chewing on a piece of pork when he heard Jackson's voice. "Ob, any word from Charleston?"

"The marshals or General Travis?"

"Six of one, half dozen of the other."

There was a low chuckle, followed by Jenkins' voice. "Lamont says the United States Marshals from the South Carolina district are still crawling over Charleston. Best as we can tell, they know the boy was moved through the area, but that's all."

Jackson said, "Why haven't we heard anything from Travis yet? Heaven knows it's been five months since we took the boy."

"Last I heard, the Texian army has only just been recalled from Mexico now that what passes for government in Mexico City has ratified their treaty. Rumor is, Travis left the army a couple of months ago. With any luck, we'll be hearing from him soon."

A boot scraped across the dirt, "Damned if all this waiting isn't taking a toll on us all."

Williams' sharp laugh cut through the night air. Jackson added, "Especially Hiram. He keeps carrying on like this, it ain't going to matter about the consequences to these darkies, he's going to wake up with his throat cut. And us with him."

Jenkins' laugh sounded hollow, "Lamont won't let that happen. We're safer here than we were in California."

Jackson's voice was cut off by a disturbance by the cooking fire. Charlie turned to see the slave named Winnie hurrying into the firelight followed by Williams. As he grabbed her by the waist, her hand reached out and slapped him. The sound of her palm on his cheek rang across the slave quarters.

"Bitch! I'll learn you not to slap your better!" Charlie cringed as Williams knocked the woman to the ground. He grabbed her by the hair, as she struggled to keep on her feet. Half dragging and pulling, he took Winnie into the cabin Charlie shared with his captors.

Charlie found himself on his feet, his hands clenched, as the telltale sounds of a one-sided fight emanated from the crude cabin. He glanced to his side and saw Cuffey. The young slave shook his head, as he wore a look of hopeless frustration.

Charlie turned until he saw Jenkins and Jackson. The half-breed from Florida was visibly agitated while Jenkins returned to eating his dinner. There was a scream and the ripping of clothing. Jenkins started shoveling food into his mouth, and Jackson swung around and walked into the darkness.

From the cabin, Winnie cried out, "Let me go, sweet Jesus, please, let me go."

Another slap and Charlie felt his face redden as Williams said, "Lay on back, missy. Or I'll give you another beating."

From within the cabin, the sounds of struggle lessened. Charlie was fifteen. He knew what was happening behind the closed door. The tears at the corners of his eyes burned as they streaked down his cheek. If his pa were here, he'd put a stop to that. Winnie was half Henrietta's age, but Charlie couldn't imagine Pa letting anyone lay a hand on the freedwoman housekeeper. His eyes swept across the circle of firelight and saw the slaves were agitated but afraid. He didn't see Joe, Henrietta's husband often, but he was sure that just like his pa, Joe wouldn't stand by and let some bastard abuse his wife.

Winnie's cries grew louder, and Williams laughed at her. Without realizing he was doing it, Charlie stalked over to the cooking fire and yanked a cooking knife from the hand of one of the women. He was halfway to the door, the dull blade in his hand gleaming from the glowing firelight when a sharp report from a gun broke the tension.

"Obadiah Jenkins, surrender or die!"

Will's knees were sore when he saw shadowy figures running low toward the cattail-lined river bank. Over the past couple of months' traveling, he had become close with the men with whom he traveled. Part of that was recognizing them or their shadows at night. Realizing he'd been holding his breath, he relaxed as one of the figures materialized into Jesse Running Creek.

The young Cherokee Ranger slid down the bank until he was next to Will. "Damnation, the Lamont plantation is big, General. The main house is nearly a mile away. But we found the slave cabins around eight hundred yards that way," he said, pointing into the inky night toward the south.

Will wanted to strangle the rest of the information from the young man. "Are they there?"

"Your boy's your spittin' image. Shock of red hair was what gave it away." Running Creek peered into the night, "Mostly a bunch of darkies fixing dinner like they was at a church social. Your son sticks out like a sore thumb."

The weight of three months of worry and fear lifted, as Will processed the news. He hadn't realized how tense he had grown until he was on the cusp of recovering his son. Lighter though the weight on his soul had become, there were still several men who needed to answer for their crimes. "Did you see his captors?"

"Yeah. There were four other white men with him in the slaves' quarters."

Will flexed his legs, kneading his calves as he stood. "What are we waiting for? Let's get this done."

Lobo, who had crouched beside the Cherokee, said, "The *güero* who owns this place is not at his *hacienda*. He and several of his men are on horseback hunting. Do they have *javelinas* here?"

Will shook his head. "Javelinas? No. Plenty of wild boar though. I suppose they could be hunting them. How many men with this Lamont fellow?"

"Three or four."

Will felt the cold iron at his hip as he ran his fingers on the revolver. Six shots. Even if both the kidnappers and the muckety-muck who owned the plantation were together, Will's men would have more than enough firepower to overwhelm them.

"Let's do this quick. Sergeant Jensen, follow Lobo to where this Lamont fellow is. If they close on the slave cabins, then slow them down. Running Creek will take the rest of us over to those cabins and capture ourselves some kidnappers."

The kind of weather one experiences in early December in South Carolina can be a roll of the dice. Will and his companions were lucky. The humidity was low for a plantation next to the Saluda River. The temperature was close to fifty degrees. Will heard his boots crunching the dead grass as he followed Running Creek's silhouette. After five minutes, he saw the dark frames of the slaves' cabins, encircling the campfire.

As Will neared, every footstep seemed louder than the previous, but nobody turned, and he and his companions approached. He froze when he heard a woman's plaintive cry above the crackling of the campfire.

Then Will saw him. Reflecting in the light of the fire, was a splash of red hair. The memory of the last time he had seen his son leapt into his mind. It had been the day Will had led the army from San Antonio to the south. Charlie had been at that awkward stage in development where arms and legs were disproportionate to the rest of his body. How long had it been? It must have been eight or nine months. The boy was several inches taller. Despite the distance, it appeared the awkwardness of adolescence had been replaced by a youth nearly grown.

Another cry broke Will's attention, and he saw the slaves standing around the cooking fire were agitated. Charlie was on his feet, staring at the cabin from which cry had come. Another scream broke the spell, and his son was striding over to the fire and grabbed a kitchen knife from one of the women and turned and ran toward the closed door.

Without thinking, Will drew his pistol and fired into the air. He stepped in front of Running Creek and shouted, "Obadiah Jenkins, surrender or die!"

A big man was hurrying after Charlie. His pale skin reflected in the firelight. He carried a stick in one hand and had the other clenched in a fist. The boy was focused on the door he was approaching.

More than a hundred feet separated Will from his target, and the shot had sent the slaves racing for cover. He'd hit harder targets, but the humanity racing around the slave quarters interfered with a clean shot. With each step the other man took toward Charlie, the more worried Will became. But he sighted down the barrel and fired at his human target.

Nothing. Will swore while offering a silent prayer he hadn't hit any bystanders. He fired again. "Dammit!" The second shot missed, too. He took the pistol grip and held it with both hands, sighted down the barrel and lined up the shot. The man was only a step behind Charlie and raising the stick to strike.

Will exhaled and pulled the trigger. The stick fell to the ground, and the man clutched his chest and collapsed. A moment later, Charlie disappeared through the door.

As he rushed forward, Will became aware one of the kidnappers had a gun when he felt a hot rush of wind buzz by his ear. He heard a grunt and turned. Lieutenant Morales grabbed at the side of his head as he fell to the ground.

A swarthy, black-haired man, smaller than the first to fall, stood between two cabins, a revolver in his hands, smoke curling from the barrel. The sight of the pistol was a shock. No other nation had adopted Colt's firearm for military use, not even the United States. Outside of Texas, the guns were expensive and hard to find. Yet one of the kidnappers snapped off another round in Will's direction.

"Shit!" He ducked. It was stupid, he knew. Although the ball missed him, his reaction was instinctive. The kidnapper spun around, the pistol flying out of his hands. Running Creek stood, his smoking weapon in hand as he approached the fallen bandit.

From the shadow of one of the cabins, a figure flew at the Ranger. Too slow to swing his gun up, Running Creek was bowled over in the collision. His assailant was easily twice the young Cherokee's age, and even though he had the drop on the young man, Running Creek was fighting back.

As Will approached, there was a muffled gunshot, and the older man rolled off the younger. The Ranger still held his pistol, although the gun and his hand were bloody. The older man clutched at his stomach as Will stood over him. Will recognized the man's face from wanted poster from California. It was Obadiah Jenkins.

He still had a round in the cylinder. And Will wanted nothing more than to put a bullet in the body of the mastermind of his son's kidnapping. Instead, he reached out and pulled Running Creek to his feet.

In the distance, he heard the unmistakable sound of a shotgun. He had left Jensen and Lobo to hold off Lamont and his men, but with things growing quiet, he said, "Go help Jensen."

Will knelt by Jenkins and studied the man who had forced him to cross a continent. He could hear the labored breathing and see the mess of the man's chest rise and fall. His breathing was shallow and labored. Grinding his teeth in frustration, Will climbed to his feet. He'd get no answers from Jenkins.

Ignoring the flurry of gunshots from the other side of the slave quarters, Will raced toward the cabin Charlie had enter only minutes earlier. He heard sobbing as he stepped across the threshold. Nearly a year older, but he instantly recognized his son's voice as the youth cursed through the sobbing.

There was a lone candle on a table in the cabin. Wax pooled on the table, as the nub cast a feeble light. But it was enough for Will to see. Charlie sat atop a smaller man, who lay face down. The handle of a kitchen knife protruded from the man's back. The dead man's shirt was torn from where the blade had ripped open his skin, and blood soaked the material.

Beneath the body lay another. A black girl, perhaps a couple of years older than Charlie, struggled under the dead weight. She whimpered as she pushed against Williams' corpse.

Will gripped Charlie's shoulder, "Son, it's over. He's dead." He helped Charlie to his feet, then rolled the body off the girl. She scooted away from them until her back was against the wall. Purple welts were rising on her throat from where her dead assailant had attempted to choke the life from her.

Will had seen the look in his son's eyes before. It took him back to before the transference, during his first tour in Iraq. During one of the battles in Fallujah, as his fireteam cleared a house, a member of his team had secured a room when an insurgent stumbled into it from a hallway. The soldier's rifle jammed when he fired on the intruder. He finally killed the other man with his M9 bayonet after a short but fierce scuffle. When Will pulled his friend from the dead insurgent, he's eyes were dilated and he moved slowly, as though in a trance. The shock of killing the insurgent wore off, but it took time.

"Come on, Charlie, let's get out of here." Will guided his son from the cabin and as soon as they stepped into the firelight, he called out, "There's a girl in here, she needs help."

An older slave woman, who had been hiding behind one of the building ran past him, into the cabin.

Charlie released his grip on the kitchen knife as he felt Williams shudder beneath him. He looked at his hands, covered in blood. Williams' blood. The rage of the last few months seeped away as his tormentor gasped his last breath.

As he replayed the previous moments, Charlie hadn't realized he was standing inside the doorway with the knife in his hand until he saw Williams with his pants around his ankles, and the slave girl's dress hiked up. When he realized Williams' hands were throttling the life out of the girl, Charlie had leapt forward, plunging the knife into Williams' back.

Charlie had wanted to feel his fists smash into Williams' face and to kick and stomp on him until cried out for mercy. Instead, a knife in the back ended Williams' life. Instead of rage or fear, there was nothing now except the release of months' worth of fear and anxiety.

He felt a gentle hand on his shoulder, "Son, it's over."

The voice he had longed to hear for months shocked him out of his stupor, and he climbed off the body. He tried to say something, anything. But the words were stuck in his throat.

Although the empty pain threatened to overwhelm, Charlie clung to his father, scalding tears streaking his face.

"Merciful God, I feared I'd never find you, Son."

The words were a balm. His pa had crossed thousands of miles to rescue him. As he wiped at his tears, Charlie became aware of the banging of guns. "Did you get them all?"

His father nodded. "Yeah. Jenkins and the rest of his men are dead."

He followed his father into the firelight. The cooking fire had spread. Flames were licking their way up the side of one of the cabins. There were a few bodies on the ground, but most of the slaves were nowhere to be seen.

His pa knelt beside slave. A gaping wound had disfigured his face. Travis swore as he climbed to his feet. "I guess we'll not be taking him with us, after all.

Travis turned to Charlie and said, "He told us where to find you, son. I'd told him we'd take him away. He must have been hit by a stray bullet."

Charlie stared at the dead slave. He'd known very little about him other than he was a skilled carpenter.

From out of the gloom, he saw one of the Rangers he recognized from the Alamo garrison, from what seemed a lifetime ago, prodding a middle-aged man before him. Jason Lamont bled from a gash above his eye. Blood seeped from between his fingers where he held his right arm. His lips were twisted in a grimace as he looked around the slave quarters.

"Who the hell do you think you are?"

His pa stepped forward and struck him square in the face, "I'm the man who holds your life in his hands." He stepped back and waved toward the ground behind him. "Jenkins and his group of murderers are dead. Why shouldn't you join them?"

Lamont spat on the ground between them. "To hell with you, Travis. I've heard about your abolitionist ways out in Texas. You'd destroy everything we've built if given half a chance."

Charlie had heard his pa say as much in the privacy of their home on more than one occasion. Now, Lamont was met with silence.

"If you're smart, you'll tell your man to release me. My men will return with the sheriff, and I suspect he'll have more than a few words for you about killing my guests."

The sound of his pa's harsh laughter echoed off the nearby cabins, "Aiding and abetting murderers and kidnappers? Normally, I'd take you up on that, but we're done here."

He pulled his pistol from its holster and shot Lamont in the knee. The planter collapsed, cursing at his pa.

Travis said, "You deserve to die for helping Jenkins. But I'm feeling merciful. Maybe the sheriff will get here before your slaves realize you're helpless and alone. Maybe he won't."

As his pa turned and walked away, Charlie had to hurry to catch up. Part of him wanted to go back and finish what Travis had started. Lamont deserved to die. But as Pa receded into the shadows, Charlie, without a backward glance, followed.

Along the bank of the Saluda River, a boat was staked to the shoreline. Two men, Mexican by their appearance, were already in the boat. One was wrapping a bandage around the other's head. As Charlie climbed into the skiff, a voice called out, "Mister Charlie!"

Poking through the cattails was Cuffey. "Take me with you, please."

The slave had scrapes and cuts along both his arms and his homespun shirt was torn. He stepped into the shallows, next to the boat, "I seen what your pa done to Marse Jason. When the sheriff come, there's gonna be hell for us to pay."

Charlie glanced at his pa, who gave a curt nod. With hands still stained with Williams' blood, he helped the slave into the boat, as it was pushed away from the shoreline. The men dipped their oars into the water and rowed to freedom.

Chapter 14

9 December 1843

Her hands were cold as she pulled the wet clothes from the wooden bucket's soapy water. Although the sun was shining, the biting north wind cut through her woolen dress. She grabbed the wet clothes and took them to a flat wooden platform, where she spread the material using a wooden rolling pin to squeeze out the water.

"Becky, you nearly done? Dinner will be ready soon." Elizabeth Crockett stood in the doorway, blocking Liza, who was trying to move through her legs. Approaching two years of age, the toddler was confident she could skootch by her grandmother if she just pushed hard enough.

Without missing a beat, Elizabeth used the spoon in her hand and landed it on the backside of her granddaughter.

In the midst of the child's squalls, Becky smiled. "Just a few more minutes. I want to get these hanging on the line before dinner."

The door closed, muffling the sound of her daughter. Things could have been worse. When she and her family had arrived, Don Garza hired her to handle his household's laundry. Word traveled fast around West Liberty, and in less than a week, she had as much work washing clothes as she could manage.

Becky was swapping out a shirt on the board when she heard a high-pitched voice in Spanish, "Señora Travis, Don Garza sent me for his laundry."

Becky wiped her hands and turned around. A Tejano child stood on the porch of her house, swinging his arms in wide arcs, trying to stay warm. She spared a smile for the boy. As she gathered Garza's clean laundry, the boy said "Did you see the train? There was a couple of cars full of soldiers getting off."

As she handed him a bundle, he continued, "There was a whole company of men from Gulf Farms getting off the train. Don Garza said the rest of the men ought to be returning before Christmas."

She handed him the second bundle. He said, "Won't that be a wonderful Christmas gift for all the families in town?"

Laden down, the boy moved away, toward Garza's hacienda. As Becky watched him leave, she leaned against the porch and grabbed at her arms, shivering.

The idea the army's reserves were being demobilized should have filled her with joy. It meant an official end to Texas' war in Mexico. Instead, she felt a tear slide down her cheek. It was hot against her icy skin. She missed Will; her war wouldn't be over until he returned with Charlie.

After saying a prayer for her husband and stepson, she finished the laundry before going inside.

"Becky, do we have any more sugar?" Elizabeth said from the corner of the one-room house that served as their kitchen.

"No, ma. A pound was thirty-five cents. That's highway robbery."

Elizabeth grunted as she stirred the pot, "I can't bake my Christmas cakes without something sweet. What about molasses?"

"Sixty cents for a gallon."

The spoon rattled in the pot as Elizabeth said, "I thought we'd won the war. What with prices three or four times more expensive than before, how are we supposed to eat."

Becky hid her smile as Liza pretended to be her grandma, stomping across the floor, while babbling. "It could be worse. At least flour and cornmeal are close to the same price as before. It's not like we're going to starve."

From her place on the floor, Liza stomped and twirled, squealing, "Not starve!"

Both women forgot about the high cost of luxury items as they laughed at the toddler.

"We'll be getting underway in an hour, sir." Captain Thompson said as they sat in the captain's cabin. He glanced at Charlie, who had taken the chair next to Will's. "I confess, I wondered if you were on a fool's errand, General, but damned if you don't show up with your son and prove me wrong."

"Let me know when you're putting this boat through the Bolivar Roads, then I'll consider celebrating." The Bolivar Roads, named in honor of the South American liberator, was the narrow channel separating Galveston from a peninsula with the same name.

"With any luck, I'll have y'all home before..."

Will heard a shout from the ship's deck and a moment later the heavy pounding of shoes racing along the narrow hallway belowdecks. A midshipman stood at the door to the Captain's cabin, "Beg your pardon, Captain, but a boat's hailing us."

Will followed the captain topside where he saw a small dinghy bobbing in the water. On the little boat, a man stood in the bow, balancing against the low gunwales. "United States Marshal TJ Condy, permission to board the *Nueces*?"

Several more men were crowded into the small boat. Captain Thompson glanced at Will, "It seems you may have been right, General. I can't refuse them permission." He turned to the midshipman and said, "Get them onboard and send for Lieutenant Porter."

Will and Charlie joined Captain Thompson on deck, aft from the ship's wheel. Cuffey was in the ship's infirmary. A well-dressed man came up the ship's ladder. He waited by the gangway until another man crawled up beside him.

The Nueces' midshipman escorted them aft. "Captain Thompson," his youthful voice cracked, "United States Marshal Condy and Sheriff's deputy Alfred Brown to see you, sir."

The marshal looked more like a clerk than a lawman, but Brown looked like the stereotypical southern lawman minus the badge. He wore a brace of caplock pistols on his hips and a shotgun slung over his shoulder.

Condy dipped his head to the ship's captain, "See you're getting ready to head out, so we're mighty thankful for your time. Deputy Brown arrived on the train this afternoon from Richland district. Says that he's tracking an escaped slave from one of the plantations in the Midlands."

Thompson frowned, "Odd place to come searching, don't you think Marshal?"

Brown stepped forward and spat a stream of tobacco juice over the railing, "I got my reasons for wanting to check the ships in port before they sail away." His eyes slid toward Charlie.

Condy caught the motion and let his eyes rest on the boy, too. After a long pause, he said, "Well, bless my soul. It seems that you've managed to track down General Travis' missing son, and here in South Carolina no less. I guess all those notices from Washington for me and my deputies to keep an eye out for the boy had some truth behind them."

Brown tore his eyes from the boy and shifted his glare between the captain and the marshal. "The boy don't interest me none. Just want to search the ship and make sure no escaped slaves are on board."

Will wondered how much the deputy knew about the raid. He stepped in front of Charlie and offered his hand to the marshal, "William Travis, sir. I wish I'd have made your acquaintance a few days ago. Turns out my companions and I had the good fortune of tracking the murdering and thieving renegades who kidnapped my son to their hiding hole in Deputy Brown's district."

When Condy turned to the deputy, Brown shook his head, "That shit don't concern me. Just looking for runaways."

Will's lip twitched. He turned to Condy, "I doubt Deputy Brown bothered telling you that we found my son on one of the plantations on the Saluda River. The men who captured him were hiding in plain sight in the slaves' quarters. When we showed up the slaves ran one way, and my son's kidnappers ran the other."

Will might have been standing on a Texian flagged ship, but he wasn't going to admit to killing them in front of a US Marshal.

Condy turned on Brown, "That would have been worth passing along, don't you think? How many slaves have run off that plantation?"

Brown stepped back, surprised at the other man's tone, "Hell, I don't know. I was told to get my ass over to Charleston and see if any Texians were in town. That there was a slave with them."

Will nearly enjoyed watching the Marshal stare down the deputy. With a prolonged sigh, Condy turned back to Will and Captain Thompson. "I don't suppose you've seen any slaves hereabouts?"

Both men shook their heads.

Condy turned to leave, "Come on, maybe we can get you back to Columbia, and you can make yourself useful finding runaways."

Brown cursed, "I want to search the ship. They're lying. Damned if there ain't any slaves onboard."

Condy reached the ship's ladder, "Search yourself if they let you. Unless you can part the Red Sea or walk on water, you're on your own for a ride back to shore."

Fuming and swearing, Brown followed the marshal over the ship's side.

Once the boat pulled away, Captain Thompson turned to Will and with a wink, raised his voice, "Hoist the anchor! Next stop, Galveston."

The dolphin leapt into the air in front of the *Nueces*, splashing back into the water of Bolivar Roads. Charlie leaned over the gunwales and pointed, “Look, Pa. There’s a whole family of them!”

His pa laughed and leaned against the side of the ship, “They’re called a pod. Magnificent creatures.”

More of the dolphins leapt from the water, racing ahead of the steamship. “Why do they do that?”

Travis shrugged, “Who knows, maybe they’re bored. Racing against the ship has got to be more fun than searching for their next meal.”

Charlie hadn’t felt as free since the night he slipped out of the house so many months before. The cold northern breeze bit at his cheeks, turning them a bright, rosy red. His pa had already ignored the dolphins at play before the ship. He’s seen Travis wear that expression during the ten-day voyage home.

“Merry Christmas, Pa. I can hardly wait to see Liza, David, and Becky. I bet they’ll plant wet kisses on us.”

His pa turned away from the bow and tousled his red hair, “I imagine they will. And, yes, it’s going to be a very Merry Christmas. The whole family will be together in just a few days.”

From the narrow channel to the port of Galveston was but a distance of a few miles, and they were soon standing near ship’s pilot as he edged the *Nueces* toward her berth alongside one of Galveston’s docks.

Captain Thompson’s smile was tinged with melancholy. “It’ll be good to spend Christmas with family. As a navy man that often doesn’t happen. It’ll be a quieter celebration this time around.”

Without thinking, Charlie asked, “Why?”

With a conspiratorial and exaggerated wink at the youth, “The price of whiskey is four times what it was last Christmas. Now, lad, how's a sailor supposed to celebrate his savior's birth if he can't afford to lift up a glass or two as a toast?"

Charlie was laughing at Thompson's reply as the sailors of the *Nueces* secured the ship to the pier. Even his pa wore a cheerful smile.

"General, you're welcome to join my family for dinner, if you've not made other arrangements."

Travis grabbed his gear and headed toward the gangplank, "Much obliged, I have a business associate I'd like to see before catching the ferry to Anahuac tomorrow."

Charlie watched with his pa while the other men who had been part of his rescue assembled on deck. Sergeant Jensen and Rangers Running Creek and LeBlanc were dressed in their worn and patched butternut uniforms. Javier Morales and Lobo stood off to the side. Without their help, Charlie shuddered to think how bad things could have been. They had made it possible for his pa to rescue him. Travis drew up straight before the three Rangers and gave them a crisp salute, "When there's a dangerous mission, there are no men I'd rather have at my side then Hays' Special command. Y'all went way beyond what was required and if I can ever repay you, look me up."

He turned to the two Mexicans and switched over to Spanish, "Lieutenant, it is a small measure of my gratitude, but if you or Lobo need a place to work, I can give you a letter of recommendation to the Gulf Farms Corporation. I think my word still carries a bit of weight with Don Garza."

Eventually, the other men moved off, and Charlie was alone with his pa on the dock. "Go fetch Cuffey and let's see if we can find Mr. Williams' house. He and I have some catching up to do."

The greenish-gray surf pounded the beach as Will watched Charlie and Samuel Williams' son, Austin racing along the sand. He sat in the wicker chair next to his business partner.

"You mean to tell me all of the bank's capital is holding treasury certificates, including our depositors' money?"

Williams smiled apologetically, "General, the whole house of cards our national finances are built on nearly came down around Michel Menard's ear. If I hadn't stepped in and used our reserves, the entire bond market would have collapsed."

Will shook his head, "Oh, I don't doubt you, Sam. It's just, damn, all our depositors' money? People have got to be howling."

"Your wife included." Williams explained about the meeting with Becky Travis the previous month, "You've married yourself a good one. She wasn't going to turn loose without something."

Will's heart ached at hearing Becky's name. "I miss her something powerful, Sam. When I get back to San Antonio, I don't imagine you or anyone else will be able to pry me loose for a very long time." He wasn't able to keep the longing from his voice, and he was rewarded with a poke in the ribs for his candor.

"Good news for you. I understand your wife and family are living in West Liberty. With any luck, she'll be in your arms tomorrow."

The news buoyed Will's spirit. "Don't doubt it, Sam. I'm done with the army. I'm going to focus on providing for my wife and children. I've missed too much of Charlie's life, and I'm not going to repeat that mistake with Liza or David."

Williams leaned over the chair, "A man like you doesn't just say that without something else in mind, General."

Will shifted his gaze and watched the children at play on the beach. It was the dead of winter, but Charlie and Austin Williams were far from the only youngsters racing up and down the sand dunes. "When I left off for Mexico, Dr. Smith had discovered a rather unstable chemical compound that he turned over to Gail Bordon. I want to catch up with what Mr. Bordon has been working on, but in addition to that, I've a mind to work with him and a young patent clerk in Austin. I've got some ideas that could industrialize Galveston Bay. Maybe even give Texas a second export than just cotton."

Williams whistled appreciatively, "Do tell."

The sun sank below the western Gulf before Will and Sam rounded up their sons and walked back to the Williams' home.

A squall to rival a tornado ripped through the Travis home. Becky turned around in time to see her toddler dumping the dregs of a flour bag onto her little brother, who protested with all his might.

"Liza, quit picking on your brother!" Becky's voice was loud enough to startle her daughter, who joined her little brother in a harmony of caterwauling.

"You're outnumbered, dear," Elizabeth said from the safety of a rocking chair in the corner.

Becky glared at her mother as she picked up David and dusted the flour from his powdery hair. "You could help."

She received back a raspy chuckle, "Let me know how you manage it when you've got six children under your feet. Lordy, I don't know how I managed."

Becky moved around the center of the one-room cabin until David calmed down. She saw her mother was lost in thought.

She circled around until she deposited David into his grandmother's open arms. "I miss Pa, too. I still can't imagine that David Crockett won't eventually walk through that door."

Elizabeth patted her on the hand, "Am I that easy to read? This is the first Christmas without him since he brought us to Texas. To know there will never be another, that's hard."

Becky felt the tears welling up in her eyes when there was a knock at the door. She looked questioningly to her mother. Elizabeth shrugged, "Maybe someone with laundry?"

With a shake of her head, Becky crossed the room and lifted the handle. Standing in the doorway was Will. She squealed at the sight of her husband and threw her arms around his neck. The tears which had threatened to spill down her cheeks only moments before, freely flowed. "Oh, Will, I've missed you so much!"

She felt his body as he clung tightly to her. "Becky, I don't ever want to be apart from you again." His lips searched for hers, and they clung to each other until Charlie coughed noisily. "A man could freeze standing on the porch."

Becky laughed at hearing her stepson's voice, as she swept her husband into the small cabin. "You found him." She detached herself long enough to pull the youth into the hug.

From the rocking chair, Elizabeth came over, with little David hanging on her hip. Becky reached out and pulled her mother and her son into the embrace. A tug on her dress followed by a plaintive, "Mama," from knee level reminded Becky that for the first time in the better part of a year, her family was together.

Chapter 15

Lying next to Becky felt both right and strange after so many months away. Will turned onto his side and draped his arm over her. He could hear little David tossing about in his crib. In the corner of the cabin, Charlie's soft snores added to the nighttime noises.

He drew in his wife's scent and crinkled his nose. It was too crowded in the cabin and bathing wasn't something one did outside when it was forty degrees. He could take the family back to San Antonio and pick up where he left off. The letter from Lorenzo de Zavala was still lying on the table, congratulating him on his son's safe return and offering to reinstate him as commander of the army.

Three hundred dollars a month salary was a princely sum, but he was sick of being away from his family. Liza and David needed a father, and it weighed heavily on him that Charlie's impulsive behavior the previous year may have been influenced by Will's own sense of adventure. More than that, he had left Becky and her mother in a tight spot. True, the Commerce Bank's issues were not of his making, but had he been there for her, Becky wouldn't have had to pick the family up, just to survive.

Becky snorted and rolled onto her back, and Will held his breath as he gazed at her sleeping form. Her breasts rose and sank with the deep rhythm of sleep. No, he was done with the army. He was thirty-four years old. Between his life before the transference and this one, he had spent nearly thirteen years wearing his country's uniform.

Since waking up in William Barret Travis' body, his focus had been singular. The Texian army was firmly established, and Sid Johnston was a capable officer. But with few exceptions, everything Will had tried to use his knowledge to advance had been military in nature. What could he accomplish if he worked to create inventions a bit ahead of their time?

The opportunity was there. Ten days since arriving home and Sam Williams had already traveled from Galveston and begged him to join in running the bank. Not to be outdone, Don Garza had offered him a job overseeing part of the commercial farming project. Even John Berry Sr. from Trinity Arms had offered him a job leading the armory's research and development team.

Any one of them would help to replace the income from his military salary and getting out of the tiny cabin was important, he thought, as he heard his mother-in-law's ripsaw of a snore. All of these enterprises were worth his effort, of that he was sure. But he had been mulling over something more. On a whim, a couple of years before, he had suggested of the late President Crockett hiring Richard Gatling as a patent clerk. In another world, Gatling would have invented the first machine gun. That was undoubtedly still a possibility, but he had already aided the army by developing a rocket flare. Will decided Gatling's talents were wasted as a clerk.

As he opened his eyes and stared at the dark ceiling, Will's thoughts turned to Ashbel Smith. The surgeon general of the army was back in San Antonio, running the army's hospital at the Alamo and conducting experiments. Will had grown to like the taciturn doctor and hoped he would be open to creating a teaching facility to train more doctors. There were things Will realized he knew about medicine that, if he could find a way to open Dr. Smith's eyes, could start a revolution to eradicate yellow fever and cholera, both of which posed threats to Texas.

Then there were Gail Borden and Andy Berry. The two of them had taken Dr. Smith's research on gun cotton and used it to develop TNT or at least something that worked similar to it. Will hoped they would eventually produce smokeless powder. From what he had picked up since returning home, they were already working on it.

Could he pull these disparate men together and form a research campus? Individually, they were each making contributions to medicine, science, and mechanical engineering. If he could harness their energies what could they accomplish? Which new inventions would ease the life of the people he loved?

Calling it a research campus sounded too plane. While he wanted to encourage profitable enterprises there, he also wanted to see men and women educated. Texas College? No, too generic, he thought. What about Trinity College? Will liked the sound of it. Trinity College it would be.

Becky rolled over and opened her eyes. "Can't sleep?"

"Just thinking."

She leaned in and kissed him. "If you're not going to sleep, at least hold me. I've missed feeling your arms around me."

Soon thoughts of a research campus were pushed from his mind.

The next day was Sunday. As Will shepherded his family out of the clapboard Methodist church, he spied Gail Borden talking with several men outside of the similarly clad Baptist church. His thoughts from the previous night leapt back into his mind. He excused himself and left Becky to take the children the short distance to their home, with a promise he'd not be long.

As Becky shifted David from one hip to the other, she poked his arm. "Where have I heard that before? There'll be a plate waiting for you."

As Will approached, Borden waved and broke off his conversation with several men. "General Travis, I trust this first Lord's day of eighteen forty-four finds you well."

Will tugged at the scarf which hung around his neck, "Having my family back together was the best Christmas present I could have received, Mr. Borden."

"Terrible situation, sir. But it's testimony that the Lord answers prayers."

Will's thoughts ran toward the image of him waking up in the body of William Barret Travis and wondered whose prayers had been answered by that cosmic event. "I understand you and young Mr. Berry had good luck building off Dr. Smith's discovery."

"Ashbel's discovery of nitrogenated cotton has opened many possible areas of research, General. I wish I had more time to dedicate to research all of them."

Will smiled. "Funny you should mention that. I've been thinking," and with that, Will launched into his proposal.

Later, when he arrived home, Becky was lying on the bed between Liza and David, who were both napping. She glanced at the table, where a single place setting was set. Softly she said, "Just about what I expected. Did you solve all the world's problems?"

Will took the plate over to the fireplace where he ladled a spoonful of stew from a pot. He lifted it to his face and sniffed. Bits of chicken and sausage were mixed in with the stew's vegetables. As he sat at the table, he said, "Probably not. Mexico still hates us, slavery still plagues us, and my mother-in-law sleeps on a pallet in the same room we share. But if I can get Sam and a few others to work with me on some finances, maybe we can make the world a better place."

27 January 1844

Erasmo Seguin tugged his hat low over his ears. The open field outside of Harrisburg was crowded with tents and people despite the cold northern wind. He walked by a tent, where a tavern keeper from Houston was selling beer and whiskey. As he stepped around a pile of horse droppings, he thought the day's event was turning into a carnival.

Part of him wished he had been able to bring Maria, but his wife of forty years was back in Austin, sick with a cold. She would have enjoyed the carnival-like spectacle on the fields east of Harrisburg. At least more than him, he thought as he stepped around a mud puddle. He wished he had been able to send his son, Juan, to do the business that brought him to the windswept prairie. But his son was busy touring the supply depots on the military road between San Antonio and Santa Fe.

Despite the reduction in the army's size, Juan still commanded the small battalion of regular cavalry employed by the Republic. Their mission had grown; no longer only patrolling between the Gulf of Mexico and Ysleta, they now had to cover the entire border to the Pacific Ocean. Less than three hundred cavalry were inadequate to the task, but his son soldiered on, happy to focus his energy on the daunting challenge.

Seguin sighed as a group of boys raced across his path, chasing after a dog that was chasing after a cat. More than he wanted to admit, he wished he was back in Austin with Maria.

The San Jacinto River came into view. If it were possible, the tents along the riverbank were packed more tightly together than the tents further away. The milling mass of humanity was thicker. Even so, a few minutes later he stood on the shoreline and looked at what had brought thousands of people out on this cold, wintry day.

Stone pilings raised into the air on both banks of the river. Atop the pilings, wooden trestles stretched across the river. A glance at his pocket watch told him less than an hour remained before a locomotive would thunder across the bridge, connecting Houston and Harrisburg to West Liberty and Anahuac. More than seventy miles of railroad tracks now connected towns around Galveston Bay. Turning away from the river, Seguin couldn't help but wonder how long before the railroad snaked westward, connecting the eastern part of the Republic with its western cities of Austin and San Antonio.

From a nearby tent, Seguin recognized a voice. It was nearly shouting. With a grimace, he made his way toward the tent. While the railroad across the San Jacinto River was a noteworthy reason to have a carnival, it wasn't enough to make him leave his Maria and travel two hundred miles. The men arguing in the nearby tent, however, were enough.

As he approached the closed tent flap, a man wearing the silver Ranger star from the Republic's frontier battalion, nodded and flung the flap open. In accented English, he heard, "By reducing the flow of cotton-backs into circulation, we're strengthening our economy. I'm not going to stand by while you push to devalue our currency."

Seguin saw Sam Williams, the president of the Commerce Bank, wagging his finger under Michel Menard's nose. "That's easy for you to say, you're not the one whose depositors are left holding the bag."

Menard shot back, "You shouldn't have used money that wasn't yours, Sam. You're the bank president, you knew better than to tie up your depositors' money."

Williams turned to Seguin as he entered, "Erasmo, would you tell your thickwitted counterpart in the Treasury that he was the one who came knocking on my damned door, begging for me to help keep the war bonds afloat?"

Menard offered a weak grin in Seguin's direction, "Ignore Sam's theatrics, Erasmo. He's just upset that there are no loans to be had for bankers."

Williams stalked over to the wall of the tent and lifted a flap, revealing the carnival-like atmosphere outside, "Theatrics be damned, Michel. Your refusal to give me a loan affects these people more than it will ever affect me. The ones who didn't risk it all in Mexico worked hard to keep the economy floating along. They're the ones who trusted their hard-earned dollars to my bank. And I'm the sucker who trusted you with their money so Texas could win the war."

Seguin took a seat and said, "Michel, what's the harm of a loan for a few thousand cotton-backs? I've seen his bank's balance sheet. It's not like he's not good for it."

Menard scowled. "We have twelve million dollars in debts. The interest on our outstanding debts in eight-hundred thousand this year alone. Even after we pruned the army back to an acceptable level, our military costs are still more than three and a half million dollars."

Seguin said, "That's half of the equation. If my clerks' estimates are correct, the land bank will receive nearly four million dollars in payments this year. Our other sources of revenue should bring in nearly a million dollars, too. A loan that has the advantage of restoring confidence among our country's depositors seems sensible."

Williams wore a triumphant smile as he added, "What about the sale of Alta-California to the United States? Won't we receive the first payment this year?"

Menard stomped over to a table and filled a shot glass with an amber liquid from a crystal decanter. He took a sip and turned back to face the other men. "That money is earmarked for payment to Mexico. Our treaty to buy Alta-California from Mexico and our treaty to sell a good chunk of it to the United States are a wash."

"Not in the short term," Seguin said. "We pay Mexico a million dollars a year for ten years. The US pays us a million and a half for six years and a million in year seven. Seems to me, at least for a few years, we have some flexibility."

Menard growled in frustration. "Why, Juan? We need to rein in our spending and pay off our creditors. I don't want it to be us with French or British warships off our coast demanding payment for unpaid bills."

Seguin winced. A few years before, in 1838 the French had sent a squadron to Mexico to force payment of debts. Editorials in Texas' newspapers had been less than charitable to Mexico during that period of unpleasantness. The idea that the shoe was on the other foot didn't appeal to anyone in the tent. But he held up his finger in response. "One, we're secure within our borders and two, most of our loans are not held by the Europeans, and three, with you in the treasury department, I've no doubt we'll make our payments timely."

Menard cut in, "That's what I'm trying to accomplish by not adding anything else to the Republic's balance sheet."

Seguin held up a fourth finger, "One last thing to remember, is that we can't afford to lose our only functioning bank. A small loan and the people who have their money there will have confidence not just in their bank but in the nation's economy. Access to their money means that they'll spend it and add to our economic activity. I don't need to tell you how anemic that is today."

With the glass still in his hand, Menard returned to his seat and sagged into it. "Damn the both of you. I'll do it, but if you miss a single payment, Sam, I'm going to come after your bank for everything. How much do you need?"

Williams said, "Fifty thousand should let us return to normal business operations."

Menard visibly relaxed and took a sip. "I guess that's not too…"

Williams interrupted him. "I wasn't finished. Regarding the bonds we're holding. I want first rights on coupon redemption."

Menard's eyes bulged. The ground beneath their feet started shaking, and a loud steam whistle cut loose close by. Seguin couldn't hear his counterpart's words as the locomotive rumbled across the river, ushering in a new era of travel in the Republic.

Chapter 16

29 February 1844

Will was exhausted as he walked down the brick path from the Capitol Building toward the Stagecoach Inn. He'd rather have been back in Mexico, facing an army of *soldados* than negotiating the redemption of war bond coupons with Erasmo Seguin and Michel Menard.

As he waited for a wagon loaded with lumber to pass by on Congress Avenue, he thought back over the meeting and decided attending it had been more than worth it. During the war, the bank had purchased almost three-hundred thousand dollars in interest-bearing bonds. While the bonds would mature in ten years, there were monthly coupon payments which could be redeemed through the treasury department. Eighteen hundred dollars paid monthly to the bank would strengthen their position. While that alone would have been enough to bring him to Austin, he wouldn't be leaving until he took possession of the fifty-thousand-dollar loan Sam had negotiated from Menard.

Congress Avenue was clear, and he crossed the deeply rutted road. His hand was on the door handle to the inn when a voice called out, "Buck, by God, that is you!"

Will turned. Sid Johnston was hurrying along the sidewalk toward him. "I thought I saw you coming from that ugly pile of stone and brick. You're not trying to talk Lorenzo into giving your old job back?"

While Johnston's voice was light with laughter, Will thought he detected a note of worry. "Heaven forbid. I was wrangling some business with the Secretary of the Treasury."

Johnston slapped him on the back. "I hope you put him into a good mood. I've got to meet with the vulture tomorrow. He says we're over budget. I think he's going to try to force us to reduce the number of Sabine rifles being manufactured for the militia."

Will cocked an eyebrow. Those contracts were turning the Berry clan into a wealthy family. A town was growing up around the gun works. He'd pass the information along.

Johnston continued, "Join me for dinner, I've read the story of how you rescued your son, but I want to hear it from you."

Will smiled good-naturedly and let Johnston guide him to a table in the Inn's common room where he spent the next hour regaling one of his oldest friends with the unvarnished account. "And, even though more than two months have passed, Charlie still wakes up in a sweat from nightmares," Will concluded.

Johnston shook his head in wonder. "Lordy, Buck. If I didn't know the man you are, I'd say you were a liar."

Chuckling, Will said, "The truth is sometimes stranger than fiction. Now, enough about me. Are you taking good care of my baby?"

"Baby? Oh, the army," Johnston said as he realized the reference. "As well as can be expected. We're stretched too thin, now that all of the reserves and militia have been demobilized."

"What has Zavala left you with?"

Johnston glanced out a nearby window. The hill on top of which the Capitol sat was framed in the twilight. "Lorenzo has been good. It's Menard that keeps screaming for more cutbacks. I've got two battalions of infantry, Seguin's understrength cavalry battalion, a few batteries of artillery, and the frontier battalion of Rangers."

Will wasn't surprised. The war had nearly ruined the nation. Keeping even a couple of thousand men under arms was still an expensive undertaking for a country as small in population as Texas. "What about Hays' special Ranger command?"

The army's commander leaned forward, "I wish to God you'd talked that boy into staying in the army. I don't know what's going on, but several men who served under Hays have also resigned. I've heard he's got a land grant in California that he's getting ready to survey. Less than a company of his men are still in the army. I've assigned them to the First Infantry for now."

Will waited for the waiter to set their food down and depart before saying, "As long as things remain at peace between us and Mexico, things should be quiet."

Johnston cut into a slab of roasted pork, "That's my hope. The Comanche don't fancy another go at us, and the Mescalero are trying to figure out if our offer of land along the bend in the Rio Grande is a serious gesture. If they stay peaceful, we'll make out alright even if Menard forces more cuts on me."

Their conversation faded as they turned their focus to the food on their plates. Before parting ways with Johnston, Will realized how liberating it felt to have left the army behind.

The next morning, Will headed over to the Treasury building. He had less than an hour before the east-bound stagecoach left and there was one other person who he wanted to see. The building housing the Treasury Department was a two-story wood-framed rambling construction. Even from the street, he could see the original building's single floor had been added onto twice more as the Treasury department grew in size and scope.

Will found a staircase and headed up to the second floor. He stared at a long hallway with doors on either side. In a proper governmental building, each door would have a brass nameplate, telling passersby who was ensconced within. Some doors had wooded nameplates tacked up while others had a scrap of paper announcing the person or department within.

Will rapped on a door with a scrap of paper on it. A voice called out, "It's open."

Will found a man, in his mid-twenties, standing in front of a long table, which ran along one side of the room. Scattered amid stacks of correspondence and forms were a myriad of mechanical devices. Nearly every inch of the long table was covered.

Will was taken aback by the room's cluttered appearance. With an informal wave, the occupant said, "You wanted to see me, sir? Have a seat."

Will had to move a scale model of a reaping machine from a chair. "Thanks for taking the time to visit with me, Dick. I wanted to tell you how much I appreciated the rocket flares you made for the army last year."

Dick flushed and offered a sheepish smile. "Truth be told, one of the patents that came across my desk last year proposed the flares." He cast a glance around the room, "as you can see, I like to model some of the patents that we receive to see if they work. The rocket was from a fellow from Philadelphia."

Will eyed several of the models. The intricate details Dick captured made him think of the DaVinci models he'd seen in museums. "Yes, but you're the fellow who put it together for us. That's why I came to see you this morning. You see, Mr. Gatling, I'm working with a few other men of vision over in West Liberty to put together something." By the time Will finished explaining, he had to hurry to catch the stagecoach. As he flung himself down the stairs of the Treasury Building, he wore a broad grin. Things were coming together.

9 March 1844

The road between West Liberty and the newly incorporated town of Trinity Park was well maintained. Charlie urged the horse to a canter. He wanted to get there before breakfast. He was glad Señor Garza had allowed him the use of his stable. The ten miles between the two towns on foot would have taken hours. Ninety minutes after leaving the Garza stables, Charlie turned a bend in the road and saw the complex of buildings that constituted the Trinity Gun Works.

The buildings were constructed on the bank of the river. Channels had been dug into the shoreline, funneling fast-flowing water through chutes where it turned massive wheels. Those wheels were connected to shafts that connected to bellows and hammering machines. Charlie tuned out the hammering coming from the buildings. The town spreading out near the factory was his destination. With every visit, more houses were filling up the grid-like township.

He rode by a general store and a tavern, where he could smell fresh pine and paint. He swung off his mount at a crude cabin on the edge of the town. A middle-aged freedman sat on the porch, smoke curling from his pipe. "Mornin', Master Charlie."

Charlie tied his horse to the porch, "Aw, Amos, don't call me that. I ain't anyone's master."

Amos took the pipe from his mouth, blew a smoke ring and used the pipe as a pointer, "Might be. But I'd be a fool of a man to go 'bout calling white boys like I'm their friend. Speaking of fools, you looking for Cuffey?"

Coloring at the conversation, he nodded.

Amos pointed at the door, "If I know my wife, Jenny'll have a plate ready for you."

Charlie found Cuffey at the table scarfing down hoecakes. "Eat up. I found a spot where I seen some deer yesterday."

Charlie thanked Jenny as she set an old worn, tin plate in front of him. He liked Amos and Jenny. Amos was the only freedman who had been working at the Trinity Gun Works before Cuffey arrived. He and Jenny had agreed to take the young man in after Charlie's pa had helped Cuffey get a job at the gun works.

After breakfast, Charlie said, "Where'd you see the deer?"

"Upriver a way."

The young men hurried out of the house. Charlie swung into the saddle and leaned down, offering his hand to Cuffey. "It'll be quicker if we ride."

Later, Charlie lifted his leg over the mount's head and slid off. A creek ran alongside the trail they followed. Once Cuffey had climbed off the beast, Charlie retrieved his rifle from the saddle scabbard.

Cuffey said, "Leave the horse here. It's not far."

They staked the horse to a line, and Charlie followed the young man through the pine trees.

Charlie had heard tales from his Uncle Davy about hunting blinds; those he'd use for hunting game and those he'd use to hunt men. After he and Cuffey had dragged limbs into place, he settled behind a large branch and rested the rifle across it. He carried a small knapsack slung over his shoulder and retrieved a paper cartridge.

He loaded the rifle with easy practice and fished a percussion cap from his pocket. "Have you ever fired one of these before?" he asked.

Cuffey swore. "Old man Lamont would,ve strung up a slave who'd ever tried to touch a gun."

Charlie crouched on his knees, "Was it like that everywhere back east?"

"Not everywhere. I knew a boy who belonged to another plantation, more like a farm. He and his master hunted a lot."

Charlie handed the weapon over, "Go ahead, take a look down the sight. Ain't no slaver to see you now."

He watched his friend gingerly take the gun and ran his fingers along the wooden stock. "It's just like the guns the Berrys make."

Charlie nodded. "The same. I lost my rifle in California and Pa got me this one from John Berry."

Cuffey shushed him. "Deer."

He gripped the rifle until his knuckles were white. Charlie followed the barrel and saw a buck step into the creek. He had a few points on his antlers. Just a young buck. Charlie bit back a chuckle, and thought, *"Like us."*

There was a crack of the rifle and the area in front of the blind was covered in gray smoke. "Did you get him?"

Cuffey was coughing. "Damned if I know. That's a powerful lot of smoke."

The two raced around the blind and to the young men's astonishment, the buck was thrashing in the water, as blood poured from his neck. "Hot damn! I hit him!"

Charlie was pounding his friend on the back, "Beginner's luck if I ever saw it." He was laughing as he said it.

They were swinging the carcass onto Charlie's horse's rump when they heard branches snapping nearby. Seconds later, a short, round man stumbled into the creek bed. Charlie sensed Cuffey go tense. He followed his friend's eyes and saw a whip secured to the man's waist.

"Nice buck you got there, boys," the man said as he leaned over to catch his breath.

"Thanks," Charlie said as he tossed a rope over the buck. He felt Cuffey pull the line taut and then tie it to the saddle.

Charlie grabbed the rifle and slid it back into its scabbard as he saw two black men splash into the creek behind the man. "Rufus, Cicero, take a break."

"Look at me, all poor manners. I'm Douglas Smith. I work for Mr. Talmage. He owns the Trinity Pines plantation." Uncertain how to react, Charlie took the outstretched hand and shook it.

"Uh, I'm Charlie. This here's—" Charlie started.

Cuffey cut him off, "Jack. Master Charlie, yo' momma gonna be tickled when you bring home dis here buck, yes, suh."

Charlie was nonplused by his friend's reaction. But he played along, "Uh, right, Jack. We'd best get going."

He nodded at the overseer and the slaves, "Nice to meet y'all."

Pulling on the reins, Charlie followed behind Cuffey, who set a brisk pace until they had left the others far behind. Finally, tired of the silence and pulling the horse's reins that he'd prefer to ride, Charlie blurted, "What was that about?"

Cuffey turned, "How many runaways named Cuffey you suppose there are around here?"

Charlie shrugged, "None that I know of. Pa got you fixed up with good papers showing you're a freedman."

Cuffey's laughter was haunted, "I'm gonna thank your pa for that all the way to Saint Peter's gates, but you and me know those papers won't hold up. Paying a county judge to put a stamp on them papers don't mean shit if Lamont shows up with real papers. Best some fat overseer see a white boy and his slave."

Angry, Charlie barreled around his friend, "That's stupid."

But as he hurried along the trail he realized Cuffey was right. Had he given Cuffey's real name, he could have undone all that had been accomplished since the night a few months before when his pa had told the escaped slave to get in the boat.

He apologized, and by the time they returned to Trinity Park, they were in high spirits over their kill.

13 March 1844

Will glanced at his pocket-watch as the train chuffed to a stop in front of the West Liberty station platform. Five minutes late was as good as being on time. The train had arrived from the west, from Houston. What had once taken two or three days by foot could be done in less than two hours now.

One of the men disembarking from the train wore the butternut uniform of the regular army. Will recognized him by his brown beard and receding hairline. Will smiled as he watched the major flick a bit of coal dust from the gold oak leaf cluster shoulder boards. Will saw the medical officer wore the insignia he had created for the office of Surgeon General a few years earlier. Crafted in silver, twin snakes wrapped around a winged staff were pinned to the officer's lapels. As Will had spent the past seven years building Texas' army, he hadn't been able to resist adding touches of familiarity, like the caduceus for doctors, crosses for chaplains, and a castle for engineers.

"Dr. Smith, it's good to see you." Will waved away the salute Ashbel Smith offered.

"General, I'm pleased to see you again. I confess, your recent letter intrigued me."

Will led the doctor to the coach he had borrowed from Don Garza. An older Tejano took the doctor's bags and secured them in the boot, at the back of the carriage.

The wagon lurched into motion, and Will settled back in the plush cushion. Ten miles lay between the depot and Trinity Park.

"How are things with the army?"

Smith took his hat off, setting it on the seat. "Only a few companies are stationed at the Alamo now. I suppose I have everything I absolutely must have but getting Austin to fund the research we need to treat wounds more effectively isn't going to happen, at least not until Zavala and Congress have balanced out the debt they've taken on."

Will bobbed his head. "That kind of funding is likely five to ten years away, as I understand it. It's a shame. Gangrene and sepsis kill more soldiers than Santa Anna's men ever did. I've been talking with a few like-minded men about healthcare here in the eastern part of the Republic, and I believe there's enough interest in establishing a hospital."

Smith leaned forward in his seat as the coach rocked along the road. Will let a smile play across his features as he continued, "Now that the railroad connects the Houston and Harrisburg communities with West Liberty and Anahuac, a hospital could serve most of the area around Galveston Bay."

"That's not small potatoes. More than a hundred thousand folks are living within fifty miles of the bay."

"True. I've talked with my associate, Sam Williams, and he tells me that there's a building in Houston that is available for rent. It's two stories. Wouldn't take much to have a few dozen beds set up there. We've got plans to build a college at Trinity Park with a few classrooms."

Smith blinked at the news, "Classrooms?"

"I don't want to put the cart before the horse, Dr. Smith, but wouldn't you like to start training our own doctors?"

"Now you're just playing with my affections, General. You know there's nothing more that I'd like than to improve the education of the men practicing medicine." Smith paused as he glanced out the coach. He could see the Trinity River in the distance. "But what you're talking about wouldn't be cheap."

Will acknowledged the comment with a single dip of his head before saying, "I've secured a couple of thousand dollars from Sam and an equal amount from Don Garza. The city fathers, in Houston, own the building and are willing to lease it for next to nothing for the next few years. I've sent a letter to the Methodist Missionary Society and Gail Borden has done the same with his Baptist Missionary friends."

"Why?"

Will's face grew somber, as he thought about how backward medicine remained. He knew he was ill-suited trying to speed the development of medicine along, but he knew malaria, typhoid fever, yellow fever, and cholera would kill thousands of Texians over the coming decades. If something could be done to reduce the risk, it was worth the effort, even if he had only the faintest idea of where to start.

Will weighed his words with care as he said, "I heard about what you did in Galveston during the Yellow Fever outbreak in thirty-eight. I happen to agree with you that yellow fever isn't contagious at least not like most folks think. I believe that yellow fever is caused by mosquitos."

Smith allowed a long moment to pass before he responded. "I'll allow you might have something there. Is that your goal? What would you call it? A research hospital."

Will nodded. "Exactly. What would you say if I told you that cholera was the result of contaminated water or food? What if I told you that surgeons who thoroughly wash their hands before operating on a patient reduce the chance of infection?"

Smith looked dubious. "I feel as though I am Eve and you're the great Tempter. You know I've speculated about these things, but my ideas haven't gained much ground."

He sounded unhappy as he continued, "Why are you offering this? If you tell me you're doing this out of benevolence and Christian charity, I'll believe you, or at least I'll try."

Will flushed, a part of him wished it were a simple act of charity. That it wasn't, left him feeling ashamed. "I'm probably not going to gain any angel wings for my altruism. Several projects that I'm partnering on are going to result in more workers coming to Texas. If an epidemic hits those workers, much of what we're trying to do could be set back. Also, if the hospital develops any medicines or the like, I want the right to manufacture the medicine, splitting any profit with you or any other creator."

For the first time since climbing into the coach, Ashbel Smith burst into laughter. "Lord have mercy. Sidney Johnston told me you had turned into a businessman when you surrendered your stars. But I suspect he's underestimated you."

Will smiled sheepishly. "I've laid my soul bare, Ashbel. Are you interested?"

The sound of hammers banging on iron came in through the open door as the carriage rolled into Trinity Park. Dr. Smith stuck his hand out, "I believe we have an agreement, Buck."

Chapter 17

End of March 1844

Becky picked up the sheet of newspaper and wrapped the porcelain plate in it. She added it to the stack in the wooden crate. The box was heavy; she'd wait until Will and Charlie return, before trying to load it into the wagon they were using to move the family's effects to their new home in Trinity Park.

She collapsed into the lone chair and looked around the cabin. Both little ones were asleep on a blanket in one corner. But apart from a few other boxes, the one-room cabin was empty. She was amazed that Will had been able to build a new home for her family in so little time, especially given how often he was traveling. But the construction was complete. Becky's new home was large enough for her children to have their own bedrooms. Unlike their home in San Antonio, the kitchen and dining areas were separated, and there was even a sitting room and library.

She was looking forward to getting out of the cabin she'd called home for the past few months. The previous experience had reminded too much of her childhood. Her father's fortunes had ebbed and flowed until he had risen to the become president of the Republic of Texas. There were times when his business dealings had soured, and they would lose their home and have to start over. She prayed the removal from San Antonio to West Liberty was the only setback Will would face. The speed with which he recovered had surprised and gratified her.

She wasn't sure what he had done, but she knew the loan from the Treasury Department to the bank had allowed the bank to make good their depositors' money. That had been a personal godsend, given that the Travis family had several thousand dollars deposited in the bank.

There was a heavy knock on the door. Liza tossed in her sleep. Becky wasn't expecting anyone. "Who's there?"

"Douglas Smith," there was a pause. "From Trinity Pines."

Neither the name nor the place meant anything to her. Cautiously, she opened the door. Smith stood in the lawn below the porch. When he saw her, he tipped his hat, "Ma'am. I'm right sorry to bother you, but I'm looking for an escaped slave."

Perturbed, Becky folded her arms, "I'd suggest you get to looking for him. You'll not find any slaves here."

Twisting his hat in his hand, Smith said, "Begging your pardon, but I believe your son may know where the escaped slave is. I'd like to talk to him."

Like ice filling a pitcher, a coldness descended into Becky's stomach. She had only met Cuffey a couple of times, but somehow or another the illusion Will had worked to create around the fugitive slave was unraveling.

She managed, "He's not here. He's with his pa."

Smith glared at her. "I know for a fact that your boy was hunting with a black boy a couple of weeks ago. I seen them with my own eyes. I didn't think anything of it until a couple of days ago, when Mr. Talmage received some notices of escaped slaves. Sure enough, that darky your son was with matched the description of the missing runaway."

Becky stood on the porch, her arms still crossed, "That don't mean anything. Charlie's friend has his freedman papers. That's proof your dog don't hunt."

Smith pulled a printed notice from a pocket and unfolded it. "My dog hunts just fine, ma'am. This notice also said that this here runaway could be in the company of a white youth with red hair and fair complexion."

Becky stared at him as he continued, "Seems to me, I've found myself a runaway. I think I'll wait here until your husband and son return."

Trembling with rage and fear, Becky went back inside. The children were still asleep on the blanket. She wished her mother was there at that moment, but Elizabeth was already at the new house, unpacking boxes Will and Charlie had taken over earlier.

Her purse was near the windowsill, and it contained one thing that might be of use. She tipped it onto the floor, and the gift from her husband landed with a heavy thump. She picked up the present and with a backward glance at the sleeping children, she returned to the porch.

"Mr. Smith, your company offends me. You've got until the time I count to ten to get out of my sight.

One," she said as she revealed the .36 caliber pistol her husband had given her years before.

"Two."

Smith chuckled nervously, "Listen up, Mrs. Travis, I'm in my right to demand you produce the slave your husband and son are hiding."

"Three."

"You really should put that away, I'd hate to see a pretty lady such as yourself get hurt."

Infuriated, she cocked the hammer back and made sure powder and ball were seated in the uppermost chamber. "Four."

"Don't make me go find the sheriff and make him do what you ought to do yourself. A good southern woman should know her duty to her fellow southerners, and damn it, this ain't it."

"Five."

Smith stepped forward and placed his right foot on the porch's bottom step. Becky pointed the gun into the air and pulled the trigger. The hammer slammed down, striking the percussion cap which set off the charge of gunpowder. The ball flew from the barrel at seven hundred feet per second. "Mr. Smith, if you take one more step toward me, you had best make damned sure you're right with Jesus because he's going to be the next person you see. Six."

The portly overseer retreated back to his horse. David's unmistakable caterwauling could be heard from within the cabin followed a second later by Liza's.

Smith grabbed the saddle horn and heaved himself back into the saddle with a heavy grunt. "Alright, Mrs. Travis, have it your way. I know I've got the law on my side. I'll be back shortly, and I'll make sure the law knows you were not helpful."

The word, seven, died on her lips as she watched Smith jerk at the reins, turn his mount around and ride north. She lowered the pistol and felt her arm shaking, the sound of her children forced her to push back on the emotions threatening to overwhelm her. She turned and hurried back inside.

A few minutes passed before she heard feet pounding on the porch and a heavy knocking on her door. "Señora, are you alright?"

She allowed a sob to escape her lips as she heard the welcome voice of Don Garza. Little David was clinging to her neck as she opened the door. Garza and a man she knew as Winters were standing there, Winters held a rifle in his hands. She had been around soldiers enough to see he carried it with the air of someone who knew how to use it.

She gulped back a sob as she said, "Señor Garza, thank God it's you. Some slaver was here, demanding we produce some runaway. He threatened me and forced me to fire into the air to scare him off." Her emotions were still running high, and the word scared came out skeered.

Garza stepped forward and placed a hand on her shoulder, "I take it from the gunshot you put the fear of the almighty into him? Or should we make our way to the nearest pigsty and make sure you're not trying to cover anything up?" The last was said through a chuckle.

The absurdity of the comment broke through her reserve and between sobs and choking laughter, she managed, "Would that I thought of that, but no, he said he'd be back, he was going to sic the law on me."

"I know the sheriff. I can delay him a bit if it becomes necessary. But if there's any question to young

Charlie's negro friend, I'd suggest, he seek employment elsewhere, Miss Rebecca."

She frowned at the news. It would tear at Charlie to lose a friend. But what choice was there?

Will and Charlie pulled the borrowed wagon in front of the house within the hour. Becky steeled her heart and broke the news to her husband and son.

Charlie fumed as he sat beside Becky. The wagon was loaded with the handful of boxes from the house in West Liberty. He held his little sister in his lap. His stepmother rocked little David, who appeared to be sleeping at the moment. His pa was driving the wagon. The two-horse team made good time, but it didn't hurt that the road was evenly graded and well maintained.

When he and Pa had arrived back at the little cabin she had stormed out with the baby in her arms and told them about the fat overseer showing up. He had to admit the idea of her holding a gun on the vile man still brought a smile to his face. Part of him wished she had just shot Smith. Then, at least, the problem facing them would have died with the slaver.

He shifted Liza from one knee to the other as he said, "I still don't understand why Cuffey can't stay."

Becky's response was low, "Because the law's on their side. If he shows up with the sheriff, Cuffey's papers showing him to be a freedman won't hold water."

"I don't see why not. They were sworn before a judge, they're as legal as anything else, aren't they?"

His pa, sitting on the far side of the buckboard, said, "As far as I'm concerned, sure, they're valid. I wish to God the world agreed with me."

"What do you mean, Pa?"

"I thought it worth the effort to provide papers that would allow Cuffey to work as a freedman. It wasn't difficult to get the town judge in West Liberty to agree to draft the manumission papers, he's a good man. But the truth of the matter is that both the judge and I took a risk in drafting the papers because, as we all know, they're not based on the facts."

Charlie was confused, "How can it not be? Cuffey made his escape with the rest of us. That made him free, didn't it?"

Will snapped the reins, urging the team to pick up the speed. "As God is my witness, Son, I wish that was the case. In a more just world it would be. In this unjust one, the law of Texas matches the law in the United States, and Cuffey still belongs to that jackass, Lamont."

Charlie hid a smile when Becky slapped Will's arm. "Language Will. Little ears."

"Well, it's true. Unfortunately, if Lamont or any slave-catcher acting on his warrant, shows up and can show that Cuffey was Lamont's, there's damn all I can do about it legally."

Becky frowned at Pa but held her peace. Charlie said, "That's not fair. Cuffey deserves to be free, like Joe and Hatti."

"I completely agree. If I could snap my fingers and liberate every man, woman, and child enslaved in Texas. Throw in the United States to boot. It's not natural for one man to own another, Charlie. As much as I hate what needs to be done now, I'm glad to see that this sickens you, too."

"What are you going to do, Pa?"

Will glanced at the sun as it was sinking to their west. "Tonight, we'll get the boxes unloaded."

Charlie laughed "Not about the wagon. What about Cuffey?"

His pa wore a sober expression. "I'll go and talk to him. I've got some business in Austin on behalf of Sam and the bank. I'll ask him to accompany me. Once I'm done in Austin, we'll head down to San Antonio. With any luck, Joe will still be home from his last freight haul. It's a poor choice, but I'll see if I can get Cuffey hired on with Joe. If he's gone most of the time, maybe this issue will die down, and Cuffey can get on with his life."

Charlie shook his head. "I know I done said it, Pa, but this ain't fair."

His pa reached around Becky and tousled his hair, "Not at all, son. Maybe someday soon we can do something about it. Until then, we'll do what we can to help Cuffey stay free."

Two days later Will sat in the passenger car as it rocked along. He looked out the window as the San Jacinto River came into view. Early April was the prettiest time of the year to see the riot of colors Texas' native wildflowers displayed. As the train swayed back and forth as it crossed the river, Will looked out and saw on one bank of the river a handful of farms. On the other side of the river spread a plantation, with slaves at work in the field. Before he could count their number, the train whisked the passenger car away.

Cuffey sat on the bench opposite from him. They were on one end of the car. On the other end, sat several other passengers. Every once in a while, one would cast a nasty glance their way. The railroads were too new a means of transportation for Congress to have taken time to legislate where blacks, freed or slave, would be allowed to ride. But based on the withering look from one mother of two small children, her husband would get an earful. From there, no doubt his congressman would get an earful and then a new law would be proposed removing the inconvenient eyesore of slavery and penury from sight.

There were times Will genuinely hated being transferred into the past and this was one of those. The past seven years, building and developing the army, slavery was an annoying itch. There were not many slaves or freedmen and women in San Antonio, and it was easy while defending the republic's borders to ignore slavery's blight.

He sighed as the engine's brakes squealed in protest, they were slowing as they neared Harrisburg Station. He was now a civilian, living nearer than he'd like to plantations. Were he transferred back to his old body, and William Barret Travis resumed this one, there was no doubt Travis would go on getting along with plantation owners. As he stepped off the train and waited for Cuffey to climb down, he thought, *"Dammit, I wasn't born into this body and I'm not going to pretend to like slavery just for the sake of a little comfort."*

No, he wasn't going to go along to get along now that his time in the army was behind him. He was proud of the Gulf Farms Corporation. They employed all of their farmers. No slave labor was used there. Sam Williams had been true to his word when Will had proposed their partnership. The bank refused to loan money for the purchase of slaves. Williams was a study of contradictions, though. Despite being a native of Rhode Island, he owned a couple of slaves. While Will disagreed with him on the issue, Williams had framed the subject as one of compassion. One of Sam's slaves was an elderly septuagenarian. The other was a young woman who was barren. To Williams' view of the world, he provided security to both in exchange for their labor.

Will checked behind, Cuffey was following him as they headed through Harrisburg's foot-traffic. With the arrival of the railroad, more frequent stagecoach trips were available for travel to Austin. Will bought two tickets, and they settled down to wait.

A few days later, Will stood in the doorframe of the small house, hat in hand. "Hatti, is Joe home?"

The freedwoman whooped when she recognized Will. "Lands sake, Joe! The Gen'ral's at the door."

A voice from within the house said, "What in the world would Gen'ral Johnston want with a poor wagoneer?"

She turned away, "Don't be silly. It's Gen'ral Travis!"

There was a scraping of a chair and a moment later, Travis' former slave, Joe stood behind his wife. He hadn't seen much of Joe in the intervening years since he had freed Travis' former slave. Echoing a moment the two had shared when Will had still been adjusting to the transference, he stuck out his hand. With noticeable hesitation, Joe accepted it, and they shook.

"Is you starting to make social calls to all the nigras in San Antonio, Marse Will?"

Despite himself, Will chuckled, "If that would help things, I might. The truth is more complicated."

Henrietta shooed Will and Cuffey into the house. "If you is going to jaw about things, let me get you some coffee."

Will waited until Henrietta had placed a few steaming mugs of coffee in front of them. "It's the real stuff. Stores are starting to carry everything they did before the war. Prices are starting to come down, too."

Will sipped the coffee. He savored the drink. It had been more than a year since he'd sat at home in San Antonio and ate her breakfasts. Joe set his cup down, "What brings you back, Gen'ral?"

"This young man is Cuffey. When I found Charlie and was able to free him from the men who kidnapped him, this young, strapping fellow came along, too."

Joe stared at the young man for a long moment before shifting his gaze to Will. "Slave catchers come looking for him back east? Lots of planter folk round 'bouts knows where you live now."

Will dipped his head, "I'm afraid so. Charlie took Cuffey's leaving hard, but he deserves a fresh start without some slave catcher hounding him. I figure San Antonio offers a better opportunity."

Joe's lips were pursed. He let out a noncommittal sound. "For some that's true. If I help, I risk not just my home or my wagons but my wife and my life. Why should I?"

Will blinked. This wasn't the answer he had expected. Henrietta slammed a tin pan of biscuits on the table and wagged her finger in front of her husband. "Listen to me good, Joe Travis. Wasn't the preacher man talking about the good book the other day? He said 'I was hungry and you fed me, I was thirsty and you gave me drink, and I was a stranger and you took me in.'"

"Hatti, them's pretty words, but I got to think about us."

Tears were spilling from her face when Hatti replied, "I'm thinking about us, too, Joe. I couldn't live with myself if we turned this young man away. You've been saying that the contracts to supply the depots out west getting better now that they've extended things to Santa Fe. You said if you could find another driver, you could expand. Now, God's giving you the chance to do that."

Joe bent down and picked up one of the biscuits that had fallen on the floor. "Woman, why can't you listen to me? This could cost us both our freedom. The Government don't look kindly on ex-slaves helping a runaway."

Hatti stepped in and hugged her husband, "We need to do this, Joe. If those words from the Good Book mean anything, then we must do this."

Will left an hour later. Henrietta had worn Joe down. All the way back to the inn where he'd stay, he prayed for their safety.

Chapter 18

29 April 1844

Will pulled a handkerchief from his pocket and wiped at his forehead. For what was probably the thousandth time, he thought about how much he hated the formal clothing worn by people in the mid-nineteenth century. He had dispensed with his jacket and wore a shirt and vest, and even though the temperature had yet to break ninety degrees, he was warm enough. The sun worked its way into the sky. "*What I wouldn't do for air-conditioning right now*," he thought.

Instead, he turned his attention to Clayton Wynters. A former corporal in the army, Wynters had been injured during the Comanche War and was now a partner in Gulf Corporation's farming operations. He was saying, "The mechanical cotton planter has been expanded a couple of times since we licensed it from a company in Maryland. The original device allowed a farmer to plant a single row, using handles behind to push the plow through the dirt. Now, we've got four rows, and the contraption is pulled by a team of horses. One man can do the work of four now."

Their other companion, Dick Gatling said, "It seems to me the bottleneck on cotton farming is still picking it. You can plant it faster and with fewer workers than ever before, and cotton gins can strip the seeds away from the cotton at industrial speeds."

Wynters spit onto the black, loamy soil, "Yep. A plantation has slaves to do all the work, so they don't much care about how quick they can put the seed in the ground, and we're limited to the same problem they face when it comes to harvesting it. Labor, and lots of it.

Will watched a couple of men hitch a pair of horses to the front of a mechanical planter. One took the lead, next to the team, while the other walked beside the planter as they began seeding the field. Wynters added, "It's something to behold. Some of our new neighbors have set up plantations where their slaves are also prepping and seeding their fields. Hardly any mechanized devices. We may be forced to put all our works in the field during harvest season, but their overall process is slower than ours."

Will didn't like the fact that more plantations were being built in the Trinity River's rich bottomland. But there was very little he could do directly. On the other hand, maybe there was. "Dick, you're the machinist here. What do you think about devising a machine that could pluck the cotton bolls from the plant? If we could automate that, we could expand the number of acres under development."

Gatling nodded, "If it's possible, it would be something to behold. An efficient cotton picker could drive the price of cotton down and make a lot of plantations unprofitable. But that's going to be easier said than done."

"Why?"

Wynters interjected, "The plant produces the cotton balls during the period when it's in bloom. But the bolls don't mature at the same time. We'll harvest the same plant several times throughout the harvest season. Even if you can make a machine that can harvest the cotton, how do you do it so that it doesn't destroy the plant?"

Will hadn't thought about it in those terms. What he knew about farming he could file away on an index card. He was dependent on men like Wynters for the details about agriculture. The same was true about mechanical engineering. Without Dick Gatling, he was lost. Despite sizable gaps in his knowledge, he hoped he could take what each knew and try to harness them together. After all, Will knew what *could* be done, even if he didn't know how to do it.

As they walked back into West Liberty, Gatling said, "I'll get started on it right away, but don't be surprised if it takes a while. Mr. Wynters is right. Figuring out how to make something that doesn't destroy the plant before all the cotton can be harvested is our biggest challenge."

Will left the farmer and the machinist to discuss the next step. He grabbed his jacket and headed for his horse, he had a meeting in Trinity Park later in the afternoon.

The public hack rolled to a stop next to the ornate building in Saint James. A footman hurried down the stair of the building and opened the door. Merrill Taylor handed over a long wooden box and followed the footman into the building.

The grand hall of White's Gentlemen's Club was extravagant. Paintings and marble carvings lined the hall. Taylor stood rooted to the floor as his eyes took in the opulence. "Sir, this way, please." The footman took him lightly by the arm and escorted him up a grand staircase and through a set of double doors into a coffee room which spanned the front of the building.

The footman brought him to a corner table where an officer in the red uniform of his majesty's Board of Ordnance sat across the table from his own benefactor, the enigmatic Mr. Smyth. "Merrill, my boy, take a seat." Smyth snapped his finger, and a waiter appeared at the table with near magical speed. "Tea for these gentlemen."

Merrill leaned the box against the wall and listened to his companions' small talk. The sound of men speaking the King's English after so many months away sounded at once odd and comforting to his ears. The harsh Yankee accents of men from New England grated on him. Even the soft drawls of men from the American South left him feeling like a fish out of water during his time taking care of his employer's tasks there.

After the tea arrived and they had imbibed, Mr. Smyth said, "Let's see what your man obtained from the inventive Texians, Merrill. Open the box."

Merrill released the leather strap holding the box closed and drew from it a rifle. His red uniformed companion rose partway from his chair to get a closer look. "Utilitarian construction. I've seen the like in the rifles the Yanks make at Harpers Ferry and Springfield. May I?"

Merrill surrendered the rifle to the Ordnance man, who stood up and hefted the gun. "Balance is good." He levered the breechblock open and ran his finger along the falling block. "Damned tight tolerances on the machining tools."

He held the rifle's breechblock close to his eyes, looking inside. "That's not something you see every day."

Looks of curiosity from Merrill and Smyth elicited a response from the officer, "One of the limiting issues rifles like this suffer from is too much gas escaping the breechblock. All that escaping gas reduces the punch a rifle has beyond a couple of hundred yards. A tight seal is important but hard to achieve. Whoever designed this used a small platinum ring to seal the breech. We'd need to test it, but it's likely to be a superior seal."

They were quiet as the ordnance officer studied the rifle. When he handed it back to Merrill, Smyth said, "What do you think?"

"I'd like to test it. See how it performs under field conditions. I've advocated that we examine the new Prussian Dreyse needle-gun, but change isn't exactly smiled upon in our service."

Smyth's chuckle was dry, lacking humor. "To say the least. God help the empire if we get into a shooting war with the Prussians. You're the expert, Major. But I don't think God is on the side of the biggest battalions, but on the side that can outshoot the other."

"This won't be an official study. We're too, ah, traditional for that," the officer said apologetically. "But I'll put this through the paces and see how it performs."

Merrill handed over the box, and the red-uniformed officer took his leave. Once he disappeared down the staircase, Merrill felt Smyth's sharp eyes on him. "Accept the thanks of my compatriots in providing the gun, Mr. Taylor. Pass that along to Stewart, as well. I know you've hardly had the chance to adjust to life here, but in the next few weeks, you'll be receiving new instructions at Lloyds for another trip."

Merrill stifled a groan. His employment with Lloyds Bank involved oversight on several unusual contracts. The one thing they had in common was they were underwritten by Smyth and his cabal of investors. They also required frequent travel. Smyth continued, "The late war between Texas and Mexico has resulted in several missed payments from General Travis on the considerable loan we made a few years ago. I need you to return to Galveston. Use Stewart if you need to but find out if the bank is solid or if there are problems with our investment."

"And if there are?"

Smyth's eyes drifted to a painting on the wall from the late war with France. It was from the Battle of Waterloo, showing the Defense of Hougoumont. Merrill followed his patron's eyes. "You don't anticipate intervening?"

Turning away from the painting, his benefactor said, "Let's leave military intervention for the French. That silliness down in Vera Cruz a few years ago did nothing but destabilize Mexico, and ultimately, that disorder played to Texas' benefit. No, Mr. Taylor, we rely upon soft power. If General Travis and his partners are unable to normalize payments, I expect that it would open the door to more direct management."

Merrill's smile was half-hearted. He liked "Buck" Travis. His expression must have been transparent. His benefactor said, "Many of my associates see General Travis as the best hope to turn back the American

South's slavocracy. While I agree he may be the best chance we have, we should never place all our eggs in a single basket. I hope he and his partner are able to resume payments, but if it isn't possible, we can play a long game. Texas' liberal immigration laws and land policies have allowed us to place more pawns on the chess board."

With that, his benefactor excused himself, and Merrill's meeting was over. He heaved a heavy sigh. He would need to find out if any ships were sailing directly to Galveston. If not the Texas port, then New Orleans. There was too much to do before he could leave.

18 May 1844

Will read the report from Dr. Ashbel Smith. In his letter, Dr. Smith detailed efforts on Galveston Island to eradicate mosquito nesting grounds. As he set the note down, Will questioned whether the measures would be enough to stop the frequent bouts of yellow fever the Texas gulf coast experienced. *"There's a reason we call it medical practice,"* he thought. If it didn't work, then the dogged former surgeon general of the Texian army would start over and find a new way to exterminate mosquito larvae.

From the library's doorway, he heard, "Will, are you expecting Andy Berry this afternoon? He's at the door."

He looked up. Becky stood in the doorway. Light flooded the room from the windows. Light reflected from her brown hair, giving it a golden luster. As their eyes locked, both of them smiled. She crossed the room and leaned over and placed a chaste kiss on his cheek. He reached up and gently pulled her in closer. The second kiss was longer and less chaste. Becky said, "If you would like, I can send him away." There was a purring in her voice that reminded Will of a contented cat.

"I like the way you think, dear. Regrettably, young master Berry is expected." Will stood and fastened the buttons on his vest. "Perhaps not too regrettable. This has something to do with some modifications to the army's rifle. It could be interesting."

Becky gave an exaggerated pout. "Men and their toys. I see where I rank." But as she left to fetch Berry, she flashed a smile on her way out the door.

Being home more had been good for Will and his family. Becky was much happier with his schedule. While he still traveled frequently, the nonstop requirements of the army were in the past. There was no guilt if he set aside work by dinner time.

Andy Berry strode into the room wearing a happy smile. "General Travis, thanks for agreeing to see me."

Will waved him into a padded chair and turned his own away from the desk. "How's your father?"

"As devout as ever. He's put a bit of money up for construction of the town's first church. Who'd have thought a town would grow up around our own gun works?"

They could hear the joyous sound of children running in the street. School was over for the day. Will said, "I'm glad to see your family has been supportive of a school for all the kids in Trinity Park. Speaking of which I expect the front door to open any moment and hear Charlie's voice."

Sure enough, the front door opened and slammed, and Charlie's voice echoed down the hall, "Pa, Becky, I'm home."

Will counted until three, as he expected, he heard Becky's feet on the staircase and her voice, "Charles Edward Travis, if I have to tell you one more time not to slam the door, I'll fetch me a switch and make sure you remember!"

He offered an apologetic smile to Berry, "Domestic bliss."

Berry offered a sage smile, "I sometimes wonder about the entire family settling down in one town. If me or John have a spat with our wives, damned if the whole family doesn't know about it the next day."

"Tell me about what brings you over," Will said.

Berry laughed, "Fair enough. First I wanted to let you know that me and Gail received a charter for our corporation for manufacturing nitrogenated processed cotton. We've got a backlog of orders."

"That's great news, Andy. NPC has the potential to revolutionize a lot of industries. Have you got confirmation of your patent yet from Washington?"

Berry shook his head, "Not yet. Haven't heard anything from London yet, either. Why are you worried about the patent?"

Will handed Berry a drawing of a rocket floating over a ship, with a flare burning bright. "Recognize this?"

"That kind of looks like the picture in the newspaper from the Battle of Saltillo. You used this to light up the battlefield, right?"

"Yes. But the idea was borrowed from a patent we had received in the patent office. We lifted it and used it against the Mexican army. Now, the truth of the matter is that if the inventor ever decides to make an issue of it, I expect a Texas court to side with him, against the army. We had no legal right to borrow the inventor's idea, not without recompense. That's the reason I want you to go through the process of patenting your invention. You can't stop people from stealing your ideas, but at least in Texas, the United States, and I hope in Britain, the courts will give you standing to sue."

Berry was scratching his chin, "You struck me as someone who would like to see the use of NPC spread far and wide. You said it was a game changer."

Will nodded. "It is. But industrialists in Britain and the United States can copy your patent. They are closer to global markets than we are. And they can make it cheaper than we do. If the legal protection isn't there, your new enterprise could be undercut in as little as a few years. Texas needs this industry. Not just explosive cotton or repeating pistols or breechloading rifles, but textile mills, lumber mills, and shipbuilding enterprises. Steel mills and distilleries. The ability to refine oil. All of those are things we need to master. So, for now, it's important that we protect what industry we have, no matter how small."

"You get passionate about it, General. I can see that. I'm glad you're looking out for us." Berry dug into his trousers pocket and continued, "Do you want to see the latest item from my own little project?"

With a nod from Will, he put a small, brass cartridge on Will's desk. "It's got a black powder charge. Still not happy with the results from the NPC, that stuff's too damned unstable."

Will picked up the cartridge. The brass casing was smooth and polished. The bullet was conical. "I borrowed that idea about a pointed bullet and used it here."

"Have you modified any of your rifles to use this cartridge?"

Berry jumped up and said, "Sure have. Was hoping I could get you over to the testing range and see what you think of it."

Will was on his feet, hurrying from his library, he shouted from the front door that he would be back shortly, then he slammed the door as he and Berry raced for the range.

An hour later, he looked at the table in front of the firing line. There must have been nearly a hundred spent cartridges scattered about.

He ran his hand over the inside of the breech, his finger was streaked with powder residue. But not as much as there could have been. "Not bad. We must have shot a hundred rounds, and the breech isn't badly fouled yet."

Berry handed him a grimy cloth and a flask of gun oil. "A little of this and she'll be like new."

Will took a moment to clean the breechblock before handing the rifle back to the inventor. "How many cartridges can your stamping mill make a day?"

As they started down the range to collect their targets, Berry said, "We're still working out some kinks in production. Today, we'll probably make five hundred. But once we're fully up to speed, with existing equipment, more than a thousand."

Will winced at the news. "Just a thousand? Andy, at the Battle of Saltillo, we shot off more than a hundred thousand rounds of ammo. That would be more than three months' worth of your ammunition."

When Will saw the hurt look on Berry's face, he added, "What you've done is extraordinary. I'll be glad to recommend this to Sid Johnston, in limited quantities."

"Limited quantities? You worried General Johnston won't be able to get funding?"

Will shook his head, "For a small run, he'll be able to pay for that. But you might want to consider pitching the model eighteen forty-one revolver to foreign markets."

Berry wore a wary expression, "I thought you didn't want these weapons falling into enemy hands. Won't selling them outside of Texas make that more likely?"

"Yeah, but Samuel Colt is pitching his thirty-eight-caliber revolver in Europe. It's only a matter of time before other nations start buying them or making their own. Better they buy your weapon than someone else's, especially if Sid Johnston's budget gets cut again." Will stopped in his tracks, weighing whether to offer up another solution. When Berry looked behind and saw him stopped, Will caught up with him and said, "I have another idea. I've heard the Harpers Ferry armory has started producing a rifled musket in limited quantities. While it doesn't hold a candle to our Sabine rifle, it's still way better than the muskets used by most of the world's armies. You could design a rifled musket for sale abroad. If the army loses more of its funding, something that this could pick up the slack in sales."

It took several minutes to travel five hundred yards to retrieve the last target. As Will unclipped it from the straw bale, he was pleased with how many times the bullets tore the target. As they walked back toward town, Will played with a spent cartridge in one hand. His thoughts turned to another invention Dick Gatling had manufactured in the world that lived on only in his memories.

Chapter 19

16 July 1844

Will stuffed the handkerchief back in his pocket as he felt beads of sweat reappear on his forehead. No amount of dabbing would keep the heat at bay. The gulf breeze was uncharacteristically still as he felt the vibration of the steam engine under the boat's planking.

A glance showed the boat was nearing the treacherous shallows off Pelican Island. From his place on the deck, he could see a shipwreck washed up on the beach of the small island that squatted in the bay between Galveston and the mainland. From Pelican Island it was less than a mile to the town's docks. He gripped the boat's railing with one hand and clenched a letter with the other. He reread Sam Williams' letter and felt disquieted. There was something about the note that felt off.

My dear William,

Matters of gravest concern have arisen and I require your expertise to resolve them. Unless you are able to break away from your endeavors at Trinity Park and hasten here upon receipt of this note, I fear ruin may befall our mutual financial arrangement. I shall expect you on the 16th.

Your obedient servant,

Samuel May Williams

Will was puzzled. When he and Sam were together, they called each other Sam and Buck. Given the nature of the bank, and Will's decision to build a home for his family in Trinity Park, they corresponded frequently. Their regular correspondence was warm and casual. Will looked at the script. It looked like Sam's handwriting, but the tone was completely wrong.

"Hey, mister, we're going to be docking in a short while. Stay clear of the sides." A lanky young man brushed by, hurrying to the bow.

Will stared after him. Was he one of the thousands of young men who had returned to civilian life following the end of the war the previous year or was he one of the thousands of immigrants who were arriving in Galveston?

As the boat was tied off to the dock, he vowed he would find out what was wrong with his friend and business partner.

When Will stepped onto Avenue B, he looked at a freshly painted street sign. In cursive letters was written, "The Strand." Compared to what he recalled from his own youth, the Strand of 1844 paled in comparison to the one at the dawn of the twenty-first century. The broad street was hard-packed dirt. No doubt when it rained, it turned the road into miry soup. Thankfully, the day was dry, and he was able to make his way along the road until he came to the red brick building atop which was a sign declaring to passersby the imposing building housed the Commerce Bank.

Will opened the door and found one of the clerks behind the counter. The clerk's face lit up with a smile, "General Travis, Mr. Williams said you might stop by today. He's back in his office with some gentleman. Said to send you back."

Will tried to match the young man's smile, but the foreboding he felt kept his smile from reaching his eyes. "I suppose I shouldn't keep them waiting. But tell me," Will searched his memory for the clerk's name, "Jeremiah, what kind of visitor do we have? It's not Michel Menard or one of his accountants?" After the hell Will and Sam had undergone wrestling a loan from the Treasury Department, the last man he wanted to see show up at the bank was Menard.

Jeremiah said "No, sir. He had an accent. Not a Yankee accent, but maybe English."

Will stepped behind the counter and made his way back toward Sam's office. The only Englishman he knew was Charles Elliot, the chargé d'affaires from Great Britain. While he liked Elliot, he had only dealt with him a few times.

When Will opened the door to Williams' office, he saw the graying head of his business partner at his desk. Opposite from him was another man, dressed in a black suit. He recognized the short, portly figure of Merrill Taylor. The Englishman had arranged the loan from English investors. Will resisted the urge to frown at the unexpected visitor. Instead, he forced a smile onto his face and offered his hand, "Mr. Taylor, a singular honor. When we last visited, I thought you had sailed back to England. I was under the impression our climate didn't agree with you."

Taylor had the good grace to dab his forehead with his handkerchief, as he offered a weak smile, "Were the decision mine, I would be taking tea right now in my gentlemen's club instead of sweltering here."

Williams offered an apologetic expression, "Buck, I'm sorry for the cloak and dagger mystery, but Mr. Taylor was insistent that you come without knowing the reason."

Will took a chair next to Taylor. His sense of foreboding remained strong as he said, "You've got my attention. What could have pulled you from your rustic English living?"

Taylor looked toward Williams, "Perhaps we could discuss the matter in private?"

Perturbed, Will shook his head, "If you have a message to pass along, I trust Mr. Williams' discretion. What's on your mind?"

"My employer understood during your late war with Mexico that repayment of the loan might be delayed, but it has been more than a year since interest payments have been received by Lloyds. This is most irregular, and I am here to find out."

Will had not given the mysterious loan a second thought since the end of the war. His gaze shifted to Sam. Williams looked perplexed as he said, "We made payments through the end of the summer last year. A disproportionate amount of the bank's balance sheet has been made up of treasury bonds since then. I sent a note explaining the delay. Did you not receive it?"

Taylor shrugged. "Not to my knowledge. My employer expects the repayments to start back up now or if you're unable to make payments, other measures may be necessary to secure the value of the loan."

Will's voice was dry, he didn't care to think about other measures Taylor had in mind. "I hadn't thought about this while I was in Mexico. Sam, how quickly can we pick up payments?"

Williams picked up a pen from the desk and made some calculations before saying, "We can pay the twenty-five hundred dollars by the end of the month. Continuing monthly after that, we should be able to make the payments. I notice, we've only been paying interest. If we were to amortize the loan, how long of a payment period would your employer require?"

"My employer views this as a long-term investment. While it is important that you pay the interest, the principle can be paid later. As such, gentlemen, he's willing for you to take the prior year's missed payments and make those up over the span of a couple of years."

Will's eyes drifted over to Sam, who was staring back at him. The expression on Williams' face was clear. No words were necessary to say, *"What kind of mess have you entangled us?"*

The sun was still in the sky as Gail Borden stepped onto the patio of his new home in Trinity Park. He could hear his children playing inside as he settled himself into one of the chairs. He lit his pipe and rummaged in his pocket until he fished out the crumpled envelope. He tore it open and smoothed the letter he'd pulled from within.

His longtime friend, Ashbel Smith, had been in Galveston, working on a project over which he and Buck Travis had been theorizing. It had been more than a month since Ashbel had been gone and this was the first letter he'd received.

My dear Gail,

As I measure the spread of yellow fever that has gripped the town of Galveston, I thank God daily you moved your family to Trinity Park. I shudder to think how terrible it would be if I had to treat any of them for yellow jack.

Between you and me, I am perplexed that Buck Travis' ideas about suppressing the mosquitos was not more successful. Despite the failure, I strongly suspect he is right about the mosquito, and it is likely the carrier of both yellow fever and malaria. Of course, more study must be done, and I am determined to test his hypothesis.

There are times Buck is so ignorant about the details of medicine and then, there are times, like now, where his insight is prescient. I have long been convinced yellow fever is not communicable through contact between people, and despite that, I am growing in conviction Buck's insistence in quarantining those who fall ill from the fever is the right decision. We isolate our patients and hang muslin shrouds over their bedding, keeping mosquitos from getting to their victims and flying away with bad blood to infect someone else.

There has been some success in fumigating our hospital. It stinks like rotten eggs, but the mosquitos appear to hate it worse than we poor humans. I have poured a measure of sulfur onto a metal plate. I then set the sulfur on fire with wood alcohol. It is effective at keeping the legions of mosquitos away from the hospital. I intend to order its use in public houses, including the orphanage.

We may not have found a way to destroy their larvae, but I am discovering new ways to combat their presence.

There have been deaths, unfortunately, but in comparison with the epidemic of 1839, the number of fatalities is a small fraction. Even if it takes several more years, I will prove the detestable mosquito's connection to yellow fever. Then I will share with other doctors my conclusions. I hope that within a decade we'll have eradicated yellow fever from the hemisphere.

The letter continued, but Gail set the message down beside him. It was just like Ashbel to see the problem, identify it, and then share his findings with the world. How different was the life of an inventor! The porch under which he sat was paid for from the sales of NPC, as was the house.

While his friend wasn't ashamed to charge what he thought his services were worth, when it came to plague such as yellow fever, Ashbel never thought to profit from a discovery. If he could prove the disease was caused by the bite of a mosquito, he would share the discovery in every scientific and medical journal that would publish his theory.

In the distance, Borden could see the wide expanse of the Trinity River flowing toward Galveston Bay and the Gulf of Mexico through the smoke of his pipe. He enjoyed escaping the noise of his children at play after dinner and sitting on the porch let him think. Thoughts of Ashbel Smith slid away as his mind drifted toward his own invention. The process of making NPC involved slowly drying sheets of nitrogenated cotton. The drying process was similar to that used in drying meat in a smokehouse. Dried meat would last longer than it would if fresh. But what if one boiled the meat down to a paste? If the paste could be mixed with flour, could it be baked into biscuits that would last even longer than jerky? An invention like that would allow the army or navy to save on the various types of foods needed when in the field or at sea.

He envisioned the process as he stretched his legs and set his pipe on the small all-weather table by his side. He closed his eyes and let his mind consider the steps he'd need to take to produce the meat biscuit.

A bit later, his wife, Penelope came out onto the porch and found her husband asleep in his favorite chair.

1 November 1844

The walk from his house to work took less than ten minutes, and rain or shine, if he were in town, he'd make the trek each day. Every day was something new. The nucleus of Trinity College was slowly attracting new talent. There were times where Will felt like a fish out of water as he poked his head in on the various projects.

He drew in a deep breath of cool morning air as he walked and enjoyed his stroll. His path took him by the extensive gun works. While the government had reduced the military's budget, they were still arming the army's reserve corps with the Sabine Rifle, and Andy Berry had taken his advice and the gun works was producing a rifled musket for export. Sales orders remained high. Will wondered what would happen when the government decided they had bought enough guns. The gun works were not part of the research campus, but nevertheless, the inventions Andy Berry was working on were critically important to the next evolution of weapons, and they could ill afford for the government to close the spigot.

A few hundred feet past the gun works was the modest building housing the production of nitrogenated processed cotton. Although Will's investment in the venture was small, he was happy for the success Gail Borden and Andy Berry were achieving. He wasn't sure when they would crack the formula, but Will was confident the two inventors would eventually develop a stable chemical compound for smokeless powder.

Farther past the NPC facility was the campus with a few small buildings. One building housed a couple of classrooms. Ashbel Smith had returned from combating the deadly yellow-fever-carrying mosquito. He spent part of his day training would-be doctors in one of the classrooms and the other part of the day either writing about his research or actually conducting it. Will spent a few hours a week talking with the doctor. He was amazed how much information he remembered from before the transference about basic science and health, and those conversations with Smith helped to uncover things in his memory he hadn't thought about in fifteen years or more.

As Will approached the college, he wondered what Smith must think of him. His understanding of germ theory, while no more knowledgeable than that of a high school senior in the world before the transference, was twenty or thirty years ahead of the eighteen forties. When he was with Dr. Smith, he spent as much time trying to figure out how to avoid giving away things he couldn't hope to explain than he did pointing the doctor in the right direction. He couldn't imagine explaining the truth. *"You see, Ashbel, the fact is, while I might inhabit the body of the William Travis, by a process I can never explain, my mind and soul were transplanted from the twenty-first century."* He chuckled at the idea. He'd long ago decided if God wasn't going to put his mind back in his own body, he'd take the secret to the grave.

Thoughts of Dr. Smith were driven from his head as he heard a crash in the building housing a machine shop. Will raced into it and found Dick Gatling standing in the middle of a room. A twisted mess of metal was at his feet. He started in surprise when Will ran in.

"What the hell, Dick?"

"Ah, General Travis, I didn't think anyone was around. What you're looking at is my last model for a cotton harvester." Gatling's face was flushed with anger as he stared at the mangled mess.

Will came over and knelt by the twisted metal. "Where's the problem? I thought you were making progress."

Crossing the room, Gatling picked up a broom and began sweeping the destroyed model into a pile. "The problem is that most of the ways we've come up with picking the cotton bolls destroy the plant. That won't cut it. The bolls on the plant grow at different speeds. That's why pickers will sweep through a field three or more times until all the cotton is harvested, after which the plants can be destroyed or plowed under."

Will grabbed a bucket and dragged it to the pile where the young inventor swept the detritus into a dustpan and dumped it into the bucket. "This was a pneumatic picker. The idea is that we could use compressed air and blast the cotton loose from the boll."

"What kept it from working?"

Gatling took the bucket from Will and set it by one of the walls before he said, "Imagine an air gun because that was basically the idea. You'd pump the device and build up a charge of air. Once a charge of air was stored, you'd use the device and blast the cotton fiber from the boll."

"That sounds pretty ingenious. What happened?"

"The damned thing takes more time to pump air into it than it takes for someone to pick a boll from the plant. Do you really think Don Garza or one of these planters would use it when it takes more manpower than picking cotton by hand?"

Will saw the problem. The pneumatic element required pumping to build up enough air pressure to do the job. It reminded him of his first pellet rifle as a teenager. He would have to pump the gun several times just to shoot one pellet. The principal was the same with Gatling's device. "Is there any way to build a generator that could pump the air into the device?"

Gatling stroked his bearded chin, "I don't know. The easy solution was a self-contained device. I've considered begging off this project, but I hadn't thought about a generator. I guess I can see what's possible."

Will offered a smile. He *really* wanted a cotton harvester. There was nothing guaranteed to disrupt the slave economy than a device that could automate their jobs.

Chapter 20

The bronze star was placed on top the Christmas tree, and three-year-old Liza squealed as Will lowered her to the ground. "Again Daddy!"

Little David giggled as he raised his hands up, "Me, Papa!" A few months shy of two years, the toddler was at that age where his waking moments were spent keeping his parents on their toes. Will swept down and swung his younger son over his head.

After the toddler screamed "Down!" Will set him on the floor and retreated to the library as Becky called out, "Don't forget, we've got church this evening."

Will eyed the papers on his desk as he settled into a chair. Work could wait. He picked up the latest newspaper and unfolded it. The headline read, "Clay Wins 2nd Term!" He had already read the article on the first page, but he flipped to the back of the paper, where the newspaper's editorial position was stated.

President Clay's reelection gives hope that soon he will arrange a suitable treaty, settling once and for all, resolution to the Oregon problem. Despite supporting the Whig platform limiting our presidents to a single term, much remains incomplete and a second term may result in new states out of the Texian Cession...

A noise alerted Will, and he turned and saw his oldest child, Charlie. Not a child anymore, he was sixteen. Will was no expert, but the boy might still have a growth spurt in him, yet. His son was a few inches short of six feet while Will was an inch over. A year had passed by since he had rescued his son from Jenkins' crew of murderers and since then, Will had been beside the boy's bed most of the time through the nightmares haunting Charlie's sleep. The boy was more studious and introspective since then, and his awareness of the world beyond his home had grown by leaps and bounds.

"Is that from Philadelphia?" he said, pointing to the newspaper.

Will flipped the paper over, revealing the name, *Pennsylvania Inquirer*. "Yep. Was curious to see how the Whigs viewed Clay's reelection last month."

He handed the newspaper to the teenager and gestured to an empty seat. "Do you recall what he campaigned on?"

Charlie glanced at the headline on the front page. "The gold discovered in California was on everyone's lips. But the Indian territory and the dispute with Britain over the Oregon territory was what I read about."

Smiling at his son, Will said, "I'm glad that Jack and his companions were fortunate to discover gold, although part of me wishes they had found it in Texas instead of what people are calling Jefferson now. As I understand it, a handful of men have hazarded the

Indian Territory to get there next and lay down their stake. Without a railroad or even a decent road, the trek is dangerous.

"The discovery of gold out west adds another reason for President Clay to reach an agreement with Britain on a common border. Lorenzo offered to host a meeting between the US and Britain a couple of years ago, and Clay's stubborn refusal was a mistake. If the British were of a mind to, they could demand everything north of the Columbia River."

Charlie looked at a map of North America, west of the Mississippi River and said, "Would Clay accept that?"

Will shook his head, "I doubt it. Clay may have a reputation of being a compromiser, but he wouldn't submit a treaty to the Senate he knows wouldn't pass. And a boundary line at the Columbia River wouldn't work. Seven Americans are living in the Oregon Territory for every one British. I think Clay will settle for the forty-ninth parallel. North of there, it's mostly Canadian fur companies. Below the forty-ninth is where most of the Americans are carving out their farms and towns."

Charlie stood and walked over to the map on the wall. After studying it, he asked, "You said earlier you thought there might be gold in the part of California we're keeping. What's to keep President Clay from trying to take it from us? Now that war with Mexico is unlikely, our army is small."

Will came over and stood next to the map, "I wasn't in favor of the boundaries that Mr. Wharton negotiated, but he's got a point. Rivers make better boundaries than a simple line on a map. Also, Clay doesn't want anything to do with Texas that draws the attention of Southern Democrats. With annexation dead as a doornail, he's interested in opening the western territories to expansion while balancing the interests of the slave states."

Will pointed to a painting of a warship at sea on another wall and continued, "And, we've got two first-rate warships in addition to our current fleet. The *Montezuma* and the *Guadalupe* are good warships, and once Texas can afford to crew them, they'll be added to the fleet. Lorenzo will put a couple of ships on the Pacific coast to protect Texian interests. When I talked with Sid Johnston, he said once the Military Road is finished to Santa Fe, he'll task the company of engineers and workers to start surveying the road between there and the Pacific Ocean. By the end of eighteen forty-six, we'll have a well-maintained road running from San Antonio to Los Angeles."

Charlie pursed his lips as he swiveled his gaze back to the map. "I know you want me to continue my education, Pa. But when I'm old enough, I want to help protect Texas."

Will's heart sank. His life until the previous year had been solely about protecting Texas; first from the Mexicans, then from the Comanche, and again from the Mexicans. He was glad to have turned the command over to Johnston. It wasn't a profession he'd wish for his son. The research campus, Trinity College, was coming along nicely. He would rather Charlie study science or business. He was about to tell him that when he saw the young man's face was set and determined. Charlie had run off and joined Crockett's expedition against Will's wishes, and now as the boy approached adulthood, Will felt his ability to rein in Charlie's desires was limited at best.

Forcing a smile, he said, "Since the end of the war, the army's pretty firmly set on only accepting recruits over eighteen. Focus on your studies for now, and I'll write to Sid and see if he can find a place for you. Alright?"

With a noncommittal grunt, Charlie took the newspaper and left the library. Will sighed as he watched the redhead go. Before Charlie could do something rash, Will decided he would write to Sid. There hadn't been time before the recent Mexican War to do anything about forming a military academy, but now, with the Republic at peace, perhaps Sid would be receptive to the idea.

3 April 1845

The Colorado River flowed along the south side of Austin. To look at the water, one might think it ran languidly by the capital of the republic. Will's eyes were drawn to the brick and stone pillars embedded in the river. Water rushed by either side with overwhelming force. His eyes followed the pier upward until they rested on the iron and wooden trellis spanning the river.

Will caught a glint of silver in the corner of his eye and turned and saw the sun reflecting on Sam Williams' premature gray. "I see you found the bridge."

Williams clapped him on the back affectionately. "I'd have to be blind to miss this monstrosity. It took long enough to see this completed."

Will turned, following the tracks off the bridge and to the edge of town. He was worried about the Bexar & Austin Railroad. "How much stock did we end up buying?"

Sam said, "More than we should have. I sold one of our larger war bonds to an investor in Mobile and used the cash from that sale to invest in this. On paper, this looks like a solid investment. A railroad between the capital of the Republic to the largest city should make sense. But it doesn't connect to anything. At least not yet."

Will grimaced. "I read about how they had to haul the locomotive engine in parts to Austin and then reassemble them here."

"It's hardly the first railroad engine to be hauled somewhere by wagon. Won't be the last either."

"It shouldn't be long now," Will said, as he glanced at his pocket watch. Over the rooftops of nearby houses, he could see sooty clouds rising heavenward. The thought of losing money on this had been in the back of his and Sam's mind since they decided to invest in the project.

Now that the train was about to make its maiden voyage between Austin and San Antonio, Will felt jittery. "What happens if we've picked wrong, Sam? Can we ride a loss of a hundred thousand dollars?"

Williams blanched, "That hardly bears thinking about. But the truth of the matter is our balance sheet looks okay. With the Treasury Department paying interest on the war bonds, we're getting a few thousand dollars each month. We're also issuing new loans and getting more depositors. A loss like that, might not kill us, but I can't guarantee we'd not get another visit from your mysterious Mr. Taylor."

Sam stared at the bridge as a crowd grew around them. It wouldn't be long before speeches were given and the train took off. Eventually, he continued, "Success here is more likely if someone were to build a railroad between Harrisburg and Austin, connecting all of Texas' railroads into a single network."

Hearing that was like biting into a lemon. Will said, "Something like that is going to be expensive."

"Very. As much as a million dollars, depending on the type of bridge construction chosen."

Will dug into his trouser pockets and pulled them inside-out. "I'm afraid I don't have that kind of money."

Sam chuckled, "While the bank has more than enough to cover it, unfortunately, it's largely tied up in other investment projects. We may need to pitch a project like that to other investors."

Will turned on Williams. "You just said, we. What do you mean?"

Sam pointed to the east, where the nearest railroad ended more than two hundred miles away. "No one else has committed to building a railroad between here and back east. We have the contacts to do it, and if we build it, I think the flow of goods, services, and people between here and Galveston Bay is such that whoever builds it will be rewarded generously."

Taking charge of developing a new railroad was daunting and risky. The men who had started the Austin to San Antonio route had taken several years to develop it, and it had been more expensive than they originally planned. So much so, that Sam had bought out several smaller investors as well as purchased new shares of the company. For a new railroad, all of those risks would ride on their bank.

Feeling his own reservations, Will asked, "How long will this take?"

Sam said, "Three years, Buck. But think of it. If we can do this, you'd be able to get on a train in San Antonio and ride it all the way to the Sabine River. Or your goods could travel three hundred miles in less than a day. Think about how much money a railroad company could make transporting the wealth of a nation across its rails."

A whistle blast cut through the morning air, and after several men gave speeches before the crowd of more than one thousand Austinites, Will and Sam watched the first train slowly build up speed before it rattled across the bridge, heading south.

August 1845

The smell of rotten eggs was nearly overwhelming throughout the hospital on Galveston Island. Dr. Ashbel Smith stepped around a ceramic pot, where wood alcohol mixed with sulfur burned. More pots had been set around the hospital as well as in many of the public buildings on the island. There was no denying it, mosquitos didn't care for the odor.

He coughed. People didn't care for the stench any more than mosquitos. But the ubiquitous pots were doing what nothing else had done before, and that was keeping the mosquitos away. Dr. Smith closed the door to the hospital behind him and sat on one of the chairs on the veranda. He pulled his pipe from a white jacket and lit a lucifer and puffed on the pipe until the fragrant odor of tobacco filled his senses, driving the worst of the burning sulfur from his nose. He liked good Virginia tobacco, and as he blew a ring into the air, he allowed the first smile in many days to light up his stern features.

He had left his lab and classroom at Trinity College when news of yellow fever in Galveston reached the town. Although San Antonio was larger than the port, the coastal town was the lifeblood of trade and immigration for the Republic. The longer the disease ran unchecked on the barrier island, the fewer ships would call upon Galveston.

He had been in Galveston more than two weeks and this night was the first time since the start of the fever he had taken time to look into the night sky. The full silver moon was high overhead. It seemed as though a halo ringed it. He was tired from too many long days and too many sleepless nights, and he wasn't sure if his mind was playing tricks. Even so, he allowed his eyes to stare into the heavens until he finished smoking his pipe.

He knocked the ashes out of the pipe and returned it its pocket. He heard a rustling and turned and saw a sheet of muslin balloon from one of the hospital windows. Every open window was covered with the light material. If mosquitos couldn't get into the building to feed on his sick patients, then it stood to reason, they couldn't pass on the fever.

He had long been convinced the fever and vomit were not how the disease spread. It was only after many long conversations with Buck that Smith turned his attention to the common mosquito. It had taken months of research over two yellow fever seasons for Smith to confirm, by following infection patterns, the mosquito was the carrier.

The hospital was far from the only building fumigated with the stench of burning sulfur. Many homes used the noxious powder, mixed with wood alcohol to chase away mosquitos. Smith had gone another step and covered the cots of his sick patients with muslin tenting. If mosquitos couldn't bite the infected and carry the contaminated blood to another, then there was hope the fever wouldn't be able to spread.

It had been a bad day for him when he figured this out. Since the epidemic of 1838, he had advocated against quarantining, because he knew neither the vomit nor the patients were contagious. Now, he knew enough to understand that a quarantine kept the mosquitos from transporting infected blood. Telling people he was mistaken about a quarantine earlier had been hard. When he had told Buck this, the general had laughed and said, "Doc, there's a reason they call what doctors do 'practice.' Over time folks will appreciate it more if you admit your earlier mistake."

As usual, Buck had been right. Yellow fever scared people worse than a rumor of Comanche on the warpath. Their natural instinct was to quarantine sick folks. Even though folks who had caught yellow fever were not contagious, the ever-present mosquito was an effective transmitter. Their rationale had been wrong, but their instincts had been dead on.

There had been no new victims within the past couple of days. The infected in the hospital would be allowed to heal or die as God willed. As a good Baptist, he had prayed until words failed. A dozen had fallen to the fever this year. While it was the fewest he'd seen, it was still too many. It galled him to know that without his conversations with Travis he might have remained blind to the role of the humble mosquito.

He shuddered to think of how much he didn't know. If there was a way to treat the illness, not merely contain it, but to destroy it, he wanted to find out how. Quarantining the victims was well and good, but it was a half measure. If a cure could be found, he was determined to find it.

He looked forward to returning to the small lab and classrooms at Trinity College. He had ideas he wanted to research and letters to write to colleagues back east. He would get the news out. He now knew the mosquito's role in spreading the fever. He knew how to destroy their nesting spots and how to prevent the spread of the disease.

It was a start, and with any luck, he intended to write up everything he had learned. While some departments at Trinity seemed determined to find new inventions and spin them off into profitable corporations, Ashbel Smith wasn't worried about making a dime from what he discovered. This information could save thousands of lives across the warm, swampy regions of the South.

Chapter 21

1 September 1845

The faint blast on the steam whistle echoed over the walls of the Alamo. Cadet Charles Edward Travis stood at attention in the plaza, as he recalled his recent trip from Trinity Park. For part of the journey, the stagecoach rolled alongside the graded railroad bed from Houston to Hempstead. He knew his pa had invested heavily in the construction, but it was a small portion of his holdings.

Over the past couple of years, Charlie watched as new businesses were built in the growing towns of Trinity Park and West Liberty. Although most of the cotton in the area was exported to the United States and Britain, a bustling textile mill produced cheap cloth. Spreading alongside the Trinity, more mills were producing farming implements for export to the United States. Trinity College boasted a small medical school and a new school of agricultural science, in addition to mechanical engineering. Dozens of men and even a few women were studying there. The inventions they had created over the past few years were fueling development around Galveston Bay and bringing in immigrants from the United States and Europe to work in the mills, factories, and foundries.

Charlie didn't care about all of that. After his pa had said he would contact General Johnston about securing a place for him in the army, Charlie kept reminding his pa of the promise. The result was why he stood in the Alamo Plaza with a dozen other young men, all wearing the butternut uniform of the Republic's army. The signs of the siege of 1842 were long gone. Behind the thin line of cadets, the western wall, where the Mexican army had surged into the compound, was rebuilt. Barracks and administrative buildings lined the twenty-foot tall wall, and heavy guns were positioned on reinforced rooftops.

To his right was the Alamo chapel's courtyard. The low wall between the courtyard and the plaza remained, but the dirt between the low wall and the chapel was replaced by gardens running alongside a paved path to the chapel's double-doors. It was a fitting memorial to the dozens of riflemen who had died defending the courtyard wall against Woll's overwhelming force. In his mind, Charlie was back in the chapel, standing behind the makeshift barricade, where the fort's survivors prepared to make a final stand. He blinked and realized a tear was trickling down his cheek. Even though three and a half years had passed since General Woll's failed attempt to capture the Alamo, for a moment, it had felt like only yesterday. He stole a glance to either side; neither cadet appeared to have noticed him, and he looked forward and waited.

He didn't have long to wait. An officer emerged from the southern barracks, crossing through the garden in front of the chapel. With a purposeful stride, he passed through the courtyard gate and came to stand before Charlie and his cohorts. His red hair stuck out below his black, wide-brimmed hat.

"You'll come to attention when in the presence of an officer!" he bellowed.

Having grown up around the soldiers of the Alamo, Charlie snapped to attention, ignoring other cadets' efforts.

"I'm Captain Sherman, and I'll be your commandant for the next two years. I don't give a damn who you knew to get into the cadet corps or who you're related to. If you can't cut it, none of that will matter. The only thing that matters is knowing the man standing next to you has your back and that you have his. You'll learn to follow orders, and eventually how to give them. But if you fail, you'll be gone faster than a scalded dog."

Sherman walked down the line of cadets, eyeing each one. "When I'm finished, you'll learn how to fire a rifle faster than the men you'll command, how to clean your rifle faster than them. You'll learn how to march further and longer. You'll learn how to care for your horse before you're even awake, and long after you're asleep. How to use that pig-sticker called a saber, and how to sight one of my artillery pieces better than my gunnery sergeants. Before you're commissioned officers, you'll demonstrate proficiency in every branch of service and study the art of engineering. You'll build field fortifications and learn how to construct bridges with whatever is available. And you'll do all that before you ever command men."

Sherman turned and walked back to the center of the short line and came to attention before the cadre of cadets. The hospital building was in front of the cadets and from an office above the medical facility another officer appeared. Charlie recognized Albert Sidney Johnston. The general wore shoulder-boards with the single star of a brigadier general on his brownish uniform. A glance at the stern expression on Captain Sherman's face and any temptation to wave at his father's friend died. Johnston had been one of the first faces Charlie had seen when the relief force had arrived at the Alamo, rescuing the survivors in the chapel.

With an informal wave at the cadets, Johnston said, "Officers and gentlemen are what West Point turns out. You'll not get a better education at what it means to be an American engineer than that. That's what Captain Sherman and I experienced as we learned the art of soldiering."

He paused, as though searching for something among the cadets. "Some of you were born in places where being a gentleman was more important than any other character trait. Rather expected if your future involved running your family's plantation. That spirit infuses the officer corps of the United States."

Johnston gripped the wooden railing as he stared down into the plaza. "To Hell with all of that. Texas doesn't need more gentlemen. We need officers with a sense of duty to the Republic and a moral responsibility to the men they command. The Republic doesn't need more men trained to die for their country, but men trained to kill. Make the other bastard die for his country while you live for yours."

Charlie joined the other cadets clapping and shouting their approval.

"Captain Sherman isn't here to teach you how to lead your regiments by line into battle. Our experience with Mexico has shown that kind of war is behind us. He'll teach you the role of rifleman, cavalryman, and artillerist and how they work together. While the United States may look to Europe when it comes to how they train their officers, Texas will take the lessons learned from the Comanche and Mexicans and use them to whip any who oppose us. No, cadets, we'll not turn you into gentlemen. When we're done, your duty to Texas and your responsibility to your men will be your guiding principle when called to ruthlessly defend our country."

Johnston's eyes seemed to bore into Charlie, and the young man's heart stirred with adventure. The general turned and a moment later, the door to his office closed behind him.

Mid-September 1845

The crane creaked under the weight of the five-hundred-pound cotton bale as the laborers used hooks to swing the bale from the platform onto the flatcar. As soon as the bale was unhooked, the crane pivoted back, and the laborers latched another bale to it.

Will watched the team hoist more bales of cotton. Most of it was wrapped in burlap wrapping with the Gulf Farms emblem. Some were stamped with nearby plantations' markings. He was unhappy knowing the other bales were produced with slave labor but there was nothing he could do to stop it, at least not yet, he swore to himself.

"Those micks know how to move the cotton, almost as well as the negro."

Will turned and saw the president of Gulf Farms approaching. "Señor Garza. It looks like a bumper crop this year. Hard to believe we've come back so quickly from two years ago."

Garza clasped Will's hand and said, "Peace agrees with us, Buck. Having all our employees back from their militia duty helps a lot. Are you telling President Zavala to keep things peaceful?"

Will laughed, "God help me, but Lorenzo didn't talk to me for six months after I resigned. He was convinced I was abandoning my duty when I put my duty to my family above my country. But he's come around as of late. I received a Christmas card last year, so that's progress."

"Lorenzo's a good man, but the presidency changes a man. He's singular in his service to Texas. I worry his sense of duty will steal his health," Garza said. "Had I been in your shoes, I hope I would have done as you did."

Will was uncomfortable with the praise. He had done what needed doing, nothing more. He pointed to the men loading the flatbed railroad car. "I've noticed a lot of the men we're hiring are Irish. I would hope they work as hard as," he couldn't bring himself to use the other word, "blacks."

Garza offered a small smile, "I suppose. I'd gotten used to the freedmen who'd been loading freight. After the spring expansion in our acreage, most of them chose to work the fields. Wages aren't any better, but we provide housing to the families who work the land."

"Why the Irish?"

Garza turned his back on the laborers, "Some of the Irish are telling of famine. Potato crops are blighted and hunger stalks the land. You may want to pass that information along. I've talked with Andy Berry and several other mill and factory owners in the area and they could use more men. The Irish problem could be a blessing to us, Gulf Farms isn't the only enterprise short of good workers."

He studied the men loading cotton bales. "Of course, that will depend on prices. Last year, we were able to sell our cotton in New England and to the textile mills in Britain for upwards of twelve and a half cents per pound. My factors in Philadelphia indicate there is a bit of a glut, and the price has fallen hard."

Will frowned. "How badly have prices fallen?"

"Eight and a half cents on the New York Commodities Exchange according to the most recent newspaper from the empire state."

Will shook his head at the news. He cursed the wide gaps in the knowledge he brought with him in the transference. Someone who had studied the antebellum cotton economy might have known about the sharp drop in the price of cotton, but Garza's information was news to him.

Another thought made him feel even worse. What if his actions over the past few years had changed things so much the drop in price wasn't something he would have known about, because he had created it? The thought left him sick to his stomach. He had lived the past nine years pushing Texas away from the American South, sowing seeds to weaken slavery within the Republic. But until the past couple of years, most of his efforts were designed around building a military that could hold its own against Mexico, and he hadn't considered how the changes made would impact the world beyond.

He said, "What's the lower prices mean for us?"

Garza stared at the laborers as they hoisted another cotton bale onto the flatbed car. As the silence lengthened, he eventually said, "We'll hemorrhage money this year. Oh, it won't drive us out of business. We sold at twelve cents a pound last year and have a small amount of savings. But if worse comes to worst, I may be coming hat in hand to you and Sam for a short-term loan."

Despite the development of the railroad, the effects of the war lingered on. Will wondered how much healthier Gulf Farms would have been were it not for the war's lean year. Very little cotton had been grown two years earlier, and the company had used up the earlier years' profits. The company had barely returned to profitability in 1844, and now the price of cotton was plummeting.

He smiled wryly, "I'll talk to Sam about it. I'm sure something can be arranged." He still struggled to wrap his mind around the complexities of industrial cotton production. Despite the improved seed drills used to plant the cotton and the water-powered cotton gin, Gulf Farms faced the same limitation slaveholding planters faced. Picking cotton was still by hand. While Will yet hoped Dick Gatling would come through with his pneumatic cotton picker, his optimism was fading.

Because of the wildly fluctuating price of cotton, few small landholders could risk their farms on more than a few acres of cotton production. Truly profitable cotton production required large, industrial farms, plantations. Aside from Gulf Farms Corporation and a few smaller free labor enterprises, much of the cotton grown in Texas was on plantations by slaves.

Plantations of dozens or even hundreds of slaves could ride a poor harvest even better than Don Garza could. If a planter needed quick cash, his first options were bankers in New Orleans or New York. Most bankers were happy to accept slaves as collateral. If loans were not available, then the planter could sell a few slaves. When Will mentioned that to Garza, the old Tejano said, “Maybe, but we can fire our unproductive laborers, and we don’t have to hire men with whips or guns to keep an eye on them. We may pay more for each laborer, but with the devices we’ve patented or bought from young Mr. Gatling, we’ve made our employees more productive.”

Will added, “Except for the picking season. Despite thousands of dollars thrown at the problem, we’ve yet to find a solution to the worst part of growing cotton.”

Garza shrugged, “It might not happen this year, Buck. But if not your young inventors, someone will figure it out. Let’s focus on surviving this year.”

There was a crash. A cotton bale collapsed, the twine holding it snapped, sending tufts of cotton blowing across the depot. Will turned and saw two of the Irishmen pointing at the crane. The stout jib hung at a drunken angle. The stone counterweight rolled from the platform, landing with a thud next to the flatcar.

Don Garza’s bitter laughter rang in Will’s ear, “Of course, before we can sell at a loss, we have to get it to market first.”

Chapter 22

15 November 1846

Will opened the door to little David's bedroom. The lamp in his hand chased the shadows away as he watched his three-year-old's small chest rise and fall. The boy looked like his mother, with brown curls covering his forehead. His youngest seemed to have only two speeds. Full-tilt ahead or asleep. Will closed the door, thankful it was the latter at that moment. Further down the hall, he repeated the process at the door to Liza's bedroom. His five-year-old daughter's room had an elaborate dollhouse in the middle of the floor, but thankfully, she was also asleep in her bed.

He closed the door and shook his head as he followed the lamplight down the hallway. His children were growing up so fast. Had it really been ten years since the transference? He'd never forget his life before, and God alone knows all the things he still missed. But he was happy with his life and even happier with his family.

"A smile like that, I hope I'm the one you're thinking about."

Will looked up as he walked into the dining room. Becky sat at the table with a cup of coffee, smiling. He took a seat next to her, leaned in and planted a kiss on her lips. "Only you, love."

An envelope lay on the table. "Open it, Will. We haven't heard from Charlie since he graduated."

Will tore the end of the envelope open and unfolded the single sheet of paper. "Alright. Let's see what the boy's got to say."

Becky took a sip of coffee. "I can hardly believe he's eighteen already. Where do the years go?"

Will moved the letter to catch the light from the lamp and began to read.

> *Dear Pa and Becky, I've missed you since the graduation in June. I thought Captain Sherman had marched me into the ground while I was still a cadet. But now that I've been assigned to command a platoon, I'm marching and drilling even more now than I did before. It's not as bad as it could be. The shoes from the factory at Trinity Park are a real improvement over the old leather soles we used to wear. If I ever see this Goodyear fellow, I'll buy him a drink.*
>
> *Tell Mr. Berry that his M46 Sabine rifle is an excellent weapon. I spent some time with Lt. Running Creek on the firing range, and we managed to shoot ten rounds in a minute! It was a caution. Jesse says his special Rangers have taken to it like a duck to water. I wish you could talk Gnl Johnston into equipping the rest of the army with these new rifles.*

I'm not sure I'll get leave to come home for Christmas. I've heard rumors that our company will be deployed to Monterey. The gold rush in Franklin, across the border, is spilling into Texian California. Gnl Johnston wants soldiers to show the flag and remind folks which country they're in. We're not going to tolerate the lawlessness taking hold over the border. If that happens, we could be marching west along the Military Road before the new year.

Tell Liza and Davy that I love and miss them. I love you and will post a letter once our marching orders come through.

Love, Charlie.

As Will set the letter down, he felt Becky's hand on his cheek. She wiped the tear away. "He's turning into a fine, young man, Will. You should be proud."

Feeling his emotions threatening to overwhelm him, Will nodded, taking her hand in his and kissing it. "We did well, Becky. But God knows, he's had to endure more than most boys, and despite all of that, he's doing so well."

Becky scooted her chair closer and held his hand, "While he may turn out to be the career soldier, I'm so grateful your soldiering days are over. Those days of you burning the midnight oil, going over paperwork are gone. Now, you've got time for the little ones."

Will pulled Becky closer and leaned in, nuzzling his lips against her neck, and whispered, "And for you."

Becky let out a squeal, "You'll wake my ma."

Will chuckled. "Maybe we should retire to our bedroom. I don't know what I'd do if Elizabeth found the two of us trying for another child on the kitchen table."

Despite her laughter, Becky looked slightly scandalized as she made to slap at his shirt. “Will Travis! The scandal it would create.”

Later that night, in their bedroom, Will stared at the ceiling. The sheets rustled and Becky leaned against him, “You’re supposed to be smiling, Mr. William Travis.

Will turned his head and saw his wife was still undressed. “You know how to put a smile on my face, my love.”

Becky snuggled against him, “What’s wrong? I can tell when you’re distracted.”

“It’s probably nothing. But I got a letter from Erasmo. Lorenzo is sick. Every time Erasmo tries to go visit him, Emily has kept him and anyone else from seeing him.”

Becky ran her finger along Will’s cheek, “If more wives did that then more husbands would recover faster. The president needs to rest if he’s sick.”

Will said, “I know. But the lack of news is troubling. I pray you’re right, and Emily is just trying to let Lorenzo recover. But if something happens, I worry.”

“Why?”

Will sat up and grabbed a nightshirt. The room was growing chilly, despite the fire burning in the hearth. As he slid the shirt over his head, he said, “I’ve never warmed to Richard Ellis. I know Lorenzo needed the vote of some of the planter types, but I don’t know if he’ll continue your father and Lorenzo’s policies.”

After putting her own nightgown on, Becky said, “You’re worried Richard will try to cozy up to the United States and get us annexed?”

“I married a smart girl,” Will said with a broad grin. “That could be a problem for us. I don’t think the Whigs will win the White House, not after eight years of Henry

Clay. The Democrats will win in two years. And if we've got Ellis banging the drum for annexation here and the Democrats in Washington, that could destroy everything we've worked for."

A short while later, Will heard even breathing next to him, signaling Becky was already asleep. The idea of Richard Ellis replacing Lorenzo de Zavala kept Will awake long into the night.

The glass panes rattled in the window frame as a cold, dry western wind blew through the nation's capital. John Wharton ran his hand through his brown hair, brushing it out of his eyes. The past week had been one of the most stressful in his life. The death of Lorenzo de Zavala had caught everyone by surprise. Lorenzo's wife, Emily, had kept her husband's sudden illness private until his passing forced her to break the news.

Richard Ellis, who had been a nonentity in the Zavala administration, had been sworn in by Chief Justice John Birdsall a few days before. Now, a man who had been an outsider was the ultimate insider in Austin, and men who had relied upon their relationship with Zavala were plunged into uncertainty as they waited to find out what kind of executive Ellis would be.

Wharton ignored the papers on his desk as he swiveled his chair to look out the window. When the structure housing Texas' state department had been built, he could still see the prairie from his desk. Now, construction blocked his view. More than just Austin had changed since 1841. He had first been appointed Secretary of State under David Crockett. When the formidable frontiersman resigned, Lorenzo had reappointed him to the post.

By any standard, as secretary of state, Wharton had been successful. Under his guidance, Texas had received recognition from France, Belgium, the Netherlands, Russia, Prussia, several other German principalities, and Great Britain.

He had established consulates in a dozen countries and negotiated trade agreements with most of Western Europe, all on a budget that had only inched over a hundred-fifty thousand dollars in the current budget year.

But now he was worried. Michel Menard, from Treasury, had left his office an hour before and he had been only slightly less livid leaving than when he had arrived. Menard had stormed in, saying, "That bastard is going to destroy everything we've built."

When Wharton asked who he was talking about, Menard continued, "Richard Ellis wants to shut down the land bank."

More than half the government's revenue came from the land bank. The brainchild of Erasmo Seguin, the land bank extended credit to all new settlers who wanted to build farms or ranches. Nearly two million acres had been financed through the land bank, and millions more were possible over the next decade. All that money flowed into the Republic's coffers. "What's he thinking?" was all Wharton had managed to ask.

Menard, cheeks flushed with anger, said, "He wants to expand the number of plantations, and wants all available tracts in the east that are suitable to cotton sold directly to planters able to buy more than two hundred acres."

Wharton had asked, "Won't that still bring in revenue?"

"What it will do is hang out a sign to the thousands of European immigrants that Texas isn't open for business anymore."

Wharton had gone pale at the news. 1846 had been a record year for immigrants from Ireland, as the Island country was gripped by a famine made all the worse by Britain's Irish policy. These people were flowing into the handful of manufacturing jobs available around Galveston Bay, but many times more of them were homesteading farms on the frontier, pushing the civilized part of Texas westward.

After Menard left, Wharton digested the news. If Ellis was interested in dismantling the land bank, what else was he going to try to change?

He turned away from the window when he heard the doorknob turn. His clerk poked his head in the doorway, "Sir, President Ellis has requested your presence."

The Secretary of State for Texas reluctantly stood and grabbed his coat from a rack as he left. If Menard was correct, Ellis was changing direction, and it bode ill for men who had skillfully directed the last two presidents' policies.

Despite taking less than five minutes to cross the street to the Capitol Building, it felt like the longest five minutes in his life. In less time than he would have liked, Wharton found himself sitting in a comfortable chair across from Richard Ellis.

"John, glad you were able to come for a visit." Ellis' smile was warm. A fellow Virginian by birth, like Wharton, he had been in Texas since before the revolution.

"I serve at your pleasure, Mr. President."

"And a damned fine job you've done for my predecessors, John. Over the past couple of years, I have advised Lorenzo on some budgetary concerns. At times he has listened to me, and other times he's followed his own counsel. In some ways, Texas is like a ship at sea, following a compass heading that is taking it toward dangerous shoals. We must chart a new direction and steer Texas away from the dangers ahead."

Wharton stared back, impassively, saying nothing.

Ellis said, "I need you, John. The recent war with Mexico nearly destroyed our economy. For years, like David and Lorenzo, I thought we could chart a path wholly our own. But this war showed me the folly of our ways. We are balanced between the Yankees in Washington and John Bull in London, and a fractious, dangerous and unstable Mexico to our south. Safety for our people is my highest goal."

Wharton broke his silence, "I thought our army, though small, is more than a match against Mexico. I was under the impression our people's safety was protected."

Ellis dismissively waved his hand, "Pure luck. Things could have been much worse. I want you to begin laying the groundwork with our friends in the United States for a closer relationship. I don't think the Whigs can control the White House after the next election. Mark my words, by eighteen forty-nine, a Democrat will be president. When that happens, I want their first order of business to be the annexation of Texas. By joining our lone star to their constellation, we will gain strength and protection."

Wharton sat, stunned by Ellis' declaration. In his mind, he saw everything he had worked for going up in flames. "But, President, the Crockett doctrine has worked well for Texas for more than a decade now. Why change?"

Ellis' eyes turned hard, "Hogwash, John. Every year, David and Lorenzo have moved the nation further away from our foundational institutions. A planter pays more taxes in Texas than he would in Alabama, and not by a small margin. My predecessors' policies have done too little to encourage a strong cotton economy. We're going to change that. By seeking union with the United States, we'll open up our public lands to even more cotton production and a flood of immigrants will come from the right sort of places."

Wharton had heard enough. He rose to his feet. "I think you'll need to find another man for the job, Mr. President. You'll have my resignation on your desk before the sun sets today!"

Without waiting for Ellis' response, Wharton was out the door and racing down the stairs. He didn't stop until he was standing in the middle of Congress Avenue. Out of breath, and out of a job for the first time in years, he didn't know what he would do next. He stepped out of the way of a freight wagon and looked around. Down the street from the Department of State, he saw the Commodities Bureau. If anyone knew what to do about Ellis' radical changes, it would be Erasmo Seguin.

A red cord separated the gallery from the chamber of the House of Representatives. A few dozen chairs were available for the public to use in the gallery, where they could watch the House conduct the People's business. A few wives watched their husbands, and a couple of men waited for legislation to be introduced affecting their own interests.

In a way, Wharton was there for the same reason. He was focused on one Congressman, with whom he traded looks as the morning wore on. These were the last few days Congress would be in session before taking off for Christmas. He heard the chair next to his scrape the floor and turned as Erasmo Seguin sat. The elder Seguin was showing his age. His black hair had given way to a mane of white, and the wrinkles on his face were more profound and the dark circles under his eyes more pronounced.

"Has Francisco spoken yet?"

Wharton pointed to the man with whom he'd been trading looks, "He was waiting for you."

The man about whom Wharton was whispering, rose and approached the Speaker of the House. He handed a sheaf of papers to him and waited.

The Speaker turned the pages, skimming as he flipped. "The chair recognizes Congressman Ruiz of Bexar."

Francisco Ruiz, a long-time friend of Juan Seguin, Erasmo's son, and an ardent supporter of Texas independence turned and faced his colleagues. In a voice with a lilting Tejano accent, Ruiz said, "I want to thank President Ellis for recognizing the republic's debt of gratitude to his predecessor. It's entirely appropriate to have a suitable period of mourning for one of such stature."

Continuing, Ruiz gripped the podium. "However, I am astounded by our new president's actions that undermine the gains Presidents Crockett and Zavala have won in the name of Texas liberty. I'm not telling tales out of school, everyone here knows of Secretary Wharton's resignation because he was instructed to bend every diplomatic resource toward annexation."

From the chamber, an anonymous voice called out, "If you're speechless then I'm a ring-tailed panther."

The chamber erupted into laughter as Ruiz raised his hand in mock surrender. "Fair enough. Then I will use my voice to champion the people's business. Unlike the Senate, the House of Representatives is often referred to as the People's House. Let it be said it's because we are often about the people's business. The president tells us that we should surrender our autonomy and seek annexation to the United States. I know my constituents in San Antonio, and this isn't something they would consent to without the voice of all Texians being heard.

"It is because of this, that I have offered up an act requiring a plebiscite of all voters in the republic to express their view on annexation. Should this act pass, the referendum will be binding on the government. If the people are willing that we surrender our independence then so be it. But if the people vote for continued independence, then this new administration will set aside talk of annexation and work to make our republic more secure and prosperous.

"Let the congressional record show that our Republic has been independent for nearly a decade. During that time, we have won every conflict we have had between ourselves and our opponents. Recently we forced Mexico to surrender her vacant northern territory. Before that, we bent the Comanche to our will, forcing them north of the Red River. We are secure within our borders. Our navy is second only to the United States in the western hemisphere."

Wharton resisted the urge to shake his head. The British squadron in the Caribbean was far more powerful than Texas' small navy. But of the countries wholly situated in North and South America, Texas' navy was second only to the US.

He focused on the speech as Ruiz continued, "Setting aside Henry Clay's anti-annexation policy in the US, were the Yankees to agree to annexation, we'd trade our autonomy for two seats in the US Senate. Two voices among fifty-six? We'd be drowned out by people whose interests may not align with ours. Our voice would be even smaller in their house of representatives. That's not what my constituents want."

When Ruiz wrapped up his speech, a couple of other men from congressional districts west of the Brazos River stood and seconded his motion.

One of the men who had been an ardent opponent to both the Crockett and Zavala administrations, James Collinsworth, stood and said, "Mr. Speaker, if I may."

Of the collection of representatives who were pro-annexation, Collinsworth was more diplomatic than most. Wharton bit his lip, hoping the Speaker would shut him up. It wouldn't do for President Ellis' allies in the House to persuade their undecided peers against a plebiscite. But Collinsworth was given permission to speak.

He straightened his jacket and placed his hands on the podium. "My fellow Representatives, just when I think there's nothing new under the sun, my colleague, Congressman Ruiz, surprises me. It should be self-evident our constituents sent us to Austin to do their business. Imagine the chaos if we had to present every budget to a popular vote?"

There was an uneasy round of laughter as he continued, "If the average citizen understood the challenges of governing they would probably wake up quaking at night. We are charged with protecting our voters from needlessly involving themselves in legislative issues. Every two years, we all canvass our districts and explain what we just did and what we're planning on doing next. The voters in my district expect me to make the difficult votes."

Wharton frowned; the congressman was warming to his impromptu address. "I'm shocked Congressman Ruiz seems to have forgotten it was his own town of San Antonio that was attacked by the Mexican hordes. Union with the United States would provide far greater security than what we currently possess. Instead of mustering every man and boy who can carry a weapon when Mexico rattles its saber in our direction, union with Washington would allow us to go on about our business, growing crops and making our fair land bloom while professional soldiers guard our southern border.

"Don't think of it as two lone votes in their senate. We have natural allies in Washington. As another slave state, we would champion the yeoman farmer and the planters, and seek to protect the farmer and the worker against the exploitation of monied and industrial interests.

"At a time when our peculiar institution has come under attack by folks who choose ignorance over understanding, union with the United States safeguards our institutions and provides us the ability to coordinate legislation and policy with like-minded lawmakers. The wealth of our nation hangs in the balance. Turning a vote over to the mob defies our duties within our democratic republic. I urge you, my colleagues, to vote down Congressman Ruiz's bill."

Wharton scanned the room, as a smattering of applause greeted the end of the speech. The proposed bill wasn't likely to come up for an immediate vote. The foreign relations committee would want to study the proposal.

A couple of weeks later, Wharton sat in the same chair in the gallery. Several pointed editorials had been published in newspapers across the Republic, advocating a plebiscite. Even pro-annexation newspapers favored a vote, and when the vote came to allow a referendum, of the one hundred men in the House, sixty-eight voted for it. The margin in the Senate was similar. Wharton smiled at the results. Even if Ellis were to veto the bill, there were enough votes to override the promised veto. The vote by the people of Texas on the issue of annexation would be held the first Monday of February of 1847.

Late December 1846

Will stared at the iron contraption setting on a field near the research campus. Metal pistons poked out of the contraption, and a long rubber hose lay on the ground, connected to the device.

"Stand back, sir. I've got to power up the compressor."

Will stepped away from the contraption as Dick Gatling fired up the loud steam engine. Raising his voice over the compressor, Gatling said, "It'll take a few minutes to build up pressure. I wasn't getting anywhere with my research into air guns, like that Austrian one we looked at. But I had read about pneumatic pumps used in mining. From there, it was easy enough to harness a steam engine to an air compressor."

Gatling grabbed the rubber hose and connected one end to the compressor. "Turns out that was the easy part. Rubber gets brittle in the cold and can melt in our hot southern sun. But I had some luck. I was reading a new publication from the United States, *The Scientific American*, and ran across a fellow named Charles Goodyear. He's developed a process called vulcanization, that makes rubber treated through his process resistant to extreme temperature. This hose was ordered from his factory back east."

Stretched to its maximum length, the hose was nearly a hundred feet long. Gatling said, "This is just a prototype. We'll need a hose twice this length to cover few acres."

He produced a cotton boll from a burlap bag and secured it to a wooden board. "Obviously, the boll would still be on the plant." He handed the hose to Will, continuing, "Hold this and point it at the boll. I'll open the valve, and you'll see what I've been working on for so long."

A moment later, Will felt a slight vibration in his hands, and the end of the hose jerked as a blast of compressed air hit the open cotton boll. Tufts of cotton flew away until the boll was an empty husk.

"Dick, you're a lot younger than me," Will said, dryly, "I'll let you chase after the cotton."

Gatling laughed. "Not to worry. I've created a catcher that extends from the end of the hose. All the loose cotton will get captured there."

Will swiveled his eyes between the tufts of cotton blowing across the ground and the compressor. It wasn't the cotton-picking machine he'd envisioned. He had reservations it would be as fast as picking by hand, but it was the first prototype that actually worked. And that was something.

"I'll talk with Don Garza. I'm sure we can test it in the fall."

Gatling turned the compressor off and banked the fire in the steam engine before running a grimy hand through his hair. "I appreciate it. Between now and then, I'll see what improvements can be made in the design."

Will turned to go. Living and working in Trinity Park, he enjoyed dinners with his family, and he had time to get cleaned up before Becky set the table.

"There was something else I wanted to show you, General." Gatling wrung his hands, smiling mysteriously.

His curiosity piqued, Will turned around. "You've not been holding back on me, Dick?"

Smiling sheepishly, Gatling waved for Will to follow as he turned and walked toward the gun works. "It's a surprise."

Will followed the young inventor past the gun works' spinning waterwheels. Beyond them was the testing range Andy Berry used to test new weapons. A white chalk line marked the firing line. A contraption, covered with a canvas tarp, was parked next to a table. Will found his steps were quicker the closer they came to whatever was under the tarp.

Breathlessly, Will said, "Take the tarp off, I want to see."

With a dramatic flourish, Gatling swept the canvas away, revealing a contraption as unique as the compressed air machine. Resting on an artillery caisson was a contraption with six barrels connected to what looked like a coffee grinder.

A voice from behind called out, "Dick, I thought you said, you'd not start without me."

Andy Berry approached, carrying two long, metal magazines in his hands. "I confess, General, when you talked to us about making a gun that could fire hundreds of rounds per minute, I thought you were pulling our legs. But Dick's a mechanical genius."

Gatling waved away the compliment. "Without Andy's brass cartridges, this would have stayed on the drawing board. Give General Travis one of the magazines and let's see how this works."

Will took the cool metal magazine and seated it above the cartridge chamber. There was a snick as it slid into place. He made sure his companions were behind him, and then he gripped the crank handle and slowly turned it. The gun's heavy frame and caisson absorbed the recoil as he turned the crank. Like a cosmic ripping noise, the barrels rotated around its central shaft and sent a steady stream of bullets downrange.

The spinning barrels hit an empty chamber, and Will stopped turning the crank and Berry removed the magazine and inserted a fresh one. Will couldn't resist a feral grin as he resumed turning the crank until again the gun emptied the magazine in just a few seconds.

Gatling said, "Depending on how fast you turn the crank, you can fire up to two hundred rounds in a minute."

There was a harsh tone in Will's laughter, "As God is my witness if we'd had these in the war with Mexico, we'd have swept the enemy from the field in no time."

Berry said, "It's a fine demonstration. But you fired ten percent of our daily production in less than a minute. Until we get our cartridge production up, it's a great idea, but it will deplete our reserves faster than we can replenish them."

Will helped the other two men cover the weapon with the tarp. "Andy, you need to find a way to increase your production of brass cartridges. In the short term, though, I think we're going to keep this between us. If Lorenzo were still alive, I'd take this to Austin tomorrow to demonstrate it. But damned if I trust Richard Ellis. All this talk of annexation is idiotic. The fool is even talking about reducing the size of the army and their budget further than Lorenzo did after the Mexican war."

By the time Will parted ways with his companions, twilight had fallen. The new weapon had caused him to forget about dinner. He tightened his scarf against a cold breeze and hurried home.

Chapter 23

7 February 1847

"David Stern Travis! Come back here and put your clothes on." Will winced as the words pierced his consciousness. He opened his eyes and saw Becky running out of their bedroom. He heard the pitter-patter of little feet racing away followed by his wife's exasperated voice, "Ma, can you comb Liza's hair? I don't want to be late for church this morning."

A moment later, Becky came back into the bedroom. She had a handful of clothes in one hand and a half-naked toddler in the other. "Good morning, sleepyhead. What time did you get in last night?"

Will stretched, "Too late. Sometime after midnight." He sat up and watched Becky put the clothes back on his younger son, who twisted and turned, making Becky's job harder.

"I don't wanna go," David protested. "I wanna stay home with Pa!"

Becky swatted his bare leg, and he squealed in protest. "Stop twisting around, or I'll give you something to howl about."

A moment later, he was scowling but dressed. She patted him on the backside, "Go find your grandma and help her with Liza's hair."

With a glint of mischief in his eyes, the little boy scampered from the room.

"Lord have mercy." Becky sat next to Will and leaned over and kissed him. "Why don't you get some more sleep. Me and Ma will take the kids to church."

Will yawned until his jaw popped. "Thanks. We didn't get away from Lynch's Ferry until well after dark. There were a couple of hundred people who came to hear us speak. Your husband's becoming quite the raconteur."

"Heaven forbid," she said as she stood and grabbed a cloak from a closet. "Pa was enough of a talker for the whole family. Were the folks in favor of continuing independence?"

"Some were. Some weren't. There are quite a few plantations along the San Jacinto River. I think we'll carry Harris county when the vote is taken. But there are plenty of places further east I'm not so sure about."

Becky dropped her gloves when there was a loud knocking at the door. "Expecting company?"

The insistent knocking echoed in Will's head. "No. Make them stop." He pulled his pillow over his head as Becky went to check.

He could hear a muffled voice and then Becky's. "No, he's resting. He'll be glad to see you tomorrow."

More muffled voice, followed by Becky's. "I'm sure it's important, Mr. Borden, but Will's been on the road all week."

Will pulled the pillow from over his head. Why was Gail Borden on his porch on a Sunday? The devout inventor should have been at church already. Will called out, "I'm coming, Becky."

He pulled on his old army greatcoat and shuffled to the front door. Becky and her mother corralled the children past Borden. "Gail, just remember, Will needs his rest."

A moment later, Will was alone with Borden. He nodded toward the kitchen, "Come on in. Let's see if Becky left any coffee brewing. What's keeping you out of your pew this morning?"

Borden was as excited as a schoolboy, "Take a look at this," he said, as he brought a brownish-colored biscuit from a pocket. "This will revolutionize how armies feed themselves on the march."

Borden had been experimenting with boiling meat down to an extract for several months, in addition to several other experiments designed to extend the life of food. Despite his exhaustion, Will was curious about the small, flat squares. "What's it taste like?"

Taking one of the biscuits, Borden broke it in two and handed half to Will, "It's mild."

Will bit into the biscuit. It was bland, nearly tasteless. He swallowed the dry morsel and chased it down with coffee. "Mild? Gail, it's got no taste."

"You can boil it, use it as a base for soup. Add all the spices you need."

Will remained skeptical, even as Borden set a pot over the fire. Thirty minutes later, several biscuits were dissolved into the boiling water. Salt and pepper were liberally added. Finally, Borden dipped a cup into the liquid and handed it to Will. "Taste it."

Will blew on it until the rim was cool enough to not burn his lips. A meaty aroma rose from the broth, and when he sipped it, the beef flavoring was notable. He had tasted worse. "What do you want to do with this, Gail?"

"I'd like to pitch it to the army and navy. They need foodstuffs that won't spoil, and this will last for years."

Will worried it might last for years because the soldiers wouldn't touch it. But he refrained from saying that. The premise was good, even if the biscuit was unappetizing. Briefly, Will wondered how a biscuit mixed with lemon peels or limes would go over with sailors. Long-term storage of food heavy in vitamin C could be even more marketable. But Borden's excitement was such that Will didn't have the heart to stop him.

As he set the broth down, Will said, "I'll write a letter for you. Have you considered other applications?"

Borden said, "I used an evaporator to dry out the meat before boiling it down. I've been thinking of trying it with milk. If I can remove the water from milk, we could greatly increase its storage life."

Forcing a smile onto his face, Will said, "Let's see what we can do to sell the military on your meat biscuits. We've got some men who are doing well selling some of Dick Gatling's farming equipment, I'll see if we can get them to help market this. If I can do that for you, can you move forward on condensing milk?"

After Borden left, Will took the pot behind the house, and he dumped the meat biscuit broth onto his mother-in-law's flower garden. But he had a spring in his step as he walked back into the house. The meat biscuit was nothing compared to the prospect of canned milk. If Borden could invent condensed milk,

Will was determined to fund it, certain its future was bright.

26 February 1847

The crowd spilled onto the beach away from the platform. From where Will sat, he could see over the heads of the men and women of Galveston who had braved the uncertain weather to hear him speak. Some in the crowd waved the lone star flag about as if both sides in the annexation debate didn't fly the same flag.

A cursory review of the crowd showed the men of the Texian navy in their blue uniforms were in attendance. As the Republic's sole naval base, Galveston hosted scores of sailors at any given time. Will irreverently wondered if the bars were closed given how many blue-jacketed sailors he saw mixed into the mass of people. Here and there, a few men wore the army's butternut uniform. A battery of coastal artillery also called Galveston home. There was little doubt many of those men had served in the Mexican campaign a few years earlier. How many of the rest of the crowd had worn the army uniform then? More than ten thousand Texians had served in the army during the war.

Erasmo Seguin was addressing the crowd. Will had heard this particular speech more times than he was willing to admit, and he tuned out the elder statesman. Despite the gray sky, a light breeze came in off the Gulf, turning the February afternoon into a balmy day. Growing up in Galveston, he had fond memories from before the transference of time spent playing on the beach in the long coastal summers as a child.

In moments like this, Will let his mind wander. He had long ago decided the transference had been something different that simply being transported back in time. Given how much he had changed things in Texas, everything he knew from his own memories would, in this world, be completely different. He recalled reading about a time travel paradox, if someone made a large enough change to the past, it would result in a history so different their ancestors might never meet, resulting in the time-traveler never existing. The fact Will still lived in William Travis' body was a good indicator something else had happened. He had overturned the applecart of Texas history, which led him to believe the transference had created a parallel universe.

As Seguin talked about the freedoms experienced by newly arrived immigrants and Tejanos, Will found himself nodding. The reason to maintain independence wasn't some nationalistic fantasy. Folks like the Seguins had fared far worse in the history before the transfer. An independent Texas was an opportunity to do things better. A Texas annexed by the United States would fall squarely within the slave states' sphere. And no matter what Will could do in Texas, he didn't see any way to destroy slavery in the United States short of a civil war. The last thing he wanted was to tie Texas to a South that couldn't change without violence.

Even beyond slavery, Will thought about the US' enormous bureaucracy of the twentieth century and later. Liberty had become nothing more than a political slogan. In the America Will had come from he felt the county was slowly dying from overregulation and government control. He didn't know if an independent

Texas could avoid all the pitfalls the United States of the future, but his only choice was to try.

The crowd's applause drew Will's attention back to Seguin, who was saying, "And it gives me great satisfaction to introduce someone who needs no introduction. The hero of the Battle of Saltillo, help me welcome General William Travis!"

Will waved to the crowd as he traded places with Seguin. "Howdy, folks," he used a voice suited to the parade ground, reaching the back of the crowd.

"Until that fellow Senor Seguin introduced shows up, I'm glad to tell you what I think about President Ellis' desire to quit and give up on the grand experiment we call Texas."

The boos in the crowd when he mentioned Ellis' name brought a smile to Will's face. "Were you to believe the president, you'd think we are overrun by Mexicans and Indians. Nothing is farther from the truth. The Mexicans who live in our country are loyal to Texas. If I was in a scrape, there's nobody I'd rather have at my side than Senor Seguin's son, Juan. Like thousands of other Tejanos, they gave their blood, sweat, and tears for Texas. Just like you.

"Let's talk about the Indians. How many of you joined me in our late war with Mexico? No doubt you remember the gallantry of the 8th infantry. Perhaps you recall their nickname? The Cherokee Rifles? I favor the continued policies of Presidents Crockett and Zavala regarding the Indians. We have thousands of Cherokee, Creek, Choctaw, and Chickasaw living in towns and villages and on farms and ranches across Texas. I believe it is far better to find common ground with our red neighbors, many of whom worship in the same churches as you than to chase them from the homes they bought, same as you."

The crowd was quiet. While many were European born, many more had immigrated from back east, lured by cheap land and a chance to start over. Their conflict with the American Indian was two centuries old. Will faced an uphill battle to win them over. "I can see the looks on your faces. Why am I talking about the Indian when you came to listen to me talk about why I'm against annexation? If we surrender our independence, we abandon the right to determine how we'll relate to our native neighbor. Washington would decide that. After watching Andy Jackson, God rest his soul, chase the civilized tribes out of Georgia and the Carolinas, against the ruling of the Supreme Court, I have no faith in the US to seek just compromises with the Indians living within our borders.

"We are a moral people. We all worship the same God and trust in His providence. What Jackson did to those folks is a travesty against natural law. We can do better. We must!"

Will's voice rose over the crashing of the waves on the beach. The crowd was silent, but the faces he could see were thoughtful, not angry. If he were going to lose his audience, it would be now. "In the United States, they have done everything in their power to ignore the elephant in the room, slavery. But every year, the relations between the North and South gets worse. Why would we want to tie ourselves to that mess? To the politicians in Washington, Texas represents two more senators from the South. To the South, Texas is the gateway to the west, more places to extend slavery to balance against the fast-growing Northern states. The compromises that hold that union together will eventually fail. When that happens, a sea of blood will cover that nation. For the sake of our families, for the sake of our children, we must stay clear of that."

A smattering of applause greeted the remarks.

"Forgive the allusion, but I feel as though I am like Paul of old, looking through a glass darkly at what is to come, east of the Sabine River. Out of that conflict, I see a federal government powerful enough to crush opposition to it. And that's what you'd get if Texas ever joins the United States. A vote for annexation is a vote against our liberty and freedom."

Will hid his disappointment at the crowd's polite applause. His job was to stir the crowd's emotions and motivate them to vote against annexation. He worried he may have failed.

Later, over dinner in one of Galveston's restaurants, when he mentioned this to Seguin, the old Tejano said, "Buck, you did more than just stirred their emotions, you got them to think. I watched them while you were talking and you challenged their assumptions and their beliefs. You made them think about the future, and you made sure they understood their future under the stars and stripes would be much worse than under our own banner. Keep giving speeches like that, to borrow an expression I've heard you say, you're going to have to put your money where your mouth is."

Will sat the wine glass down, and with a sinking feeling, asked, "What do you mean?"

Using his fork as a pointer, Seguin said, "You need to run for the presidency."

5 March 1847

Will winced. It seemed as though a hundred burning kerosene lamps bathed the ballroom of the Hotel Lafitte's ballroom in a harsh light. Despite one last cold front attempting to grip the bustling town in winter's embrace, the room was stifling, as more than a hundred people waited anxiously for the latest telegram with vote tallies to arrive.

"Juan, how the hell are you doing?" Will said as he pounded Colonel Juan Seguin on the back.

"Begging my poor father to resign. His grandchildren miss their *abuelo*."

The heavy demands of campaigning against annexation had taken their toll on Erasmo Seguin. His normally swarthy skin was pallid. Dark circles caused his eyes to appear sunken. If anything, the elder Seguin looked worse now than he had when they had finished their campaign circuit a couple of weeks before.

"Erasmo, at least take some time to rest."

"Papa, listen to Buck. You're all skin and bones."

The elder Seguin glared at his son, "If we win, there is still so much to do in Austin. President Ellis' overtures to the US has created uncertainty in the commodities. The bureau will have to act to shore up confidence."

Will cringed when Juan said, "And if we lose, what then?"

"I'll retire. If the people favor annexation, staying in the government would be reefing the sails on a sinking ship."

Will moved around the room, shaking hands and exchanging pleasantries with the attendees. He felt a tug on his sleeve. "A moment of your time, General?"

John Wharton beckoned him to a corner. "How is private life treating you now that Ellis has brought Lamar back from France?"

"Mirabeau's a good sort, Buck. If there's another diplomat in our stable that can ride herd on our overseas missions, Lamar's the man."

Will wasn't sure if he agreed with Wharton. Years earlier he had talked President Crockett into appointing Mirabeau Lamar to serve as Texas' chargé d'affaires to France. Getting the nakedly ambitious politician out of Texas had seemed prudent. "I hope you're right. Lamar is a bit of a loose cannon."

Will had to lean in to hear Wharton's next words. "Mirabeau may love the sound of his voice more than most, General, but he's not one of Ellis' supporters. He's as ardent a supporter of independence as any of us."

"Then why'd he accept your old post?" Will asked, confused.

"Don't forget, Mirabeau's favorite person is Mirabeau. Secretary of State is a step up, and he's nothing if not ambitious."

As he wound his way through the sea of tables and chairs, he spotted the British chargé d'affaires. "Minister Elliot, how nice of you to join us, tonight."

Charles Elliot dipped his head to the woman by his side, "General, allow me to introduce my wife, Clara, to you."

The trappings of polite society bemused Will even after more than a decade, but he took her offered hand and brushed his lips over it, "The pleasure is mine, Mrs. Elliot."

The British minister said, "Of all the votes counted so far, your independence party trails by a few hundred votes, yet there is an air of celebration. Do you think you'll make up the balance when all the count is in?"

That was the ten-dollar question. "I hope so. There are thirty thousand people who are now Texian citizens in what was once New Mexico. By the Treaty of Saltillo, they're all citizens. The results have raced across the desert of west Texas by courier and with any luck, will arrive in San Antonio today."

Elliot furrowed his brow, "Why do you expect people who only a few years ago were loyal Mexicans to support Texas independence? Wouldn't they rather trust the United States than Texas?"

"I'm hoping they'll accept the devil they know over the one they don't," Will said before taking his leave. He didn't want to say more, but funds contributed from the Commerce Bank and several other enterprises, allowed several of the Texas Congress' more eloquent Tejano members to spend the last two months canvassing the people of the Northern Rio Grande district, as New Mexico was now called. The plan was to use the US's Indian policy as a stand-in for how the US would handle the thousands of newly minted Texian citizens. Time would soon reveal if it were the right strategy.

He had come full circle, arriving back at the table where his family sat. Becky sat with Liza on one side and David on the other. Six-year-old Liza gave her little brother a nasty look, contrasting poorly with her elegant, frilly dress. Three-year-old David wore a triumphant look as though he had managed some nefarious victory against his older sister.

"Thank God you're back. These two heathens have just about found my last nerve." Becky was stunning in a velvet dress, bought especially for the evening's festivities. The necklace sparkled in the lamplight. He swept David out of the seat and plopped down beside his wife. Letting the toddler ride his knee, Will leaned in and nuzzled his wife's neck, propriety be damned.

"If you should see my hand, I think one of Sam Houston's Cherokee cronies may have shook it off."

Giggling, Becky said, "You're a martyr for the cause, love."

He glanced at a blackboard, which had been brought in to track the vote. All the ballots from eastern Texas were tallied there. In the heavily pro-slavery part of Texas, independence had lost by a margin of two to one. In the area around Galveston Bay, the forces of Independence had eked out a small victory. In west-central Texas, in the area between San Antonio and Austin, the vote favored independence by a large margin. In northeastern Texas, near Arkansas, the vote had split nearly even.

Except for Santa Fe and everything west of there, the vote was in. More than sixty thousand votes already counted. Less than a thousand votes separated annexation supporters from those favoring independence. The result would hinge on the far west.

A commotion arose as a courier burst through the ballroom's doors. The young man held a telegram over his head. "The results are in! Santa Fe and Albuquerque have reported their returns."

Will gripped Becky's hand and gently squeezed as the courier handed the note to Erasmo Seguin, who unfolded it and quietly read it.

Will heard the ticking of his timepiece in his vest pocket as time seemed to slow to a crawl. The elder Seguin clutched the crumpled note to his chest and called out, "We did it! The Rio Grande District backed independence by a margin of three to one."

Will felt Becky's hands grab the lapels on his jacket and pull him into a passionate kiss. Any sense of decorum was gone. Independence had won and annexation had been defeated.

Chapter 24

7 October 1847

A film of dust lay on the desk as Lieutenant Charles Travis collapsed into the camp chair. A light breeze riffled the pages of an open book; the sides of the tent were rolled up, allowing the cool air to waft through the tent.

Charlie examined the letter from Captain Orwell Jackson, the company commander. In it, Jackson told him the expected ammunition wagon was again delayed. Charlie crumpled the note and left it on the table. How the hell was he supposed to keep his men trained if the army wouldn't give him the tools to do his job? He gripped the wooden tent pole at the front of the tent and glared across the small camp for which he was responsible.

A half-built adobe wall surrounded nearly two dozen tents. The northernmost post in Texian California was home to a platoon of riflemen tasked with monitoring the coastal road between San Francisco in the Jefferson Territory and Monterey, to the south.

The scowl fell from his face as he saw Bill King, the Customs agent emerge from another tent. “Mornin’ Bill. I hope you have better news than me.”

Using a cane, King hobbled over. “If I were any better, the good Lord would have to make two of me.”

When Charlie stopped laughing, he said, “Liar. The way you were walking, I’d have thought you were a drunken sailor instead of Texas’ chief customs officer for San Jose.”

“I was fifteen when I was shot at the Battle of the Nueces. I nearly lost my leg but got a comfortable job with Customs. At least until we took California from Mexico. I must have pissed on somebody’s boot to get stuck here with you.”

Charlie gave him a rude gesture.

Smiling, King said, “Treat the man who supplies your food a bit nicer. Next time I find a barrel of rancid meat, I’ll send it your way.”

Charlie held his hands up in mock surrender. King collected the tariff on all trade crossing the border. When merchants couldn’t pay with cash or specie, they paid in-kind with a portion of their supplies. All of the food Charlie’s platoon ate came from King’s collections. “You win. I don’t suppose you’ve collected any gunpowder as of late?”

“No. But I’ll add it to the list of things to take in lieu of payment.”

A gunshot echoed through the camp startling the two men and, a moment later, one of Charlie’s riflemen raced up to him, “Lieutenant, sir. There’s some coolies on the road. We stopped ‘em but damned if not a one of them speaks a lick of English.”

Charlie cringed inside. He hated President Ellis’ latest executive order, banning immigration from the

Orient. Since the beginning of the gold rush into Jefferson and to a lesser extent into Texian California, laborer's from China had trickled into the region, working for low wages.

"God save us from idiot politicians. I doubt there are more than a hundred of these coolies in the entire country. Why in heaven's name does Richard Ellis think we need a law against them?"

King followed Charlie toward the road. "You know the answer to that. Ellis has offered to prioritize claims this side of the border to any slaveholders who bring ten or more slaves. These Chinamen pose a real risk, given how little they'll work for."

Charlie glowered at the customs officer. "Not you, too, Bill?"

King shrugged his shoulders, "Don't ask if you don't like the answer."

When they arrived, Charlie found one of his rifle teams corralling a group of Asian men. He demanded, "Who fired their gun?"

One of his men said, "That was me, sir. One of them tried to run around the gate. I fired a warning shot and he decided he didn't want to run no more."

Satisfied no one had been hurt, Charlie turned on the group of Asians. "Any of y'all speak English?"

He scanned the faces of the men. The oldest was probably no older than his father and the youngest a few years younger than his own twenty years. But to a man, they wore confused looks. He tried again in Spanish, but with the same luck.

Down the road, toward San Francisco, he saw a man riding a horse, wearing the blue uniform of the US army. While the US chose to not patrol the border, a small garrison protected the peninsula. By the time

Charlie could make out the shoulder boards and see the captain's bars, he could also see the red piping of the artillery on his uniform.

The horseman stopped on the US side of the gate spanning the coastal road. "I heard the gunshot, thought I'd see if you people had a problem. Do you?"

Charlie eyed the officer. He didn't envy the horse his heavy rider. "Howdy. As much as it pains me to say, these coolies aren't allowed across the border."

Was there a spark of anger in the officer's eyes? It was gone as soon as it appeared. "You people were shooting because of that?"

Charlie wanted to curse. He hated Ellis' executive order. He hated the slaveholders the order was meant to profit. He hated the rifleman whose excitement had brought the American officer here. And most importantly, he hated the pompous ass sitting on the other side of the gate.

God dammit, I'm the officer. I'm in charge. His thoughts were scarcely framed in his mind before his father's cool reasoning came to mind. *Before an officer can master his men, he must first master himself.* He bit the inside of his lip until the iron taste of blood filled his mouth. In a voice he considered measured, he said, "Just a warning shot, Captain. You wouldn't happen to know any of the coolies' language by chance?"

"Just enough to get my laundry done."

Before Charlie could respond, King said, "I happen to have a bottle of whiskey imported from Ireland for you, if you could help us let these poor lads know that the border's closed."

The captain appeared to weigh the prospect. It was evident he knew of Texas' closed door policy regarding the coolies and didn't care for it. But the temptation of a bottle of whiskey tilted the scales the other way.

He turned to the Asians and spoke in a language that rose and fell almost melodically. The expression on the men's face changed from confused to angry, and several of them responded harshly to the captain. When he spread his hands, he turned and said, "Lieutenant, I'll thank you for that bottle of whiskey. As you can see, they don't care one whit more for your policy than I do."

A few minutes later, as King handed over the bottle of whiskey, Charlie said, "Duty is a double-edged sword, Captain. As soldiers, we must carry out unpopular but lawful acts with the same diligence as we carry out the orders we like."

Uncorking the bottle, the captain raised it to Charlie in salute. He upended the bottle and drank.

8 April 1848

Will checked the door before he swore at the newspaper in his hands. The article on the first page proclaiming President Ellis had won his case before the Texas Supreme Court was the source of his ire. At the first whiff Ellis was thinking of running for election in his own right, his opponents in Congress had filed a lawsuit against him, claiming the constitution's prohibition against multiple terms denied him the right to run for election. After all, each president was limited to one six-year term in office.

Will missed Lorenzo. Zavala had been an able president, following in President Crockett's footsteps, pursuing policies that strengthened Texas' independence. Will had always viewed Zavala's recruitment of Ellis as a necessary evil to win the presidency, peeling just enough votes away from the pro-annexation Sam Houston to win the election of 1842. But since Zavala's untimely death, Ellis' true colors had come through. As a condition to being Zavala's vice president, Ellis had pledged to support Texian independence, even though he was pro-slavery.

Zavala's body had barely cooled before Ellis declared support for annexation. Will had hoped defeating annexation in the plebiscite the previous year would have ended Ellis' political fortunes. Instead, the president had continued wooing Southern Democrats in the US. Some, like John Calhoun, from South Carolina, had scorned Ellis' entreaties. He had said, "The people of Texas have spoken. If they change their mind, and if there is a Democrat in the White House, we can talk of this again."

Now, Will thought, the Supreme Court had cleared the way for Ellis to run for the presidency in his own right. He scanned the newspaper and reread the offending paragraph.

> *Quoting Chief Justice Birdsall, "The constitution assumes the president must be elected in his own right in order to serve a term. The constitution also establishes the vice president will act in the capacity of the president if he becomes incapacitated. When President Zavala succumbed to pneumonia and Vice President Ellis became president, while he completed his predecessor's term of office, he did not trigger the one-term requirement.*

Will rolled the newspaper into a tight roll and dropped it into a wastebasket. He muttered, "Here's what I think of your election chances, Dick."

He sat in his chair and was deep into reviewing the quarterly finances of the farm machine company he and Dick Gatling had founded when he heard a voice, "Will!"

Thoughts of balance sheets fled as Becky's voice registered. He found her in the kitchen, where she was standing over a heavy iron skillet. "You've got to try this." With a large spoon in one hand and the other covered in flour, she looked happy as she said, "Those jars used to store food are a real marvel. Those peaches I preserved last year were perfect for this dessert. And you won't believe how rich and tasty it is. Try it."

Will waited as she dished out a serving. The smell of cooked peaches brought back memories from his own childhood. The flaky crust smelled heavily of cinnamon mixed with peach. With Becky standing over his shoulder, he picked up a fork and took a bite. The sweet peach flavor filled his mouth. He resisted the urge to swallow and sat there, savoring the taste. Rich desserts, like peach cobbler, were usually reserved for the harvest time when the peaches hung heavy from their branches.

With the canning made possible with sealable glass jars invented by one of the mechanical engineering students from Trinity College a couple of years earlier, fruits and vegetables could be stored for months. He swallowed and spooned more into his mouth, it was like eating a little bit of heaven.

"Don't eat it all. We'll save some for after dinner this evening. Is it sweet enough?"

Will nodded; he had a mouthful of cobbler.

Becky held up a tin can. "Mr. Borden brought this over yesterday. It's that condensed milk he's been working on. I used a bit of it in the cobbler. It's like having milk and sugar all together in one can."

Will swallowed and smiled. It wasn't like that. It was exactly that. More than a year of Gail Borden's life had been poured into discovering how to condense milk into something marketable. As Will grabbed another bite, he was happy to see Borden seemed to have worked out the kinks.

Becky leaned down and used her finger to wipe a piece of peach from his lip. Will tilted his head up and grabbed her by the arm, pulled her down until their lips touched. It was the peachiest of kisses.

The following Monday, Will leaned against one of the tables in Gail Borden's lab. Behind him was a stack of tin cans. Borden stood behind a large vat, and said, "I'm glad you liked the condensed milk. I've been handing it out to the women in town hoping they would use it in their cooking. I've not been disappointed. If we were set up to commercially produce it, I could sell a hundred cans tomorrow."

Will asked, "What do you need for us to start manufacturing it?"

Borden's smile evaporated, "I'm not sure we can. We need a steady supply of tin and a company who can make our cans. We need more sugar and more milk than what the cows around Trinity Park can produce. We need access to transportation networks and access to markets back east. All of that is available back in New York."

Will's mouth sagged. "New York City! You've got to be kidding me. Texas needs this invention, Gail. For Texas to grow into a vibrant country, we need things like your condensed milk."

Borden's shoulders slumped, "I've been here nearly twenty years. Texas is my home as much as it is yours. But if we want to make this work, how can we do that so far away from eastern markets?"

Will paced across the room, thinking. "We can do a railroad easy enough. We can build you a factory in West Liberty or even Houston. That'll put you on the railroad. If you put out the word you're buying milk, we can probably get enough milk from farmers located near the railroad to meet demand."

"What about manufacturing? We still need a supplier for tin cans and we're going to need a factory big enough to hold the vats in which we'll boil down the milk, machines that will transport the tin cans to the vats where the milk will be poured into them and machines to remove the air and seal the cans." Borden wore a forlorn expression as he continued, "Then we need access to those eastern markets. We're too far away."

Unwilling to let the production slip away from Texas, Will said, "The railroad connects to Anahuac. We can ship from there if we have to or ship it to Galveston. We have seven hundred ships a year come through Galveston. We can move the product anywhere in the world from there. We're closer to New Orleans and the river shipping here than you'd be in New York. We can make this work."

"What about production? Buck, there's are not a lot of options here."

"Give me two months, Gail," Will said, hoping he wasn't grasping at straws. "I've got an idea for producing the tin cans. If I can make that work, then I think we can probably get the tools necessary to build your factory in Texas."

1 July 1848

"Every time I come to Austin, it seems as though it's twice as large as it was before." Will wasn't sure he agreed with Andy Berry, but it was plain to see the capital of the Republic was a fast-growing town.

Sam Williams grumbled, "I still don't see why in the hell the railroad couldn't have had its maiden run begin in Houston. By God, why in the hell we rode a stagecoach to hear a bunch of politicians bloviate just so we turn around and take a train ride back to Houston is beyond me."

Will patted his business partner on the back, "Because we own the largest share of stock, Sam. Be a shame to miss the opening." He stopped in the middle of the street, "Think about it, gentlemen. When the Austin to Harrisburg line opens, it's going to connect more than three hundred miles of railroad. You'd be able to get on in San Antonio and ten hours later, you'll be in..."

Gail Borden interjected, "Pain. Ten hours of being bounced around in one of those railroad cars will have my bones so jumbled up, I'd be useless."

Will finished, "Anahuac. Now, Gail, if you're going to be a killjoy, you're going to have to ride back to West Liberty in the mail car. Leave those of us who know how to celebrate to do so in the passenger car."

Laughing, Williams patted Borden on the back, "He can't help being a wet blanket. He was all set to go enjoy the high life back east, and damned if you spoil his plans."

"We spoiled them, Sam. You called in a lot of favors to make this happen."

Berry said, "Is that all I am? A favor? I feel cheap, like a two-dollar whore."

When they had stopped laughing, Will said, "Andy, you're probably the only man in Texas with the expertise to help manufacture the tin cans needed for Gail's enterprise."

Berry said, "Without the experience from manufacturing cartridges, I'm not sure I'd have been much help. It didn't hurt that we've a stamping mill that can cut the tin and rolling presses to turn them into cans."

"How did you ever talk your father into letting us use these resources from the gun works?" Will said.

Berry said, "Pa wouldn't have anything to do with it. I was already adding more rolling presses, to increase our cartridge production. I bought those from Pa, and we'll be setting up shop just for making tin cans in West Liberty."

They came to a cross street where railroad tracks ran east to west, down the middle of the road. They were close enough to the Colorado River to see the bridge, connecting Austin to San Antonio by rail.

There was already a crowd gathering near the depot. People spilled from the street on which the railroad ran onto side streets. Berry said, "Buck, I thought you said there were maybe three thousand people in Austin. It looks like every one of them must have turned out for the show."

Will came to the back of the crowd, and groused, "This is what passes for entertainment here."

They circled around the crowd until they came to the train's engine. A mixture of engineers, Rangers, and soldiers formed a cordon, separating the train from the crowd. Borden turned to the rest of them, "Doesn't look like we're getting through here."

Williams said, "Follow me. I've got the tickets." With that, he hurried toward one of the railroad men.

"Hey, nobody's allowed through," the engineer said.

Williams fished some tickets from his jacket and offered them to the man standing in their way.

He took them and studied them. "When the speechifying is over, y'all can get on board. I ain't supposed to let folks board until then."

Williams produced a small coin and offered it to the engineer. "Are you sure? You'll see our seats are in the salon car."

The engineer jerked his head in surprise and looked at the tickets again. He pocketed the small, gold coin and said to the other men manning the cordon, "These gentlemen are allowed through."

Moments later, Will sat in the spacious salon car, next to an open window. There were a dozen seats. A few tables were strategically placed; every occupant could conveniently set their drink on one of the tables. Bottles of whiskey, gin, and rum lined a bar, situated in one of the corners of the car.

Will watched Sam pour himself a drink, "Did you know the bank president spent money on something like this?"

Sam took a sip and allowed a contented look to play across his face. "Not until I bought the tickets. The bank owns less than a quarter of the stock. The board meetings I attended, this was never discussed. But we're here now, might as well enjoy it."

Will turned his attention to the platform next to the train. Apart from the railroad company's president, the other men on the platform were career politicians, all members of Ellis' cabinet. One face missing was that of Erasmo Seguin. The director of the Commodities Bureau had died earlier in the year from a heart attack.

The man speaking was Michel Menard. He had been in Texas for nearly twenty years, but his strong Quebecois accent was unmistakable in a land full of southern drawls. As he waxed about the financial benefits of the railroad, Will tuned him out and focused on the man sitting in the middle of the platform, Richard Ellis. The man had betrayed everything Will had worked with David Crockett to attain. Nearly weekly there was an article in one of Texas' many newspapers discussing the continual budget cuts to both the army and navy. Nearly as often, the same newspapers ran stories about meetings between Ellis' envoys to Southern Democrats. Some newspapers pilloried the president, others lauded him.

When the president rose and approached the podium, he was stooped. Grey hair stuck out from beneath his wide-brimmed hat. But his voice remained strong, and Will had no problem hearing every word spoken.

"My fellow Texans," he dropped the i, as was becoming common in some newspapers. "The railroad is the locomotion of Texas' success. With the completion of this line between Austin and Houston, we now boast more than three hundred miles of track. Before long, you will be able to get on the train, here on Cypress Street and get off the same train at the Sabine River. Eventually, the railroad will connect our resources to markets back east.

"I see a day when cotton grown on the Brazos river will be loaded onto trains and those trains will follow the tracks all the way to New York where that cotton will be turned into textiles sold all over the world. I see a day when plantations grace the banks of the Colorado River hereabouts, made possible by this railroad. My friends, that's progress. Opening up Texas to reap the rewards of her natural bounty.

"That is why I would like to take this opportunity to make public what many of you may already know. Now that the Supreme Court has cleared the way for me to serve Texas in my own right, I am announcing my campaign for president.

A smattering of applause greeted the announcement. A voice behind Will mimicked Ellis' tenor, "Not being able to destroy the republic in one term, I'm determined to do it in two."

Will turned and saw Andy Berry. "Not a supporter of our president?"

"I support riding him out of town on a rail or maybe tarring and feathering him," Berry retorted. "Why don't you run against him? You'd have my vote."

Will said, "Shush. Don't let Becky hear you talking like that." He turned his attention to Ellis' speech.

"We are bound by blood and kin to our relations in the South. We are one people in two countries, and when you elect me, I'll renew my efforts to seek union with our American siblings. As all are aware, President Clay will not run for a third term. He is old and worn out. Daniel Webster may seek the Whig nomination, but even if he does, the Democrats will nominate the next president of the United States. I pledge that I will work with that man to add our beloved lone star to the constellation on the American flag."

Will felt his blood rushing to his face, and he turned away from the window. "God damn that fool!"

Sam handed him a glass sloshing with amber liquid. "Here, Buck, drink this. If that blowhard continues, we're all going to need more to drink."

Will took a sip and let the fiery liquid burn his throat on the way down. "Ellis is determined to destroy everything we've built. He's already extended his slavocracy through Texas to the Pacific. Who does he think he is?"

Berry said, "Probably the president. Our contracts aren't getting paid quite as regularly anymore, and another six years of his rudderless statesmanship will bankrupt my family's business."

Sam said, "Take another drink, Will. Andy's right. Ellis has pushed some legislation that could cripple banking. Between Michel in the Treasury Department and our allies in Congress, Ellis' banking ideas haven't made any progress. But God help us all if he wins in September."

Will squeezed his eyes shut, willing tears of anger away. "I get it. He can't be allowed to win. We've got to find someone who can run against him and win."

Borden sat in the chair next to Will and leaned in, "Buck, what Sam and Andy are trying to say is that you're the man who needs to run against Richard Ellis."

Will jerked away and stepped to the other side of the car. "I'm no politician. I was a soldier because that was what was needed of me. Since then, my family has first claim on my time. Sure, I love working in business with you, Sam. And Gail, helping to provide you and other men with vision has been rewarding. These are things I will do until I can't. But I don't have the right skills to be the president."

Williams broke the silence. "Buck, without you, I'm not sure if we could have won our independence. Most people in Texas think the same thing. Add to that, you beat Santa Anna's army in Mexico and captured his bastardness, ending the war and wrangled hundreds of thousands of miles from Mexico. The only people who won't vote for you are Richard Ellis and the village idiot."

Will shook his head. "Sam, you know that's not true. If I run, I'm not going to hide my candle under a bushel. Slavery is what has Ellis so worked up over joining the US. Slavery is the millstone around our country's neck. If I run, I would run on a platform of gradual emancipation."

Sam took Will's glass and drained it. "I think it's a mistake and will only make getting you elected more difficult. But if that's what it takes, then fine."

Will said, "Good. Then it's official, gentlemen. I am running for President."

Chapter 25

4 July 1848

A single kerosene lamp burned in the hallway, casting enough light for Becky to see the sleeping form of her daughter. Liza tossed in her bed, rolling onto her side. She was getting so big. Already attending the small school in Trinity Park, learning her letters. She closed the door, *How many more years before boys stop pulling her ponytails and start trying to steal kisses?* The image of a young man standing before Will asking permission to take their daughter for a walk brought a sad smile to her face. No doubt Will would terrify the first boy to come calling on Liza. Thankfully, something like that was still more than a few years away.

She cracked open David's room. Painted tin soldiers were scattered around the floor. The five-year-old loved his little soldiers and was at that stage where he'd play with them all day if he could get away with it. Now, though, the festivities of the evening in town had worn the little boy down. Despite living in another country, the former citizens of the United States had gathered in the town square for an impressive fourth of July celebration. Now, David lay in his bed. The sliver of light fell across him, and Becky gazed on her son, watching as his little chest rose and fell in the rhythm of sleep.

She closed the door and moved down the hall. Her life had never gone as well as now. While she always knew her pa had loved her, he had been gone far more often than he had been there. When she was growing up, before her father had won his election to Congress, he had been gone often, hunting, running his own enterprises, or serving in the Tennessee legislature. In contrast to her pa, Will was as stable as a mighty oak. She loved him for his commitment to her and the children. Adding to all of that, she loved living in Trinity Park. The town had grown from a few buildings centered around the gun works to a bustling town of hundreds. It had all the comforts she could desire. There were three churches, the same number of stores, a couple of saloons, and the college. Yes, she thought, Trinity Park was a place on the rise.

And that's why she worried about the future. She found herself standing in the doorway of her husband's library. Despite the late hour, he had several lamps, bathing the room in a warm light. In some ways, Will had never stopped being a soldier. As she stood there, quietly watching him, he said, "For a dyed-in-the-wool Baptist, John Berry knows how to throw one hell of a party. Did you enjoy it?"

Becky came over to him and hugged and kissed him. "I'd have enjoyed it more if I knew you weren't running against President Ellis."

Will swiveled around and faced her. "What's bothering you, Mrs. Travis?"

He had a way of turning her name into a term of endearment, and it melted her heart every time she heard him say it. "I wish you'd reconsider running for president. You'll be gone more than you'll be here over the next couple of months. And if you win, you'll be in Austin all the time. For six years. Think about that. Liza will be thirteen and David, eleven by the end of your presidential term. I don't want you to be like my own pa, gone so much that you don't recognize your own children."

Will ran his finger along her chin, caressing her. "Is that your only reason, love?"

Becky frowned, "My reasons are like the sands on the seashore, Will. We don't need more money. To hear Sam talk about it, the dividends you receive from the railroads you own parts of are more than enough to provide for me and our children. Add to that all the money you're making with your partners on those products spun off from the college. We have a good life. Why risk all this by running against Richard Ellis?"

Will snaked his arm around her waist and pulled her close. "At least they don't make you get rid of your businesses here if you run for president." The comment didn't mean anything to her, but she stayed quiet, waiting.

It seemed like minutes passed as he struggled with his thoughts. "Every few years the Northern states and Southern states find something to fight about. If Ellis wins, Texas will be the next political battle between these factions. If that happens, I fear Texas will be forever linked with the Southern faction."

Becky let him pull her into his lap, and as he ran a finger along her chin, he added, "Slavery's a terrible institution, but as bad as it is, I don't think the Southern states will give it up without a fight. Too much of their way of life is wrapped up in it."

Becky took his finger and pushed it into his chest. "Don't distract me, Will. Surely it won't come to fighting between North and South."

Will's smile was sad. "May it not be so. But I wouldn't count on it. That's why it's so important that Texas stay out of the United States. If I can convince enough people to elect me, I can put a stop to this annexation talk from Ellis and his planter allies."

Becky took Will's arms and wrapped them around her waist. She felt safest when he held her so close. "Do you really think you can convince people to let slavery die out in Texas while it's still so powerful just over the border in Louisiana?"

He nuzzled against her neck, and she felt his lips graze her ear. Damn, he could distract her! "I hope so. A lot more people have come to Texas from places not called Virginia or Alabama. Did you know last year more than four thousand Irish came to Texas? As a matter of fact, only a third of people who came to Texas were from the South. There are less than thirty thousand slaves in Texas now. Perhaps there are five thousand slave owners. Against that, there are more than sixty thousand men who own no slaves. If I can convince enough of them that it is to their advantage to kill off slavery, then Louisiana or the other slave states, won't matter."

Later that night, Becky snuggled up to Will, he was still awake. "Just promise me one thing, Will. Be careful."

31 August 1848

Broadway Boulevard was a far cry from the central thoroughfare through Galveston Will recalled from his own time before the transference. In 1848, the best Will could manage was to call it pretentious. Sam Williams chose the intersection of Bath Avenue with Broadway for the day's speech. The only thing making the sultry weather bearable was the breeze blowing from the gulf.

It was times like this Will hated the mid-nineteenth century the most. Social convention demanded men wear jackets regardless of the time of year. Granted, Will's summer jacket was made of cotton rather than wool, but still, it was intolerable. *One of these days, I'm going to invent an air conditioner*.

From his place on a raised platform, he saw traffic was completely blocked by the gathered crowd. Beyond the crowd, men sat on top of wagons, waiting to hear him speak. Boys wound their way through the crowd, hawking brass buttons with a fair likeness of Will and his running mate, Juan Seguin.

Once Will had decided Ellis must be stopped, and he came to accept he was the best man to make that happen, he considered men he knew well in addition to men he knew only by reputation. He knew enough of twentieth- and twenty-first-century politics to know a vice president needed to add something or create a balance in a presidential ticket. Will felt confident he could sell himself to Texas' immigrant communities as well as appealing to thousands of people who had come from the North over the past decade. Given Texas' recent conflict with Mexico, he feared many of the folks who had their citizenship forcibly changed from

Mexican to Texian in the former New Mexico territory would sit out the election.

Seguin could appeal to those voters in a way Will never could. *"And,"* he thought, *"it doesn't hurt that he's a damned fine friend."*

Getting Seguin to resign from the army had proved easier than he had expected. Since Erasmo's death, Juan had been forced to spend more time on the family ranch, taking more time away from his post at the Alamo than he wanted. When Will came calling, the Tejano listened to his pitch and then resigned within a week. Since then, Seguin traveled to Santa Fe and Albuquerque where he had campaigned for the newly minted citizens' vote.

Will used a handkerchief to battle the sweat pouring down his face. From somewhere in the crowd, he heard a voice, "Ellis must go!"

Another called out, "Down with Ellis! Restore the navy!"

Will winced at the last comment. Ellis had forced the navy to mothball three warships. This left only two warships for the entire Gulf of Mexico and two for California.

A church bell chimed, announcing to the crowd it was noon. Will stood and approached the podium. As he gripped it with his hands, another voice could be heard as the applause died. "You're trying to destroy our institutions, you nigger-lover!"

People in the crowd turned on the hapless heckler, and Will could see him beating a hasty retreat.

"Folks, thanks for coming out on such a hot day. Days like today make me think that if the devil had the choice between hell and Texas, he'd rent out Texas and live in hell," Will warmed to the laughter of the audience. "In eight days, you'll go vote in the third presidential election since we won our independence and, when you do, you have the chance to decide on the kind of Texas you'll hand to your children."

He wiped at his forehead as he continued, "In all my years in Texas, there has never been a choice as stark as the one you face today. You can vote for Richard Ellis, and he will try again to suture us to the United States, like some kind of political Frankenstein."

Will wasn't sure if the allusion to Mary Shelley's book had an audience in Texas, but as he watched the crowd, the remark found its target, as heads bobbed in agreement.

"The President will continue to weaken us, as he prays for a Southern Democrat to sit in the White House. He'll allow our army to wither away on the vine and for our navy to rot in port, convinced a weak nation will have no choice but to seek protection under the American eagle. Under Ellis, cities like Galveston are nothing more than waypoints for the plantation economy, like feudal lords of old, to ship their cotton to world markets. Industry, merchants, and businessmen have no place other than to offer their wares to rich planters and to do as they're told."

The cries of "No," from the audience fueled Will's passion as he continued. "Under Ellis, Galveston will become be a tiny port amid a nation with many larger ports. He'll happily watch trade languish here as long as his planter friends can build bigger plantations and import more slaves."

Then, more like a mob than a political rally, the crowd began chanting, "Down with Ellis!"

Will let them chant, as he swept his gaze over the crowd, confident he wasn't losing control of his audience. He finally raised his hands and waited for the Galvestonians to quiet down. "That's Richard Ellis' vision for Texas. Now, let me tell you about mine. In the Texas that I know and love, a man's worth is measured by the contribution he can make to his family, community, and nation, not by the number of slaves harvesting cotton under the hot autumn sun, while he sits in his mansion sipping mint juleps. The Texas I love is a strong nation with a strong army and navy, able to deter Mexico from getting uppity. The Texas that I love is a beautiful mosaic, made up of folks who fled their places of birth, looking for a fresh start. Whether you came from Tennessee or New York, Dublin or Belfast, Bremen or Copenhagen, or San Antonio or Vera Cruz, you all came for a better future.

"The Galveston I know and love is the gateway to a healthy and vibrant Republic. Galveston is the jewel of the gulf. If you trust me with the presidency, I will pursue domestic industry, exported through this fine port, reasonable tariffs that provide for our common defense, and better charts of the bay so that captains can rely on our charts to sail their ships safe into port.

"The Texas that I love knows that slavery devalues the labor of all men. My opponent would have you believe that you can't get the genie back in the bottle, but my friends, we can create a vibrant economy of free labor and let the South's peculiar institution die of old age. As I have said before, as president I'll lead Congress to pass a free birth law, that everybody born in Texas after eighteen fifty will be born free, no exceptions! And there'll be no more slaves brought into Texas after that date. If you send me to Austin to do the people's business, my priority will be to provide every Texian the opportunity to prosper by their own hands, whether they be farmers, machinists, merchants, or laborers. You and me, together, we'll create a golden age of prosperity for Texas!"

Will ignored the sweat pouring down his face as the crowd cheered. He hoped there were more folks like the sea of faces before him. He'd need them to offset the tens of thousands of transplanted Southerners Ellis was courting.

11 September 1848

Samuel Williams helped his wife onto the porch of the Liberty Hotel. Light spilled into the night, illuminating their steps. "Oh, Sam, General Travis has gone all out tonight."

"Buck isn't one for all this show, but Señor Garza loves to put on a display. Heaven knows how much money he spent to help Buck's campaign, but win or lose, tonight's party is just a drop in the bucket." Sam had a fair idea the amount Garza had funded had exceeded ten thousand dollars. His own pocketbook was lighter by a similar amount.

As they stepped into the hotel's lobby, it was nearly bright as day; Lamps chased shadows away revealing wooden paneling hung with paintings of the late Mexican War. Sarah cried, "I've heard of this one," she pointed to a piece of art depicting Mexican *soldados* swarming up a Texian redoubt. A brass plate below the picture read *Defense of the Cherokee Rifles*. To Sam, it seemed the artist had taken liberties with the defenders' uniforms. The Cherokee had worn the same butternut uniforms like the rest of the army, yet in the painting, they were adorned in the traditional Cherokee garb.

"You've got to commission one of Mr. Wright's paintings. They're so patriotic."

Sam found himself agreeing the art was patriotic if a bit melodramatic.

A voice from behind caught him off guard, "Sam, you shouldn't have."

He turned and saw Buck standing in the doorway to the hotel's ballroom. "And miss the celebration? All of Texas is waiting to find out how bad you'll trounce Ellis.

The former general took his wife's hand and kissed it, "Mrs. Williams, as always a pleasure. Becky is simply dying for more civilized company than a bunch of men poring over telegrams."

Sam waited until his wife, Sarah, hurried away before saying, "What's the latest?"

Travis pointed to a slate board someone had borrowed from West Liberty's schoolhouse. "All the vote has been counted in east Texas and along the gulf coast. Everything Between Laredo and Austin has reported in. We're still waiting for the northeastern portion to report and also the area in the Rio Grande district."

Sam walked over to the blackboard. Close to seventy thousand votes had already been counted. Ellis led by a few hundred votes. "Any idea how the Red River area will vote?"

Travis said, "Best case, we'll match Ellis' vote in the area. Lots of folks from Tennessee and Arkansas have settled there over the past few years."

Sam raised his eyebrows, "I didn't think there was much plantation farming that far north."

"There's not. But those folks reckon the best way to get ahead is to save up and buy a slave. With any luck, the towns settled by the civilized tribes will break our way, and enough Irish and Germans are living in the area to give me hope we won't slide further behind."

Sam noticed at the bottom of the board a large blank spot next to the words *Rio Grande district*. "So it all depends on a bunch of former Mexican citizens in Santa Fe?"

Travis motioned him to join him at a bar, where a bartender served up a couple of shot glasses. "Pretty much. The ten-dollar question is will they see their interests best served by being annexed by the US or by making the best of Texas' annexation of their territory."

Sam took a sip, pursed his lips as the alcohol burned his throat on the way down. "What a bargain. They get to choose between the devil they know or the devil they don't know."

Travis chuckled. "That's exactly what I told Juan before I asked him to spend a bit of time campaigning out there."

They turned toward a ruckus coming from the lobby. A young man wearing the peaked hat of the telegraph office held up a telegram, "From Austin, more results are in!"

Sam watched Travis hurry through the packed room and take the telegram. After opening the note, he called out, "Bowie, Red River, and Harrison counties are in."

He wrote the results on the board. Sam shook his head, discouraged. More than three thousand new votes and Ellis extended his lead by more than a hundred. When Travis joined him at the bar, he took a bottle from the bartender and filled both their glasses again, "What do you think happened, Buck? I thought you might regain some votes."

With a shrug, Will took a sip. "Harrison County is on the Sabine River. Lots of prime land has been picked up by planters. I imagine they made me out to be Beelzebub in the flesh."

Sam said, "Someone might think you intend to upend their applecart. I've read what the pro-Ellis newspapers have said. They claim you'll try to free their slaves and destroy their livelihood."

Travis grimaced. "We've been over this before, Sam. Any system built on one man owning another deserves to collapse. It's a cancer in our nation. But I know the difference between what I'd like to do and what I can get away with doing, provided Juan and I do better with the folks in Santa Fe."

There was a lull as the two men nursed their drinks. Into that Travis said, "What about you, Sam. You still have those two slaves?"

Sam laughed into his glass, haunted by the answer. "Probably until they die, Buck. Billy's getting pretty long in the tooth. He's almost seventy now. He can't do much anymore. To borrow one of your expressions, I'm his pension plan. I don't know what I'm going to do about Chastity. She has been a tremendous help to Sarah with the children and the housework. We've been partners long enough that you've reminded this Rhode Island-born man that my views on slavery should evolve again. Enough so that I've taken to giving Chastity a small salary. It assuages my conscience a bit."

Sam averted his eyes, embarrassed. Chastity was barren, unable to have children. Neither Freedman nor slave were uncommon on Galveston Island, and the few black suitors who made their way to the Williams homestead beat a hasty retreat once they learned of her condition.

Sam breathed a sigh of relief when Will changed the subject. "Did I tell you that Sid Johnston has set up a relay along the military road between Santa Fe and San Antonio. He's spread our cavalry out along the entire route, a few men every fifteen or twenty miles, upwards of fifty stations. Once the vote totals are confirmed by the election judges in Santa Fe, a rider will race back along the road, trading his mount at every station. Every few stations a new rider will take over. Only four days are necessary for the results from the Rio Grande district to reach San Antonio, and then from there, they'll be telegraphed to the rest of the country in just a few minutes."

Sam said, "Makes you wish we had pushed the telegraph further west. But I can think of better uses of two hundred thousand dollars to run nine hundred miles of cable."

Travis looked at the blackboard, "Right now I can't. It's been four days since the election. We should have the results by now."

Sam looked through the hotel's plate-glass window, light spilled onto the sidewalk and attempted to pierce the darkness on the street. The courier who had delivered the earlier results was racing along the sidewalk.

The young man burst into the ballroom, waving the sheet of paper in excitement. "The results from the Rio Grande district are in!"

Travis took the folded piece of paper. Sam watched his business partner's hands quiver as he opened the telegram. Seconds dragged by as the former general digested the results. The room was silent as every set of eyes focused on Buck Travis.

After what seemed an eternity, Travis said, "The results for the Rio Grande district are eleven hundred and forty votes for President Ellis."

Sam looked at the tally on the blackboard and mentally adjusted the president's tally upward. His friend needed nearly two thousand votes to win.

Travis continued, "Thirty-two hundred and twelve votes for me!"

The men in the room erupted into cheers and applause. William Barret Travis had won the presidential election of 1848.

From the Telegraph and Texas Register

> *12th September 1848*
>
> *We are able to assure our readers that the hero of the Revolution and former general of the Texian army, William B. Travis will succeed Richard Ellis as the 4th president of our fair nation. While a few hundred votes are still traveling by mule somewhere between Los Angeles and Santa Fe, General Travis's margin of victory is sufficient to call the election in his favor.*
>
> *The republic's election commission in Austin estimates more than 80,000 votes were cast in the election. President-elect Travis was awarded 41,042 votes while President Ellis captured 39,844. Based on the voter rolls in Texian California, this publisher of record estimates no more than 500 ballots remain outstanding.*
>
> *Colonel Juan Seguin has secured the nomination as vice president. Messrs. Travis and Seguin will be sworn in on the 23rd October, commencing their six-year term of office.*

Chapter 26

Early December 1849

"What a strange custom, putting a tree in the house at Christmastime." Will laughed as Becky stepped back from hanging a tiny wooden manger on one of the branches.

He said, "It's a tradition in our German community, and becoming more popular across Texas." He picked six-year-old David up and let the boy hang another ornament on the tree. "This evening, there'll be a reporter from the *San Antonio Zeitung* here for an interview following my speech to Congress, and I thought this touch of home would put him at ease."

Becky pouted, "I don't see why you have to give a speech before Congress on the state of the country. Pa and Lorenzo sent letters. That would be easier."

Before the transference, Will had hated even the thought of public speaking, but starting with his days during the revolution and later commanding the army, he'd grown accustomed to speaking in front of his soldiers. But after campaigning against the annexation vote, it had become old hat. He still didn't like the butterflies in his stomach before a speech, but he could deal with it.

"It's a bit like this Christmas tree. We're a young republic, and we need our own traditions. This speech before Congress is a tradition I'd like to start. I want to remind people where we've come from and share my vision for where we're going."

Becky leaned over and helped Liza attach a small wire hook to a painted blown-glass bulb. "Go practice your speech, me and the kids will finish the tree."

A short while later, Will and his family crossed Congress Avenue from the hacienda-style president's mansion to the Capitol Building. Seats had been set up in the gallery for his family at the back of the House of Representatives, and Will took a place next to the Speaker of the House and the President of the Senate, waiting for the hall to fill up with more than a hundred and forty members of both houses of Congress.

After the Speaker of the House opened the joint session of Congress, Will stood behind the podium and looked out across the room. Factions had been part of Texas' Congress since the beginning, but now they were more pronounced. The Democrats, taking their name from their American counterparts sat on one side of the hall, while the Republicans sat on the other. Will had considered other names for the Republicans, but given Texas' status as a republic, the name had stuck.

"Friends and fellow Texians, I am honored to stand before you this evening and fulfill my constitutional duty to provide a state of the republic to Congress. It isn't lost on me that the last time both houses of Congress were in joint session was seven years ago when David Crockett asked you for a declaration of war against Mexico. I'm happy our circumstances are far removed from that now."

Some in the hall seemed to hang on his every word while others appeared disinterested. "Over the past fifteen months, the government has strengthened our security by expanding our military, on both land and at sea. We have three battalions of infantry and another of cavalry and artillery as well as our frontier battalion of Rangers. We have ensured they have adequate support by expanding our quartermasters' corps and corps of engineers. We have reclaimed status as the most powerful squadron in the Gulf of Mexico by expanding to five ships. We have maintained our two-ship squadron on the Pacific Ocean. Over the next two years, we will expand our combined fleet to ten ships."

Aside from the Ellis era, the military had been something to unite the nation and as Will finished outlining the state of the military throughout the room men stood and applauded. He was gratified to see men from both factions standing.

"Since the birth of our republic, we have been beholden to foreign creditors. Wars are ruinous, and our war with Mexico cost us the better part of eight million dollars. I'm pleased to say that within the next five years, we'll repay nearly all our foreign debt, leaving most of our public debt held by the people of Texas.

"How, you may ask, have we done so well at repaying our debts? At the end of our war with Mexico, we produced around twenty million dollars in goods, services, and produce. Six years later our population has doubled, and in eighteen forty-nine, we are projected to generate more than sixty million dollars. This year, more than one thousand manufacturers are doing business in Texas. They employ more than eight thousand of our fellow citizens. They produced more than fifteen million dollars in goods.

"Our farmers have cultivated almost three million acres of farmland across eighty thousand farms at a total value of nearly one hundred million dollars. Nearly four hundred thousand Texians live on these farms."

Again, a standing ovation greeted Will's numbers. "This year we imported ten million dollars' worth of goods from the United States and Europe and exported more than five million. Our tariffs collected nearly two million dollars from this activity. Between property taxes and loan repayments to the Texas Land Bank, we received more than five million dollars. Also this year, we received one and a half million dollars from the United States as part of our treaty ceding the northern parts of California to them. In all, our coffers took in more than eight million dollars.

"Against that, we spent around a million dollars on interest, five million on our defense, and the remainder on education, infrastructure, and diplomatic missions. As a matter of fact, we have diplomatic missions in the United States, Britain, France, Belgium, the Netherlands, Prussia, Bavaria, Hannover, Russia, Spain, and the Papal States.

"As we establish ourselves as a nation among nations, I hear talk from the diplomats who come calling that they would open up even more to us if we addressed the issue of the South's peculiar institution. Although it may not seem so to some assembled here, Texas is not of the South; we are a people apart, neither northern nor southern nor entirely European."

Will glanced at the four members of Congress elected from farms and towns of the Cherokee and other civilized tribes. "Sometimes that means we bring part of our heritage with us, sometimes it means we leave it behind. When the people of Texas elected me to the office I now hold, I was open about my views on slavery as well as the direction the Republic should take. Now is the time to show the rest of the world that Texas is able to shuck off the vestiges of a system that devalues all of our labor, a system that has more in common with feudal Europe of old than the modern world we inhabit today.

"As we put to rest the eighteen forties and welcome the new decade in a few weeks, it is time to put to rest slavery within our borders. Before Congress recesses for Christmas, I will offer a bill to Congress called the Free Birth bill, that every child born in Texas, without exception, after the first of January, eighteen fifty-two will be born free. Also, it will allow slaves the right to buy out their freedom or to have it bought on their behalf."

The hall erupted into pandemonium as most of the Republicans stood and applauded. Many Democrats stood and walked out. Will waited until the noise subsided before he wrapped up his speech. He couldn't help worrying about the trouble the Democrats could create. In his own history, just the threat of loss of political power had caused the Southern Democrats to split the United States in the leadup to the Civil War. He prayed they wouldn't try the same thing now in Texas.

21 March 1851

"Furthermore, by letting slavery die we poke a stick in Mexico's eye, as they continue to practice peonage, which is hardly any better than slavery, even though they sit there in Mexico City and pat themselves on the back that the negro is in chains north of the Rio Grande while he is free in Mexico. By voting for this bill, we show Mexico we are more enlightened than they."

Will felt a hand on his shoulder and hear Juan Seguin's voice, "Count on Francisco Ruiz to stir the pot. He hates Mexico with all the fervor of a convert."

Will dipped his head, agreeing. "Have we been able to peel any votes away from the Democrats?"

Seguin collapsed in the chair next to his. "One from Harrisburg. The Neches Faction, as they've taken to calling themselves, are holding fast."

Will pursed his lips, the Neches faction represented most of the Democrats in the Texas House of Representatives. They took their name from the river running through the heart of Southern opposition to the Free Birth bill.

He tuned back into Ruiz's speech, "Texas should become a beacon of hope for both Mexico and the United States, showing them both how a nation can grow out of its worst excesses. That is why I urge my fellow Congressmen to vote for the Free Birth bill."

Will watched the next speaker to approach the dais. Thomas Rusk had commanded the militia in the late Mexican War. He had left that role after the war and been elected to Congress. A South Carolinian by birth, he was one of the Democratic stalwarts in the House.

He drawled, "To listen to my colleague from San Antonio, you'd think Texas was on the brink of destruction. I was reading a bedtime story to my youngest son, about a hen convinced the sky was about to fall just because an acorn happened to fall on her head. My Republican friends sound much like that hapless chicken. To hear folks talk, you'd think slavery was some diabolical effort to hold some folks down. That couldn't be further from the truth. Slavery has been with us since the time of Abraham and is ordained by the creator. It is part of our natural order. What would negros do if left to their own devices? They are ignorant of the outside world and unable to care for themselves without the benevolence of the white race. We have a duty to care for them and guide them to work fitting for their abilities. The best social structure for this is slavery."

Will felt his jaw drop. While he'd heard such arguments before, it still amazed him men like Rusk believed it. Rusk continued, "Freeing the negro from his natural state makes no more sense than convincing yourself the sky is falling because of a single acorn. What order would President Travis want if he succeeds in freeing the lowly slave from the labor that gives him purpose? Does he see white women laying with negros? God forbid.

"No, my friends, let us nip this foreign foolishness in the bud before it takes root. Rather than letting the good institution of slavery die, I say let the silly infatuations of abolitionists die. Join me in voting against the president's bill."

Will was glad the short speech was over. As another Democrat approached the front of the hall, he motioned to Seguin, and they left.

Later, after the bill had been debated, it passed the house by a vote of sixty-two to thirty-eight. Then it moved to the Senate.

Several weeks later, Will sat in the Senate's gallery, which looked much like the one in the house, separated from the Senators' desks by a red velvet rope. Southern

Democrats had spoken for two weeks, and the Senate stayed in session for the entire time. It was only after one of their number defected that the Senate was adjourned. The next day, Republicans arrived early and locked the doors. Because they had a quorum, they could legally conduct Senate business without the Democrats. They refused to allow Democrats back into the chamber until they agreed to a vote on the bill.

Will listened to the roll call vote of the senators as they voted on his bill. With a lone defector from the Democrats, the bill passed twenty-five votes to fifteen. As the bill was read aloud, tears spilled down Will's face. While thirty-thousand men, women, and children remained enslaved in Texas, no more would follow after the end of the year. He brushed away the tears. There was still a long way to go, but the first steps had been taken. He stood and shook hands with several Republican Senators. Tomorrow, he would sign the bill. For now, it was time to celebrate.

The officer lifted the binoculars to his eyes and stared across the river. A sentry stood next to a massive stone pier which anchored the railroad bridge to that side of the river. The pier rose high above the water to the bridge deck, where iron rails and wooden ties connected two countries. As the officer watched, another person on horseback rode up to the guard.

From his place on the ferry, the officer could only imagine the conversation on the other side of the river. As the small craft cut through the water, the officer clutched his horse's reins. He chanced a look behind, and his two traveling companions were whispering. He ignored them. Their excited words were nothing he hadn't already gone over in his own mind.

While it seemed an eternity, the ferry ride only took a few minutes before the officer led his own horse from the boat onto the river bank. The sentry remained beside the pier, leaning on his rifle, staring at him. The man on horseback was an officer, wearing the butternut brown of the Texian army. His shoulder boards revealed he was a colonel.

The mounted officer leaned down and offered his hand, "General, I'm happier than a tick on a dog to see you. Colonel Gotch Hardeman of the Neches department at your service."

The officer looked Colonel Hardeman over and liked the Texian's enthusiasm. "How much land does the provisional government control?"

"Everything east of the Neches River for a couple of hundred miles. Are your men on their way?"

As if to answer the question, a faint blast from a locomotive echoed across the river. "Of course."

A rumbling trailed the engine's shriek, followed by an almost imperceptible vibration below the officer's feet. He looked at his pocket watch. *Fancy that, on time for once*, the gray-jacketed officer thought. He was glad the train's arrival didn't contradict his confidence. Black smoke curled into the clear sky and what started as a slight tremor turned into a violent shaking as a locomotive thundered onto the bridge overhead. He could feel the ground vibrate beneath his feet as the train rolled across the Sabine into Texas. From every window, gray-clad soldiers hung out of the passenger cars waving at him as they sped by. A flag stuck out of one window, flying a single white star on a blue field.

Allowing a faint smile to work its way onto his face, the officer snapped off a salute to the men on the train as they receded down the tracks toward Beaumont.

"Nice flag y'all got there," Hardeman said.

"Borrowed from the old West Florida Republic. The lone star seemed appropriate, don't you think?"

Hardeman nodded. "It's a short ride into town, won't you and your companions come with me? Officers of the provisional government are meeting there. We've been waiting for your arrival before reclaiming territory held by that abolitionist, Travis, and his supporters."

The officer swung into his saddle and joined Hardeman as they wended their way from the riverbank to the road. They passed by a farm. He saw a woman and her children working in the field. When he commented on it, Hardeman said, "We're mobilizing our militia. Once fully organized we'll have between eight and ten battalions."

They had traveled less than a mile when the officer noticed a horseman racing toward them from the west. They drew up and waited for the rider. When he reached them, he skidded to a stop, throwing up a cloud of dust, and shouted, "Colonel, the telegraph line has been cut to the west. We can't get or send any messages from anything west of Liberty County."

Hardeman swore before turning to the officer, "General Beauregard, it has started."

The Southern Cross Convention: A Short Story

The people of the Republic of Texas, in Convention assembled, on the 13th day of August, A.D., 1851, declare the frequent violations of the Constitution of the Republic of Texas by the Travis administration and its encroachments upon the reserved rights of the people of Texas, fully justify the declaration of the new provisional government of the people of the Republic of Texas. The people of the Republic of Texas, understanding their rights must be secured by the union of Texas to the United States, authorize a commission to entreat with members of the United States Government and delegations of certain states to facilitate the union between Texas and her sister states.

Early September 1851

His leg twinged as he hurried down the gangplank. Moving fast always hurt his game leg, but the other passengers behind him forced Jason Lamont to hustle along. Once on the dock's wide wooden planking, he leaned on his cane and looked behind him. More than a dozen tall-masted ships were either docked or rode at anchor in the deep-water harbor. Mobile was the largest port in the Gulf of Mexico after New Orleans.

He watched slaves transferring cotton bales from the dock onto a ship. *No doubt bound for Liverpool or New York,* he thought. He turned away from the bustle and left the dock. Twenty thousand people called Mobile home, and it seemed to the planter from South Carolina that they were all streaming one way or another in the streets.

Lamont made his way along the harborside to a small coastal schooner, moored alongside one of the docks. The stars and stripes hung aft of the ship lazily. Several men were already aboard.

"Mr. Lamont, I was afraid you'd not be able to travel in the midst of the harvest season."

Lamont glanced up the walkway at the man addressing him. The goateed man mopped at his forehead as he waited to Lamont to step onto the ship's deck. "Mr. Rhett, nothing short of the very survival of our institutions would drag me away from my fields during harvest season."

He leaned on his cane, as he adjusted to the rocking motion of the small, double-masted boat. "The news out of Texas is such news. I'm gratified to see such an ardent supporter of Southern rights onboard."

Rhett colored at the compliment. "I feel like you, that it is my duty to attend this convention. If anything can be done to aid our fellow countrymen, then we must be about it."

A deckhand removed the wooden planking between the schooner and the dock and a voice called out, "Weigh anchor!"

Inch by inch, the boat drifted away from the dock until the crew raised the sails. As the coastal schooner slid across the waters of the bay, he said, "How reliable is the news from Texas? A provisional government with the right views almost sounds too good to be true."

Rhett mopped his brow as he gripped the railing. "The provisional government from Texas has sent representatives. We'll be able to ascertain whether they are a going concern when they speak."

"I'd love nothing better than to see William Travis deposed. His presidency in Texas is a dagger to the heart of our economic interests."

Rhett chuckled, "I'm sure that cane you carry has nothing to do with the animus you feel toward the Texian president."

Lamont's face turned red. Rumors had trickled out of the South Carolinian capital in the aftermath of Travis' attack on his plantation. Even though he had buried the evidence tying him to the kidnapping of Travis' son, word had seeped out that his injury was tied to Travis' rescue. A lesser man might have quaked at the scandal, but Lamont weathered the curious stares in the years following Travis' attack, and life had continued.

"I wouldn't know," he replied, "What did General Travis do to you for your newspaper to brand him an enemy of the South?"

Rhett tipped his head, acknowledging Lamont's retort. "An abolitionist winning the presidency of a slaveholding republic was enough for me to direct my pen against William Travis."

Lamont smirked at the newspaper editor. "Seems to me that's enough for any of us."

The next day

Lamont felt the irony at eating in the hotel's restaurant called the *Texas* as he scooped up a forkful of eggs. The large circular table was crowded with other delegates, also eating. He barely tasted the eggs as he strained to listen to the delegate from Louisiana, on the opposite side of the table.

James De Bow used a napkin to clean his eyeglasses as he said, "Containment, gentlemen. That's the risk posed by the government in Austin. If President Travis is allowed to put down the provisional government of Texas and continue to push a policy of abolition, we'll be contained and cut off from the west."

Lamont set the fork down and leaned forward. De Bow continued, "Despite the Cass administration in Washington being sympathetic to keeping harmony between South and North, Massachusetts, Connecticut, New Jersey, and Rhode Island have sent abolitionists to fill their states' Senate seats. As a matter of fact, the bonds of union that have held our southern states to their northern brethren are coming undone and finding common ground is becoming harder with each passing year."

A man sitting next to De Bow said, "But Henry Clay and Daniel Webster have always kept their radicals reined in. Surely our union is safe."

De Bow used a piece of bacon as a pointer. "Not so. Calhoun is more than a year in the grave and Clay and Webster are not far behind. The men rising to prominence in the north resent the horse trading their elders have done to keep the delicate balance between our regions. Northern congressmen have reintroduced a bill to admit Wisconsin as the fifteenth free state. Twice before we've defeated it in the Senate. But for how much longer? More than a quarter of a million people live there already. Denying Wisconsin statehood is a last-ditch effort on our part to maintain the status quo in the Senate."

He ate the piece of bacon before continuing, "If Travis can defeat the provisional government in Beaumont, the South is cut off. Apart from buying Cuba from Spain, there's no place to grow. With each passing year, territories north of the Missouri Compromise line will petition for statehood, and we'll be drowned by free states, even in the Senate.

"When that happens, they'll begin to pry slave states away from us. First, it will be Delaware, and then either Kentucky or Maryland. Before we know it, there'll only be seven or eight slave states left. When that happens, the free states will force through an amendment to the constitution, outlawing slavery. When that happens, our economy and our way of life will die."

The men around the table grew quiet as they absorbed De Bow's words. Lamont swallowed a bite of eggs and said, "They'd destroy our way of life."

De Bow nodded, "And happily do it, too. The industrialist in Boston or Philadelphia sees the Southern planter as a competitor. We compete for the same banker's dollars as he does. When a bank loans you ten thousand dollars to expand your fields, that's ten thousand dollars he doesn't have to loan the industrialist. Banks know we make better partners. Our loans are secured by our property which, if we fail to repay the loan, they can seize and sell. We're a good investment. The industrialist, if he goes bankrupt, has only the machines and buildings. If the industrialists can destroy us, the banker has no choice but to lend money to the riskier industrialist. Vanderbilt and his lackeys are happy to toss money at abolitionist politicians, but it's not because they care one whit for our negroes and how we care from them. It's because they want to destroy their economic competition."

Exasperated, Lamont asked, "What are we supposed to do?"

Like a teacher educating his student, De Bow said, "That's the question we're here to discuss, Mr. Lamont. If we're to survive, we must expand. The first step has already been taken. Our fellow Southerners in Texas have formed a provisional government. Left to their own devices, I'm not sure they can depose of Travis. We must aid our fellow countrymen and defeat Travis. Once that happens, we'll petition Congress to allow Texas and Wisconsin into the union, then we'll carve as many slave states out of Texas as needed to keep parity with the north."

Lamont wanted nothing more than to get revenge. He'd dreamed of burning the Texas capitol building down with Travis trapped inside. But dreams were easier than reality. There were plenty of things that could go wrong. "What happens if the north rejects our bid to bring Texas in?"

De Bow placed his napkin on his empty plate. As he stood, he said, "Then we secede."

Lamont was glad to escape the stifling heat of the Texas Restaurant, which had been converted into the convention hall. Despite the gulf breeze and open windows, more than a hundred delegates made the large room uncomfortably warm.

He took a pail of food from a matron by the door and saw William Yancey staking out a spot under a tree. He'd been looking for a reason to talk with the Alabaman since arriving the previous day. As Yancey spread a blanket under the boughs, he said, "Would you mind a bit of company, Mr. Yancey?"

Taking a seat next to Yancey, he dug into his pail. As Lamont was about to bite into a drumstick, he saw James De Bow approach. "Would you gentlemen have room enough for a third under the shade?"

Soon the three men were drinking beer and eating lunch. When he was finished, Lamont stretched out, his feet sticking off the end of the blanket, content. Before he could drift off, Yancey said, "Mr. De Bow, what do you think Lewis Cass?"

"The president? About the best we can hope for, after eight years under Henry Clay. The question you should be asking is how does he view the situation in Texas. While I know he'd support annexation of Texas if the winds were favorable, he's not going to meddle in their affairs. If Travis crushes the provisional government, then Lewis Cass would wring his hands and moan that annexation just isn't going to happen," said De Bow.

"Why?" Lamont said. "Surely he understands that the preservation of the Union justifies the acquisition of Texas. We can't let the Yankees dominate us in the Senate like they do in the House."

De Bow offered a smile in Lamont's direction. "You'd think so. But Cass is a northern man, even though he's a Democrat. He understands the needs of the South, to a point. That's why he favors annexation. But he doesn't want to get drawn into a messy civil war in Texas. Sure, he'll cheer as loudly as any Southern man if Travis is defeated. But he's not going to let the Federal government get drawn into Texas' mess."

Yancey said, "What are the odds that the provisional government can defeat Travis?"

De Bow shrugged. "We'll hear from the Texas delegates tomorrow. But I'm not optimistic. The provisional government controls most of Texas east of the Neches River, in the southeast corner of the Republic. Maybe twenty counties. Perhaps a hundred thousand folks live in that area, and about twenty thousand are slaves. We don't know what portion of

Texas' regular army has gone over to the provisional government, but for the sake of argument, let's say that none of them do. There are two branches of the militia in Texas.

"The first is a reserve group. They get the uniforms and weapons from their armories, more drill time, and money. Most of these men served in Mexico in Texas' last little war. There are perhaps five or six battalions of men the provision government can call into service from the reserves. Then there is the second, larger group. The rest of the militia is made up of all the other men of military age. Not much in the way of uniforms or weapons from the armories. Maybe there are seven or eight battalions that can be mobilized from that group."

Lamont said, "For sparsely populated Texas, that sounds like plenty."

"You'd think," said De Bow, "but that's less than ten thousand men. They would face Travis' regular army. There are three battalions of regular infantry, another two of cavalry and one of artillery. They are well armed and well trained. If General Johnston betrays his people and stays with Travis, then they also have a damned fine commander. If he can manage to mobilize even half the reserves and militia against the provisional government, Johnston could command an army of twenty thousand."

Lamont was aghast. "The provisional government and annexation are doomed if that's the case."

"Not necessarily," De Bow said. "The whole reason we're assembled here is to discuss how best to help our fellow Southerners. Tell me, Jason, how many men are in Southern militia companies?"

"I've no idea."

De Bow said, "Two years ago, according to your state's militia report to Washington, there were more than fifty thousand men in the common militia. In my state, Louisiana, more than forty thousand are enrolled. Across the entire South, there are more than a half million men enrolled."

"I've seen the men in my county drilling," Lamont said, "and most of them aren't worth a tinker's damn as soldiers. How many of these half-million could actually be called to service?"

"Fair point," De Bow conceded. "Even so, many of the volunteer companies like the Washington Artillery in New Orleans are ready for service. There are tens of thousands serving in these volunteer units across the South. If the convention decides to aid our fellow Southerners in Texas, we can mobilize these men and send them to put down Travis and his abolitionists in Austin."

A smile creased Lamont's face. "Damn, that'd be a sight to behold. Do you think the other delegates would support intervention?"

In response to De Bow's nod, Lamont leaned forward, "What can I do to help?"

The three men discussed their strategy until the convention was called back into session.

The party in the restaurant showed no signs of slowing when Lamont felt a tug on his sleeve. William Yancey yelled above the din, "There are a couple of men who wanted to meet you."

A few minutes later, the two men were in the relative quiet of the hotel's salon, sitting across from the two commissioners from Texas. Thomas Rusk was heavyset while his companion, James Collinsworth was tall and lean. A fifth joined them. He wore the gray uniform of the Louisiana militia. He wore shoulder boards with a single embroidered golden star.

De Bow said, "I've asked G.T. Beauregard to join us this evening. He holds the commission from Governor Walker as commander of our state militia."

Collinsworth said, "How quickly can our Southern allies get men and matériel to our provisional forces along the Neches?"

De Bow's chuckle was warm and friendly. "You certainly don't beat around the bush, Mr. Collinsworth. The reason I asked General Beauregard to join us is that he's well acquainted with other militia commanders as well as the resources available."

Rusk appeared embarrassed by his younger colleague's direct speech. "What Mr. Collinsworth is saying is that our provisional government is not yet ready to move against Travis and his abolitionist forces to our west."

Lamont, hearing Travis' name, muttered a curse against the man who had crippled him. "The sooner that abolitionist is dead and gone the happier I'll be. Why haven't you moved against that traitor to our institutions?"

A shadow passed over Rusk's face. "Many of our leaders have served in Texas' Congress, and when Travis sent an envoy, they voted to listen to Travis' man."

Collinsworth spat into a cuspidor, “A few damned fools still think there’s a peaceful way out of this. Travis won’t abdicate, and we won’t relent. War is the only way forward.”

Rusk placed a restraining hand on his fellow delegate. “Not everyone agrees with us, Jim. Although I’m convinced force of arms must eventually settle the matter, time favors us more than Buck Travis. Especially given the promises this convention has given us. But if it takes a bit more time for the provisional government in Beaumont to realize it, then so be it. The question we need to know is how many men can we expect and when?”

Beauregard leaned forward, an expression like a hunting dog on his face. “While there are more than half a million men enrolled in the various state militias across the South, the reality is that only a small fraction are worth a damn. Take a unit like our Washington Artillery. There are a couple of batteries ready for service. There’s a sister infantry unit, also ready for service. Across all of Louisiana, I can mobilize a light, mixed brigade and could have them ready to support you by the end of October.”

Rusk’s smile was guarded. “On paper, the provisional government has three brigades it can call upon, perhaps as many as ten thousand. What’s your light brigade in comparison?”

“Less than two thousand. But that’s two thousand men who are trained, armed, uniformed and motivated,” Beauregard said. “More than that. Give me time to coordinate with my counterparts in Mississippi, Alabama, the Carolinas and elsewhere and I can give you ten times that many men. By the spring of eighteen-fifty-two, I can lead an army of twenty thousand men on Austin."

Rusk said, "That's a tall promise, General Beauregard. But what of your President Cass? Is he going to stand by while the Southern state militias engage in the world's largest filibuster?"

Still thinking of Travis, Lamont interjected, "He will if he knows what's good for him."

"There's a plan in place to deal with Lewis Cass," De Bow said. "We control half the Senate, and we will introduce a bill supporting your provisional government, on the grounds that Travis' ill-conceived Free Birth bill will cause servile unrest throughout our country. We'll tie the federal government in hearings and votes until long after G.T. here has defeated Travis' army. Once that's done, we'll present President Cass a fait accompli. In the Senate, we'll package Texas and Wisconsin together as a deal, one slave state and one free. Sectional balance is preserved. Northern Democrats won't be able to resist it, and Daniel Webster's Whigs won't be able to stand against it."

As Beauregard explained his strategy, Lamont let his thoughts return to that cold night several years earlier when Travis stood over him after putting a bullet in his leg. He had never felt more helpless. He wouldn't stand by and let others do all the fighting. Like a mad dog, Travis needed to be put down, and he'd be damned if he'd do nothing more than attend a conference.

As Beauregard stopped talking, Lamont said, "We'll all do our duty to seeing things put to right in Texas. I promise to raise a regiment of men for service and will personally lead them."

De Bow slapped him on the back as the others praised his commitment.

"Don't be too quick, General Beauregard, I'd like to be there at the end to see Travis get his," Lamont said with a fierce grin. He stood and walked over to a nearby bar where he liberated a tray of glasses and a decanter. As he passed the drinks out, liquor sloshed about.

He turned to the other four men and lifted his glass, "To victory or death!"

Stay tuned for the conclusion of the Lone Star Reloaded Series, book 6 in the second quarter of 2019.

Thank you for reading In Harm's Way

If you enjoyed reading In Harm's Way please help support the author by leaving a review on Amazon. For announcements, promotions, special offers, you can sign up for updates from Drew McGunn at:

https://drewmcgunn.wixsite.com/website

About the Author

A sixth generation Texan, Drew McGunn enjoyed vacations to the Alamo as a kid. Stories rattled around in his head throughout school, but as with most folks, after college the nine-to-five grind intruded for many years.

His passionate interest in history drove him back to his roots and he decided to write about the founding of the Republic of Texas. There are many great books about early Texas, but few explored the what-ifs of the many possible ways things could have gone differently. With that in mind, he wrote his debut novel Forget the Alamo! as a reimagining of the first days of the Republic.

Drew's muse is his supportive wife, who encourages his creative writing.

Made in the USA
Columbia, SC
14 September 2023